A Quarter Past Dead

TP Fielden

ONE PLACE. MANY STORIES

HQ
An imprint of HarperCollins*Publishers* Ltd
1 London Bridge Street
London SE1 9GF

This paperback edition 2018

1
First published in Great Britain by
HQ, an imprint of HarperCollins*Publishers* Ltd 2018

A catalogue record for this book is available from the British Library.

ISBN: 9780008193805

MIX
Paper from responsible sources
FSC™ C007454

This book is produced from independently certified FSC™ paper to ensure responsible forest management.

For more information visit: www.harpercollins.co.uk/green

Printed and bound in Great Britain by
CPI Group (UK) Ltd, Croydon, CR0 4YY

For

Bo Wilson

Of every creature's best

ONE

The trouble with Betty was she could never say no.

'Oh, *Betty*,' sighed Miss Dimont, looking over her Remington Quiet-Riter and pushing the spectacles back up her nose. 'Who was it this time?'

'Dudley Fensome.' Betty was sobbing into a creased handkerchief and was clearly not going to do much reporting this morning.

'But you *know* his reputation,' said Miss Dimont, who'd met the brute at the Constitutional Club. 'And a Freemason as well – what were you thinking of?'

'He said he wanted it that way and I did it to please him.'

'Surely not!'

'He made me.'

'It's a woman's right to decide for herself!'

'You don't know what it's like when they ask.'

You're right, thought Miss Dimont, I don't. The chief reporter pushed her notebook aside and got up to make the tea.

'I don't know, Betty,' she said, 'there was Derek. Then Claud Hannaford in that revolting pink Rolls-Royce – now

Dudley Fensome. All in the last few weeks. None of them seems to show you any respect.'

'I know,' wailed Betty, 'sometimes I'm just like putty in their hands...' Not just sometimes, thought Miss D. But it was true – the burning desire of a bachelor Freemason had got the better of Betty. It might have been better if she'd got a professional to take care of the problem straight away, but Betty had to go and do it herself.

She looked wretched.

'Platinum's not so bad,' said Miss Dimont finally, looking down at the disaster from above, teapot in hand. 'There are a couple of green patches over your ears, granted, but I've got that nice crochet hat the Mothers' Union gave me last winter – you can have that.'

Betty Featherstone wailed even louder.

Nobody else in the newsroom of the *Riviera Express* took much notice. It was press day, the usual hubbub of a busy newsroom augmented by the occasional bellow of anguish from the editor's office. Rudyard Rhys may once have been a naval officer, but these days he was not entirely the captain of his own ship.

'No, no, *no*!' his voice echoed out of the door, sounding as agitated as if he were trying to avoid an iceberg. '*Not* Sam Brough again, I simply won't have it!'

'The first mayor of Temple Regis to go to Buckingham Palace,' argued Peter Pomeroy, his deputy, perfectly reasonably, 'to be made a Member of the Order of the British Empire. That's a feather in the town's cap. The readers will expect a good show on that.'

'You mean *His Worship* will. Page Seven,' said Mr Rhys

dismissively, who hated Brough and his snobbish wife. He may dither about what to put on his front page, but when it came to pushy self-aggrandising town officials the editor's decision was final.

'There's always Bobby Bunton,' said Miss Dimont, who'd put her head round the door to see what the fuss was about. 'By the way, Betty's going to take the rest of the day off, d'you mind?'

'Rr… rrrr,' growled the editor, shuffling the page proofs in front of him.

'Bunton,' said Miss Dimont, who knew how to get a decision out of her procrastinating leader. 'He's in murderous mood.'

'Sounds good to me,' said Peter, whose responsibility it was to make sure the paper went to bed on time, and by now didn't care much what was on Page One as long as the story fitted the gaping hole in the page.

'Remind me,' sighed Mr Rhys, swivelling in his chair and eyeing the seagulls circling like vultures outside his window. One of these days he'd walk out on press day and never come back. That would show them.

'It's the latest round in his battle with Hugh Radipole. Bunton brought in a new funfair attraction and now Mr Radipole has banned him from the Marine Hotel. It's all-out war!'

'Rr… rrr,' replied Rhys and did what he always did at times of indecision. It could take a good three or four minutes for him to clean out his filthy briar pipe and load it with tobacco – precious minutes, with the newsroom clock ticking towards deadline.

Peter Pomeroy nodded urgently to Miss Dimont. 'Do it,' he said. 'Four hundred words.'

'It's written,' said Miss Dimont cheerily. 'And Betty?'

'Yes,' nodded Peter understandingly. He'd clocked the disaster on top of her head.

'Just don't *sensationalise* it,' said Rhys anxiously. 'We don't want Fleet Street picking up the story and making a mockery of this town. Bunton may be a well-known figure, but he's hardly representative of the virtues of Temple Regis – I don't want outsiders thinking we're *Blackpool*.'

Heaven forbid, thought Miss Dimont as she whisked back to her desk. Demure, discreet, desirable – these were the watchwords which attached to any story describing their adorable town. If it wanted to get into the *Riviera Express*.

In truth Temple Regis was all of those d-words. What's more it was the prettiest town in Devon; people always said that. From the palm trees which welcomed you on the railway station platform to the winding narrow streets with their interesting shops to the soothing ice-creams, the donkey-rides on the broad and beautiful beach, and the never-ending sunshine – nothing could be nearer paradise.

In the late 1950s, with the nation back on its feet at last, it was the ideal place for people to come on holiday – but Rudyard Rhys wanted to make sure only the *right* people came.

Indeed, the two people his chief reporter had just mentioned somehow summed up what was both right and wrong about the place. Hugh Radipole had bought the Marine Hotel after the war, put a not inconsiderable amount of money into refurbishing it, and to its smooth Art Deco halls welcomed some of the most distinguished people in the land. Their presence added tone and culture to the town.

But then somehow someone had allowed Bobby Bunton in, and with him he'd dragged the knotted-handkerchief brigade. The *wrong* people.

If that wasn't bad enough Bunton also brought with him Fluffles Janetti, that well-known courtesan whose shapely form was never far from a headline and whose pot-pourri of a love life kept the Sunday newspapers very busy indeed. She loved the bar in the Marine, though apparently it no longer loved her, despite her impressive consumption of its many liquid offerings. There'd been a bit of a dust-up, with bottles smashed and a quantity of blood spilt.

NEIGHBOURHOOD DISPUTE OVER FUN FAIR RIDE
by Judy Dimont, Chief Reporter

ran the headline.

Police were called after a dispute at the Marine Hotel ended in violence on Tuesday night.

The well-known entrepreneur Bobby Bunton, owner of the Buntorama Holiday Camp, has demanded an apology after he was requested to leave the building. He and a companion have threatened to sue the management of the Marine. Mr Bunton says he had

been enjoying a quiet drink in the Primrose Bar when he was suddenly asked to leave the premises and not return. His companion's garments were torn and disarranged.

'I take this as a personal insult,' said Mr Bunton. 'I can think of no reason why I should be subjected to such vile treatment.'

A spokesman for the Marine Hotel declined to comment.

Buntorama, the fifth in Mr Bunton's nationwide chain of holiday camps, opened last year on the site of the old Ruggleswick army camp. The camp is situated on land abutting the grounds of the Marine Hotel and there have been reports of disputes between the two companies running the businesses.

Since establishing Buntorama in 1948 Mr Bunton claims to have provided cheap holidays for over eight million people and has become a familiar figure on radio and television.

'People are entitled to have fun,' he told the *Express*, 'whatever they earn. My guests mean a great deal to me and I don't see why (*continued on p 3*)

Wary of infuriating her editor further by putting in the bit about Fluffles losing her clothes, Miss Dimont put the story back in her Quiet-Riter and xxxx'd out this rather delicious detail. She also refrained from mentioning that

Bobby Bunton had deliberately placed his new helter-skelter ride right next to the boundary of the Marine Hotel, so that shrieks and cries from his punters would shatter the calm and sobriety of the guests on the posher side of the fence.

'All done,' she said, handing over the copy-paper to Peter Pomeroy with a smile, and in that moment her face lit up until she looked quite beautiful. Peter often remarked to his wife how Judy could seem so plain one minute and so dazzling the next, and Mrs P agreed. They sometimes wondered why someone so worldly and so accomplished had come to Temple Regis to be a reporter on the local rag.

It remained an unanswered mystery.

Over in the darkroom Terry Eagleton was busy sloshing developer fluid into a tray, happy to be back in Temple Regis after a boring stint in the Plymouth head office. Sooner or later the images painstakingly captured from the top of a schooner's mast would appear, as if through the fog, and he would hang them up to dry. He was tough, efficient, handsome, and occupied that parallel universe where photographers exist – linked to humanity, but not quite part of it.

'I suppose it's all that time you spend peering down a lens,' Judy Dimont once observed as they sat in the Minor in the drumming rain, waiting for the Regis lifeboat to come in. 'Separates you from the real world.'

'If you want the real world,' grunted Terry, who did not squander precious time pondering the human condition, 'just look at my pictures. Pictures of real people doing real things.'

'Very fine they are too, Terry,' said Judy, and let the matter drop. Oil and water, water and oil – they'd worked together as a successful team for five years, yet neither could see inside the other's head. She admired his courage and tenacity and undeniable skill with a camera, but couldn't understand why he never read a book. Terry felt protective about Judy but when the editor called her 'Miss Dim' he could see what the old boy was getting at. She had a brilliant mind but was not altogether trustworthy in polite company.

After all, hadn't there been that extraordinary incident at the Regis Conservative Party ball? Apologies were offered all round afterwards, and everybody pretended they'd forgotten it ever happened, but you'd never catch a photographer behaving like that!

Just then the maverick in question popped her head round the darkroom door. 'All done for the week,' she said.

'My Buckingham Palace pic?' said Terry, washing the developer off his hands under the cold tap.

'Seven.'

'Ridiculous. Should be on One – the readers'll expect a good show on that. First Mayor of Temple Regis to get a gong!'

'Don't worry. Sam Brough will be wearing that medal everywhere, even on his pyjamas, I shouldn't wonder. Word will soon get about he's met the Queen, no need for the photographic evidence.'

Terry turned and looked disparagingly at Miss Dimont. She just didn't get it – didn't even try. The lighting in the Palace courtyard that day had been very tricky – up and down like a yo-yo – the trouble he'd had with his aperture!

'Coming to the Fort?'

There was only one place in Temple Regis on an early

Thursday evening if you had any connection with local newspapers and that was the Fortescue Arms, just round the corner from the *Express* offices and handily placed if you needed to be called back. As with all newspapers, things had a habit of going wrong at the last moment and there was an unwritten rule you did not stray far, even though your working day was over.

'Don't know,' said Terry. He was cross about the MBE and wanted to blame Judy.

'They've got cribbage tonight.'

'Ur.'

The pair made their way down the stairs and out through the grand-looking front hall. Upstairs the newsroom looked its usual mess – paper strewn over the floor, glue pots everywhere, overflowing ashtrays and discarded cups of tea, the cleaners as usual having failed to take away the overnight mousetraps. But down here it looked as if they were expecting a visit from the Queen Mother herself – all polished wood, copies of *Express* front pages lining the walls in oak frames, and an impressive oil portrait of the newspaper's founder above the fireplace.

Keeping guard over this shrine to the fourth estate was Joyce, the new girl who looked nice but irritatingly could never remember a single person's name.

'G'night, Terry!'

Well, thought Miss Dimont crossly, could never remember a person's name – except Terry's. The darling boy lingered, delighted to exchange a bit of banter, but Judy strode on.

Though it was still early the saloon bar of the Fort was crowded, mostly with muscular types in need of a shave and a new wardrobe. They smelt clean, though, and the racket they made was joyful: clinking and shouting and gurgling and laughing.

These ruffians were the reminder that Temple Regis was not just a holiday resort, but a fishing port too. And tonight the sailors, fishermen and ferrymen, Customs men and lifeboatmen, were here in force, bringing an energy to the place which no crowd of summertime holidaymakers could ever match.

Across the bar Miss Dimont spotted the Viking-like skipper of the *Lass O'Doune*, Cran Conybeer, and waved. His beard tilted upward in salute and as he raised his glass to her he looked even more magnificent in his shaggy, unkempt way. There had been a moment when... but somehow nothing had come of it and the two were no more now than smiling acquaintances.

As she plonked down her raffia bag on a wet table Terry meandered through the door and instantly started droning on about some new high-speed film he was going to try out – really, his idea of conversation! Severely in need of an overhaul! Miss Dimont left him boring a couple of subeditors about Tri-X and push-processing while she made her way to the bar to order him a brown ale.

'What you doin' 'ere?' said a familiar figure from the crew of the *Lass*. It was Old Jacky, a man for whom a day was wasted if he were not at sea. He must have been all of seventy-five.

'Every Thursday,' shouted Miss Dimont, gesticulating at the barman. 'Press night. What are you lot doing here? Not your usual haunt.'

'The *William and Mary,*' replied Old Jacky, though he pronounced it 'Willummaree'.

'Oh yes,' said Miss Dimont.

'Fifty yars agoo nex Sa'day.'

It remained Temple Regis' greatest tragedy, the loss of the lifeboat and a dozen souls who'd braved gale-force winds to save the crew of a merchant ship, grounded on the rocks beyond the point and breaking up in mountainous seas. What made the event such a bitter memory, even today, was that by the time the lifeboat reached its goal, the merchantmen had already been lifted off and were safe. They lived, while their saviours died.

'We'll be putting a big piece in the paper next week,' promised Miss Dimont earnestly, though she had no idea whether Mr Rhys was even aware of the anniversary. But it was the sort of thing you always said to the public when it looked like you'd missed the most obvious story in town. She backed away quickly in case Old Jacky wanted more details, the brown ale and her ginger beer slopping gently over her shoes as she went.

When she got back to the far corner there were a handful of familiar faces but no Terry.

'Where'd he go?' she shouted to one of the sub-editors above the din.

'Shot out back to the office. Someone came and told him to get up there in a hurry.'

'Why?' yelled Judy. 'Too late to change any of the pictures now, the presses are rolling.'

'No, it's a story, I think. Someone found dead over at Buntorama – you know, the place where...'

'I know the place!' rasped Miss Dimont. 'Why did he go without me?'

'Dunno,' said the sub, edging towards the door, more interested in getting home for *Hancock's Half Hour* on the radio. They worked in newspapers, these people, thought Miss D – but would they know a story if they tripped over one on the promenade?

'Here,' she said, brusquely, 'drink these!' and pushing her way back out of the door, she was just in time to see Terry behind the wheel of the Minor, gunning the motor while impatiently waiting for a couple of pedestrians to get out of his way.

'Terry!' she shouted, but the office car veered away, the photographer bent forward with a look of steely determination on his face.

Just then Peter Pomeroy hove into view. 'What are you doing here? Why aren't you over at Buntorama? For heaven's sake, Judy, I do expect more from the chief reporter!'

It was unlike sweet Peter to say a harsh word, and it hurt.

'What's going on?' said Miss Dimont, for once in a fluster.

'Woman found dead, for heaven's sake,' said Peter urgently. 'Shot. Surely you know? For heaven's sake, why aren't you with Terry?'

'He went without me.' It sounded so lame.

'Well, get over there as fast as you can. There's just time to re-plate the front page for the last edition. Five hundred words. In half an hour, not a moment later. Get going!'

TWO

Ruggleswick was the part of Temple Regis most people preferred to ignore. Just as townsfolk rarely discussed the snooty enclave of Bedlington-on-Sea, hiding behind the headland and pinching its nose in case a bad smell wafted its way, so too it was for Ruggleswick – people didn't want to be reminded of Buntorama and the type of people it attracted.

The feeling was mutual. The camp's guests had to clamber aboard a bus in order to get into a town which, on arrival, perplexed them with its prettiness. Instead they mostly idled their days away at Ruggleswick, being bullied by Redcoats and indulging in unsavoury practices.

At least that's what most Temple Regents thought. There was almost no visible evidence of moral turpitude, however, when Miss Dimont finally arrived at the holiday camp aboard Herbert, her trusty moped. Dressed in an undistinguished livery of grey-blue paint and with a gaping pannier-bag contributing an ungainly lopsided look, Herbert nevertheless was a trustworthy aide and companion – one who could be guaranteed to get her to a story far more nippily than others, like Terry, burdened with an office car.

Except tonight.

'You promised!' hissed Judy when she finally caught up with the runaway lensman. 'You absolutely promised!'

'All finished now,' said Terry, with a smarmy smile. 'I'm off back to the office. Not much to see, I wouldn't waste your time if I was you.'

This only compounded the fury she felt.

'Never mind the dead body, Terry,' she said tartly, 'what about the spark-plug? You promised me you'd put a new one in Herbert this morning. I could've got the garage to do it but you said you'd…'

'Ooops,' said Terry, carefully winding the wiggly cable of his flashgun into his camera bag, 'I'll do it tomorrow, Judy.'

'I couldn't get the engine started! And while we're on the subject of negligence, *Terry*,' went on the reporter, standing in his way with hands on hips so he couldn't leave, 'why did you just shoot off like that? Couldn't you wait just a moment for me? For heaven's sake, it was me who went to get you a drink!'

'It was an emergency.'

'You knew I'd have to come up here to get the words to go with your picture.'

'Picture's worth a thousand words,' said Terry. He often said this, and it got more infuriating each time. 'Pictures sell newspapers, not words.'

Miss Dimont shook her head so hard some of her corkscrew curls came out of their pinnings. She was lovely when she was angry, thought Terry, and he levelled his Leica at her.

'Put that down! Tell me why you shot off like that!'

'Shouldn't you be gettin' the story?'

'Tell me!'

'If you want to know,' said Terry, 'it was that look on your face back in the Fort. I came in the door and started telling you about this new Tri-X film and you just rolled your eyes up to the ceiling in that way of yours and...'

'Heavens, Terry, it's like me talking about buying a new typewriter ribbon! Tools of the trade! It was boring!'

Terry gave her a look. 'Let's see if Herbert can get you back to the office in one piece,' he replied, meaning the spark-plug. 'Lucky for you it's downhill most of the way.'

'No, wait!'

'Bye.' He clunked the door of the Minor shut with a complacent thud and sped off back to civilisation, leaving Miss Dimont with no clue as to where to start.

They'd met at the entrance to the Ruggleswick Camp – Terry on his way out, Judy coming in – so now it was her turn to make her way towards what had been, in its army days, the guardhouse. Nowadays it was the camp's reception, brightly lit with neon tubes and festooned with posters advertising Bobby Bunton's other holiday resorts, but even now you wouldn't be surprised to find a platoon of armed soldiers tumbling out of the doors to stop your escape.

'Are the police still here?' she asked a pimply youth reading a comic.

''Oo wants to know?' said the fellow without raising his eyes. Clearly Bobby Bunton had yet to include the rudiments of etiquette in his staff training.

'Miss Dimont, *Riviera Express*.' She didn't want to make it sound too important – people had a habit of saying, 'No Press!' at the slightest provocation – on the other hand, she wanted to jerk the youth out of his torpor. There were only twelve minutes left to find the body, discover what had happened, parry the stonewall response of the police, parlay a fact or two out of them in return for who knows what promises, find a phone, and file copy to the impatient Peter Pomeroy.

'Inspector Topham's expecting me,' she said, without the slightest clue whether the old warhorse was on the case this evening, or out dancing with Princess Margaret.

The lad looked up. 'Row Seven,' he said, 'only they call it Curzon Street now. Last 'ut on the left.'

Bearing no resemblance whatever to its Mayfair namesake, Curzon Street had dismally failed to shake off its resemblance to an army barracks. The best that could be said was its hutlike appearance softened in the growing dusk and the purple clouds which backlit it gave a glow, an allure, which would last until nightfall and dissolve with the morning light.

Down the end, where a Londoner might expect Park Lane to be, she could see the red tail-lights of the police car, and a pool of light spilling from a couple of brightly lit windows.

'Not now, Miss Dimont, if you please.' Inspector Topham must have turned down the Princess's invitation to dance this evening. He was never very helpful in such circumstances but at least Judy knew where she stood with him.

'Dead woman,' she said authoritatively, maximising in two words the extent of her knowledge of the case. She hoped Topham thought she knew more.

'Shot,' she added after a brief pause – just that little extra bit of info, held back for maximum effect, to help do the trick.

'Mm,' said Topham in a stonewall sort of way.

'Murder,' asked Miss Dimont, her voice rising now, 'suicide? Or was it just *an accident*?' The sarcasm was lost on the policeman, whose way of sweeping unwelcome deaths under the carpet was all too familiar.

'A shooting fatality,' came the stolid response. 'Woman of middle age, guest of the camp who had been here four days. That's it.'

It was enough, the rest of the drama would be in the writing. All Miss Dimont had to do now was find a telephone.

Herbert sensed the urgency of the moment and did not attempt a repetition of his earlier, most disagreeable, behaviour. Instead he took Miss Dimont, curls flying, on a roundabout trip through Knightsbridge, Regent Street and The Mall before arriving at a large well-lit building which clearly had been the officers' mess and now housed the camp's senior staff.

'. . . phone?' she said breathlessly to a vague-looking gentleman who poked his nose out of the door. 'Because… emergency!'

The man smiled non-committally and his eyes clouded in concentration. Finally the penny dropped, and he meandered down the hall to a cubbyhole under the stairs and within five minutes Miss Dimont had filed her story.

'Thank you so much,' she said to her host, whom she discovered sitting at a small cocktail bar in an adjoining lounge. 'I'm sorry, I didn't introduce myself. Judy Dimont, *Riviera Express*.'

'Oh,' said the man, 'you'll be here for the murder.'

It happens like that sometimes in journalism. You spend

all day knocking on doors and people won't even be able to remember which day of the week it is, let alone their mother's maiden name, then suddenly you bump into someone who knows everything.

This could be he.

'Yes,' Judy said encouragingly. It always pays to appear to know more than you do on such occasions and her conspiratorial nod, she thought, spoke volumes.

'Our first stiff,' the man said, laconically. 'Of course, there've been a few at the other camps, but this is a first for Ruggleswick. Drink?'

'Erm, that would be…'

'I usually have a gin about this time of day,' he said, though the bottom of his glass looked as though it had more recently contained an amber liquid. He was looking more than a little pink-cheeked but that could just have been the lighting.

'Lovely,' said Judy, who generally didn't trust Herbert to behave after a drink or two and usually refrained in case he took a wrong turning on the way home. 'She'd been here for less than a week.'

This reworking of Topham's bleak statement made it sound like she knew what she was talking about.

'Came on Sunday,' agreed the man, sloshing a prodigious amount into each glass.

'And should have been going home at the weekend.' It made it sound as though she had the whole story already. She hadn't a clue but it pushed the narrative to the next page.

'Never saw her. She arrived, parked her bags and disappeared. Of the four nights she was here, her bed was slept in only the once.'

Ah, thought Miss Dimont, the moral turpitude which everyone enjoys gossiping about back in town. Clearly the lady had a friend who…

'… must have had a friend who…' said the man, nodding in agreement. 'Only problem is there's no single blokes booked into the camp. I checked because the copper asked me to.'

'I'm sorry,' said Miss Dimont, suddenly collecting her thoughts, 'I don't know who you are.'

'Baggs. Under-manager. I served with Bobby Bunton in the Catering Corps. Actually not strictly true – he managed to escape with a gammy knee after six weeks while I was in for the duration, worse luck. But we remained mates and he gave me this job.' His hand shook slightly as he took another sip of gin; evidently war service in catering was not the breeze most assume it to be.

'How nice. I haven't met him but he sounds a wonderful man.'

'Mm,' said Mr Baggs.

'So who was this lady in… Curzon Street?' It never hurt to ask the extra question.

'Oh,' said Baggs, brightening, 'are you interviewing me?'

'Only if you want me to,' replied Miss Dimont. She could tell he was dying to talk.

'A strange one, that. Went by the name of Patsy Rouchos – South American by the sound of it. Interesting really. She had a cheap suitcase and cheap clothes but the rings she wore and her hair, her make-up, sort of said to me this wasn't her usual kind of place. Come down in the world, perhaps. Or found herself a boyfriend from a different walk of life and was chasing after him.'

'What did she look like?'

'Very strong-looking, almost like a bloke, but handsome. Nice manners but distant. Nothing in the way she spoke to tell where she came from, but a cut above our usual campers, I'd say.'

'So what actually happened?' This was the crucial question which had been on the tip of her tongue from the start, but long ago she had learned to choose her moment. Get them talking is the first rule in journalism, and don't ask awkward questions till you've managed to prise the door open a little.

'One shot, through the heart. Or the chest – never quite sure if the ladies have a heart on the same side as us mere males. Or at all, ha ha!'

Miss Dimont looked into her glass and let this pass.

'Elsie, the cleaner, found her late this afternoon, but I got a good look before the police arrived. She was sitting on the bed, completely dressed, full make-up, very well turned out. Almost as if she'd prepared herself for it.'

'No gun?'

'No gun.'

'Signs of forced entry?'

'Door was open.'

'Could have been a burglary?'

Mr Baggs' jovial tone suddenly deserted him. 'Here?' he said. '*Here?* Look Mrs, er,...'

'Miss Dimont.'

'People who come here have saved up all year. They haven't got pots of money. Not likely, miss, to have expensive possessions worth taking a life for.'

The reporter felt embarrassed – Baggs was right. Suddenly she saw Buntorama for what it was, a sunny haven for working people who prized their few moments in this beauteous corner of Devon just as much as the posh collar-and-tie lot next door at the Marine.

'My apologies, Mr Baggs, I'm just trying to find out why this should have happened. Who this Patsy Rouchos was. It's unusual, don't you agree?'

Baggs was quite a clever man, she could see, even if he had the weakness. And she wasn't quite sure about his eyes. He poured himself another slug of gin but seemed too concerned with getting the measure correct to remember to refill Judy's glass.

'I was on the desk when she came through the gate that first day,' he said. 'Arrived on foot – that struck me as odd, usually the campers come by bus from the station. Carried her suitcase as if she was used to somebody doing it for her. Smiled politely when most of the campers are worn out from the journey and looking for a bit of a squabble. Her clothes were ordinary, but she stood out.'

'That's why you remember her.'

'Look, we get hundreds of new faces every week, no reason to remember an individual over all the others. But she just struck me as a bit of a fish out of water.'

'Do people have to sign a register?'

'The Inspector asked me that. She gave her address as 11a Milcomb Street, London.'

'And did she take part in camp life?'

'What, you mean the sing-songs and the gym classes? No. I didn't see her at the talent show, but she did go to church the day she arrived – I saw her there when I was rounding up the collection.'

'Church?' said Miss Dimont, startled. 'I didn't know you had one of those!'

'The last hut in what we call Knightsbridge. Looks like all the others on the outside, but it's been done up all proper inside. A nice little earner.'

'Sorry?'

Mr Baggs tapped the side of his nose.

'The collection? You don't mean you…!'

'Helps keep the cost of the holiday down. Better than sending it all to some missionary in Africa to squander on beads and bells.'

Miss Dimont did not care for this and changed the subject. 'Was there anything else that struck you before the police got there? It just seems so odd she was sitting there, almost waiting for her killer to call.'

'Police said there was nothing in her handbag to give her a name. Purse and hankies, make-up, that sort of thing, but no driving licence or identity card. They did find a small photo album though. I expect that'll help them find her relatives.'

'If it had her relatives in it.'

'Ah yes.'

'Did you look inside it?'

'No.'

That appeared to have exhausted the extent of Mr Baggs' knowledge and there seemed little left to say. He eyed Judy's unfinished glass with interest as she gathered up her notebook and prepared her departure.

'Mr Bunton – where can I find him?'

'He'll be with Fluffles, I expect.'

Judy turned at the door. Writing that Page One lead on Fluffles being thrown out of the Marine Hotel seemed a lifetime ago. Was it really only an hour?

'I suppose you know about that incident in the Marine?'

Mr Baggs had got up, wandered over, and absently helped himself to her glass. The action appeared to ease a momentary stress in his features.

'Par for the course,' he said, serene again. 'Fluffles likes her presence to be felt.'

'What actually happened?' It's amazing how you can write a newspaper story and appear to know so much when actually all you've done is thrown some random facts together at top speed and crashed them out on your Remington.

'Well, you know Bobby and that stuffed-shirt Radipole are at loggerheads.'

'Evidently.'

'Yers, well, when we opened up the camp here last year, Bobby went out of his way to be nice to him – sent a bottle of champagne, wrote and offered him a free holiday, even. That man is such a snob he didn't even bother to answer.

'Now Bobby don't give up easily. So he started going into the Primrose Bar when he come down here, just to make friends like. That seemed to work OK – they didn't mind taking his money, and Bobby can splash it around when he wants.'

'Mr Radipole, I seem to remember, tried very hard to stop Buntorama opening.'

'Nothing he could do. He may run a stuck-up hotel with fancy customers and write-ups in all the glossy magazines, but Bobby has given more pleasure to more people than that stuffed-shirt could ever dream of. Eight million workers – *eight million* – spend all year waiting for their annual holiday, Miss Dimmum, and we give 'em the best they could wish for. Not just some lousy cocktail in a glass – we give 'em the works!'

'You were talking about Fluffles.'

'Ah yes,' said Baggs, nodding happily. 'She's a one!'

'I thought Mr Bunton was married.'

'Several times, ha ha! But this is one's different – she's gorgeous, don't you think?'

'I don't think I've…'

'You should, you should! Like a film-star, only she's never been in films. I guess she's just famous for being famous.'

'Or because of the famous people she's been photographed with.'

'Well, think how much nicer *they* look in the paper when they've got Fluffles by their side – I mean, that *figure*! Those *curves*! And every man loves a platinum blonde!'

I can certainly think of one, thought Miss D. And look what he did to poor Betty…

'Only sometimes she gets a little excitable after a drinkie or two. And she always wears those high high heels which she falls off.'

'I was told her clothes were torn.'

'Well,' said Baggs, enjoying himself now, 'she likes her dresses so tight she's been known to be sewn into 'em – oh, she's the one! – and you can guess what happened. A drink too many, a little arse-over-tip, her dress splits, she bashes her nose – hey presto!'

'So nobody manhandled her? Roughed her up? Kicked her out of the hotel?'

'Not likely, not her. Self-inflicted wounds, I'd say.'

Thank heavens that woman died in Curzon Street, she thought selfishly, and the Fluffles story got pulled as a result. The editor does hate a complaint.

THREE

'We're supposed to be in this *together*, Terry. Thanks so much!'

It was next morning and the dust kicked up by the spark-plug incident had yet to settle – or was it the heaven-raised eyes that had done the damage? Either way, the pair greeted each other with the bare minimum of civility.

Normally Friday was a day for writing up expenses, sending off letters to loved ones, planning holidays or phoning distant mothers, for the editor rarely put in an appearance until after lunch. But this was no ordinary Friday – the murder at Buntorama had changed everything.

'Better get over there,' said Judy. Terry looked unconvinced, he had plans to strip down his Leica and do something unfathomable with it.

'Bobby Bunton,' insisted Judy. 'The man Baggs told me he was coming down to visit the camp today, we should try for an interview. I want to get some words out of him before Fleet Street comes nosing around. Get to the bottom of him and Miss Janetti being chucked out of the Marine at the same time.'

'Yeah, but I've just got the new A-36 Infra-red filter.'

'Many congratulations, Terry.'

'That'll take me all morning to get sorted.'

'Not now it won't.'

'You don't know what it can do. Why, I guarantee…'

'For heaven's sake, Terry, toys for boys!'

Terry looked at her steadily. This was, after all, the reporter who nearly missed the scoop last night. The arch of his shoulder against the library counter inferred the superiority he felt this morning, but Miss Dimont knew her man.

She tossed out the bait.

'You always wanted to meet Fluffles, you told me so.'

This altered things. 'I could try out the Tri X!'

'Oh, do shut up about the Tri X,' said Judy. 'Let's just get over there.'

The Marine Hotel was all its rival, the Grand, was not. The Grand looked like a cake whipped up by an excitable Italian pastry-chef, smothered in icing and promising a sweet interior. Its colonnaded halls and fussy décor appealed to the traditionalist, and it was true that in its time it had attracted more than its share of the rich and famous.

After all, when the celebrated actor Gerald Hennessy decided to grace Temple Regis with his glorious presence, hadn't he chosen the Grand as his watering-hole of choice? It was a shame he had to get murdered before he could set foot in the place, but as a result of his unexpected demise the Grand's public profile took a significant upswing when his wife, Prudence Aubrey, came to stay instead, trailing behind her widow's weeds the assembled multitude of Fleet Street's finest.

And then, to top it all, it had emerged that Marion Lake – *the* Marion Lake! – turned out to be Hennessy's secret love-child. And she was staying at the Grand as well! No wonder the iced cake looked down on its smoother rival, the Marine.

The Marine didn't care. An art deco edifice of immensely elegant proportions, it looked like an ocean liner. Its rectilinear windows were painted a seafoam green, as snooty a colour as you will see anywhere, its vast entrance hall was dotted with sculpture which may or may not have been by Henry Moore. Its staff wore boxy clothes and angular haircuts which made them look as though they'd stepped out of a portrait by Tamara de Lempicka, and if you asked for a cocktail it came in a triangular glass.

Its clientele were urbane sophisticates and, not to put too fine a point on it, rich. They didn't mind paying 5/6d for a pot of tea when you could get the same in Lovely Mary's for 1/3d, and as for the price of a bottle of Moët & Chandon!

Despite the discarded front-page splash detailing the ejection of Bobby Bunton and his companion from the Primrose Bar, Judy guessed the King of Holiday Camps would be back for a drink sooner or later.

'The man has never allowed anybody to dictate anything to him, any time, ever,' she said to Terry. They were trundling in the Minor out past Ruggles Point, the stately piece of headland from which the Marine stared imperiously back at the lesser folk of Temple Regis.

''E's very short,' said Terry. 'A titch.'

'What difference does that make?' asked Judy, more interested in the flight of a cormorant, like a low-flying aircraft on a bombing-raid, dodging the wave-tops and searching for fish. The water was a dazzling shade of turquoise this morning, the sun crisping the edges of the wavelets and giving it sparkling life.

Terry, though far from immune to such beauty, was thinking ahead. 'She's much taller,' he said. 'You can tell.' Judy turned and glanced at his rugged profile hunched over the steering wheel: in his mind he was composing his picture.

'He stands, she sits,' they said simultaneously – the problem was not exactly a new one.

Finally, with this joint decision, harmony was restored. It was hateful when the competing priorities of reporter and photographer drove them apart, for they had long been a remarkable team. Terry turned and smiled at her, his gaze perhaps lingering just a shade too long as the sunlight caught her profile.

'Watch out!'

But Terry neatly swerved round the donkey being led down to the beach, and they safely turned the corner into the Marine's front drive.

As they entered the vast entrance lobby a wondrous sound came to them from somewhere deep in the heart of the building. A low, sweeping voice somersaulted over itself and performed some agile gymnastics before rising in a slow portamento up towards a thrillingly high note. Then silence.

'Moomie,' said Terry, enthusiastically.

'Mm?'

'That's the new singer you can hear – they've got her in for the season. Press call next Monday.'

'That'll be Betty with the notebook then,' snipped Miss Dimont. She didn't do showbiz.

'She's amazing – all the way from Chicago. Wonder how they got her? Normally she does West End only.'

'Everyone loves a summer season,' said Judy absently but her thoughts were on the story ahead as she strode purposefully towards the Primrose Bar. It was barely midday but there were already sounds of activity within.

Sure enough in a corner, shrouded by wafting palmettos, sat a short fat man with a pencil-thin moustache and shiny shoes. Next to him, leaning forward, sat one of the most notorious figures of the day, the platinum-haired Fluffles Janetti. Fluffles! Her rise to fame had been unstoppable, partly on account of her impossibly-proportioned figure, but also because of the number of men it had been draped around, from politicians to financiers to actors and now, the King of Holiday Camps, Bobby Bunton.

'Mr Bunton. I hope you don't mind,' started Miss Dimont. 'Judy Dimont, *Riviera Express*.'

'Get yourself a drink,' replied Bunton without glancing in her direction. He had eyes only for Fluffles.

'Thank you,' said Judy, used to such snubs. It was extraordinary how famous people treated the Press like serfs when their very fame depended on nice things being written about them.

'Miss Janetti?' pressed on Judy. The famous blonde locks bobbed and turned but did not wave, frozen in time as they were by a lavish dowsing of hairspray. Its noxious aroma just about won the battle with her perfume, thick and syrupy and speaking profoundly (so the manufacturers boasted) of yearning.

'Yes.' The voice, far from fluffy, was pure gravel. The eyes were hard and watchful. A tricky piece of work, thought Miss Dimont instantly; how can so many famous men have made fools of themselves over her?

Terry was already focusing on the answer to that question. With the unspoken compact which exists between professional photographers and famous women – of a certain sort – Miss Janetti straightened up and very slowly arched her back. For a moment her famous proportions seemed to acquire almost impossible dimensions.

'That's enough!' snapped Bunton, who hated the spotlight being turned away, even if only for a minute. ''Ere you are,' he said to Terry, straightening his tie-knot and brushing cigar-ash from his lapel. 'Local rag, is it?'

Several thoughts flew simultaneously into Miss Dimont's mind. First, why was it that reporters could be ignored, blackballed, shoved aside and generally made to feel like pariahs, while photographers were given a golden key into every rich man's drawing-room? Second, why was it that everyone referred so dismissively to the 'local rag'? Their Fleet Street equivalents were never known as 'national rags' yet they served the same purpose.

And third, Bobby Bunton had built-up heels on his shoes.

'Nice,' Terry was saying in the ingratiating tone reserved for the victims of his lens, 'now one of the two of you together. Fluffles, can you just go round behind Mr Bunton, lean over the chair, like…'

Fluffles obliged, her considerable expanse threatening to envelop the King's small head. It was an absurd pose, but one guaranteed to find space in the paper. Terry knew what he was doing all right.

Did Miss Dimont? She wasn't quite sure where to start. The small man in front of her – even at first glance – was arrogant, manipulative, a liar, a cheat, an adulterer, and a rapacious exploiter of the small incomes and high hopes of millions of working-class families.

'How lovely to meet you,' she said sweetly, and sat down.

'Everyone is so thrilled you chose Temple Regis for your holiday camp,' she lied.

'It has done wonders for the town.' Another stinker.

'All that silly opposition last year.' We nearly saw you off, but for the whopping great bribes you paid a couple of councillors.

'And look at the success of it all!' One dead body, unexplained.

'I want to write something nice about Buntorama,' not necessarily, 'so maybe we can clear up this shooting business with your help, Mr Bunton.'

For some reason the King chose not to look Miss Dimont in the eye. Instead he fixed his gaze on Fluffles.

'People get excitable when they go on holiday,' he sighed, as if having someone shot on the premises was a weekly event. 'They've been saving up all year, it's going to be the best fortnight they've ever had, then they come down here and don't know what to do with themselves. That's why I provide so many distractions – the funfair rides, the keep-fit classes, the dance competitions. These people work hard all year, they never have a moment to themselves.'

He took a swig from a heavy goblet. 'Suddenly their time's

their own and after a few days they go a bit nuts. Some take to drink, some go off with other men's wives, and a hell of a lot of them just sit down and have an out-and-out row. Men and women – the age-old story.'

He got up as if to signal the interview was over. A famous man, a rich man, he had generously given of his time and his wisdom to the local rag, and now it was time to get back to the business of making money.

Miss Dimont remained in her seat and elaborately turned over a page in her notebook, her signal to Bunton the interview was far from over. She could see him watching her out of the corner of his eye, even though he appeared to be summoning the wine-waiter.

'So that's what it was,' said Judy, 'just a domestic argument?'

'Yup.' Bunton was flapping his hand at some far-distant minion.

'Man shot his wife dead?'

'What else,' came the dead-ball reply. 'The clock ticks. He can't stand her a moment longer, it's driving him crazy. Clock chimes the quarter-hour and – bam! He's glad it's over.'

Fluffles was too busy with her powder-compact to pay attention to this shockingly arbitrary supposition. She stretched her lips and grinned in ghastly fashion back at her reflection.

'She wasn't married.'

The King spared his interlocutor a look. 'How do you know?'

'No wedding ring.'

'Proves nothing.'

'Had registered on her own,' insisted Judy. 'Had not been seen with anyone. Her neighbours in the chalets either side confirmed that.'

This was not strictly true, in fact it wasn't true at all, but when interviewees are nasty or unhelpful or contemptuous, it does no harm to give them a prod. Bobby Bunton wouldn't know what Patsy Rouchos' neighbours had seen or hadn't but he did know something, and Miss Dimont was determined to get it from him.

'She wasn't a holidaymaker in the ordinary sense of the word,' she said, half-guessing. 'Could she have been here on business? Or waiting for a boyfriend who didn't turn up – is that what it is?'

Bobby Bunton stared hard at her, as if for the first time. 'It. Really. Doesn't. Matter,' he said through yellow, oversized front teeth. 'She's. Dead. A. Tragedy. Our. Hearts. Go. Out. To. Her. Family.' The effort from issuing these words seemed to have exhausted him and he leaned against Fluffles' pillows. Fluffles looked at Miss Dimont with hatred.

'Ah,' said Judy, 'so you do know who her family is, and therefore presumably you know what she was doing here.'

She paused. 'You see, Mr Bunton, Temple Regis is thrilled to have Buntorama here but it would be a concern to townsfolk to think that people come down here with guns. And then shoot people with them. It's just not that kind of place, you know – we have a reputation as being one of the safest resorts in the West of England.

'So, you see, a simple explanation is so much better for them than a mystery. "MYSTERY DEATH" is an unsettling thing to read in a headline, whereas "DEATH AS A RESULT

OF A DOMESTIC DISPUTE" – or whatever it was that happened – they can swallow much more easily. Less unsettling. So I need your help.'

As Bunton took a swig from his glass Judy reflected, not for the first time, how difficult it was to worm information out of habitual liars. Yes, she had lied herself to wrest information out of the King, but those were white lies, little ones. Bunton's were of a much deeper hue.

Then again, she thought, looking at the pint-sized individual opposite, how much harder a reporter's life is than a photographer's. Terry just ambled in here, didn't introduce himself, got his camera out and took a picture which would occupy as much space in the paper as her words. Job over and done in a matter of seconds while she, Judy, had to beaver away at screwing information out of this tight-mouthed wide boy. It could take all morning.

It was why she loved the job so much. The challenge!

'I like to do my best for the local press,' said Bunton, who'd evidently undertaken a snap re-evaluation of the woman sitting opposite him. 'We rely on you, at each of our resorts, to maintain a connection between our business and the local folks. Even so, you won't want this in your paper.'

'What is it we won't want?'

'This woman, the dead woman, she was a prossie. A working girl. She was coming over here to the Marine from the camp, sitting in the bar here, waiting to pick someone up.'

'Oh.' Miss Dimont took off her glasses and polished them. Such things were not unknown, but here – in Temple Regis! A lady of the night!

'I saw her in here the night of the – disturbance,' said Bunton. 'You can always spot 'em a mile off.'

'Oh yes,' said Miss Dimont, recalling the scrapped front-page article from last night's paper. 'I wanted to ask you about that. Seems a little high-handed of the Marine to ask you to leave.'

'Kick me out, more like. But,' said the little man proprietorially, 'as you see, we're back here buying the Marine's drinks at their extortionate prices. Always ready to take our money!' He had more success this time when he beckoned the waiter. 'What's yours?'

'No thank you,' said Judy. 'So what exactly happened?'

Bunton threw his thumb at Fluffles' *embonpoint*. 'You tell her, darlin'.'

The courtesan straightened her hair and glanced down at her abundant heritage. 'Outrageous!' she squawked. 'You can still see the bruise if you look closely enough. They were outrageous!

'We'd been in here for a few hours, Bobs was doing business on the phone and then talking to someone at the bar, I got a bit bored. I *do* like a man to pay attention!' she said pointedly and flapped her hand at Bunton's belly. 'So yes, I'd had a glass or two and I decided to go over and break it up.'

'That'll do,' said Bunton, with a warning glance. 'What she's trying to say, Mrs, er…'

'Miss Dimont.'

'Yers. What she's trying to say is that as she got up she slipped on some liquid on the floor. I mean, they charge so much you'd think they'd have staff looking after you properly if you spill your drink – they should have wiped it up immediately.'

'Anyway, Bobs,' intervened Fluffles, not to be denied her moment, 'it was all your fault. If you hadn't spent so long chatting to that person I wouldn't...'

'What *actually* happened,' said Bunton, cutting in, 'Fluffles got up, slipped on the drink, went over. Someone came over and helped her up...'

'Split my dress,' chimed in Fluffles cheerily. '*That* got everybody's attention – including his!'

'Hardly needed splitting,' said Bobs, 'you was showing everything anyway.'

'It got him away from *her*, anyway,' she said to Miss Dimont. 'So then I told him off – look at me, I says, covered in drink, my face bashed in from falling over, one of my heels broken, my whatnots falling out – if you'd left her alone none of this would have happened.

'Then she came over, and I let her have it with my handbag. Bitch. She just stood there looking all superior, kind of looking down her nose at me, one heel on one heel off. I tell you, she'll remember that handbag!'

'Er, sorry, can we just go back a moment?' asked Judy. 'This lady we're talking about at the bar. The one your Bobs was talking to all evening.'

'Bitch!'

'Yes, I'm sure. But, she was the one from Buntorama, the, er... prossie?'

'Never seen a cheaper-looking tart.'

'She was the one who was shot?'

'A bullet never found a more deserving home,' said Fluffles magnificently, pushing out her chest as she wiggled out of the chair.

FOUR

They were in the Minor speeding back to the office, and Terry was humming to himself.

'Take that stupid look off your face. Not as if you haven't seen a woman before.'

Terry kept up the tuneless noise but now his countenance melted into idiot proportions.

'Fluffles,' he breathed to himself, breaking into a crooked smile. The pictures he'd got of the infamous beast were clearly going to be eye-poppers.

'Where d'you think she got that silly name?' said Miss Dimont peevishly. 'Fluffles Janetti?'

'Come over from Italy,' said Terry, who'd read up her clippings in the cuttings library before coming out. Actually he hadn't done much reading – mostly it was looking at other people's photographs of the minx to see how he could better the shot, for Terry was nothing if not competitive. Some of the caption information must have drizzled into his brain by a process of osmosis, though, the way that most photographers learned things.

'So that was an Italian accent she was talking with?'

'More sort of Birmingham,' said Terry after a moment's reflection.

'Just so,' said Judy, who'd done the same amount of homework but had concentrated on the words, not pictures. 'And I suppose you think that's her name, Fluffles?'

'"FLUFFLES JANETTI – THE FIRECRACKER FROM FIRENZE,"' Terry quoted a headline which had stuck in his brain.

'Janet Fludd – the bosom from Brum. Famous for the wide variety of bedsprings she has tested in her time.'

Terry turned to the reporter with a look of reproval. 'That's not like you,' he said, 'to be so snooty.'

'Oh, Terry, you're such a fool with women,' she replied, taking off her spectacles and giving them a good wipe.

'I'm a photographer,' he said, as if it were explanation enough.

Back at the office Terry parked the car and scuttled away to the darkroom to do what photographers do. Judy entered the newsroom and wandered down to her desk.

Even at a distance she could see that, as usual, it was covered with the typical avalanche of debris which forever tumbled from Betty Featherstone's workplace opposite – the discarded copy-paper, sheets of carbon, glue pots, cuttings, old notebooks and the copious contents of a handbag.

There was also a dead cat.

Still some yards away Miss Dimont stopped and stared in horror. 'Betty!' she called, '*Betty!*' She loved Mulligatawny more than life itself and could not bear the thought of poor sad corpses. And in the office, too!

The miscreant wandered over from Curse Corner where she'd been chatting to the chief sub-editor, John Ross: 'Hello, Judy, cup of tea? Your turn.'

'What on earth is this creature doing on my desk, Betty?'

Betty stepped forward and looked down in a vague sort of way. 'Oh sorry, the usual debris, Judy, I'll clear it away in a minute.'

'Not the debris,' seethed Miss Dimont through gritted teeth, 'the dead animal.'

Betty laughed, but it came out bitterly.

'I couldn't bear it,' she said. 'Try wearing that on your head, Judy, the weight of it, the sense of claustrophobia. I don't know how people do it.'

'Do what? Wear dead cats on their heads?'

Betty picked up the offending corpse and draped it over her hair. 'Honestly, d'you think it makes me look any better?' she said, and flung down the bedraggled wig with disdain.

'Gave me quite a shock,' said Judy, catching up.

'Not as much as the platinum blonde dye did me. Honestly, when I saw myself in the mirror after I'd done it – I wanted to kill myself. Look, there are still green patches!'

'You should take a tip or two from Fluffles Janetti,' said Judy, and described the frozen platinum helmet she'd recently witnessed adorning the nation's favourite courtesan.

Betty was transfixed: 'I must meet her!'

'No, Betty,' said Judy, 'I would fear for your moral compass if left alone in Fluffles' company for more than five minutes. You're better off with Dud Fensome.'

'Not any more. I sent him a wire.'

That makes a change, thought Judy. Normally it was Perce,

the telegram boy, who waylaid Betty to alert her to the latest failed venture in the marriage stakes. A wire could guarantee an end to the affair without need for the inevitable exchange of recrimination and disappointment. Betty didn't like getting them, but they were preferable to a confrontation – and always they brought with them the prospect of greener grass. She'd never had much luck in finding Mr Right.

Just then Miss D's eye was caught by the sight of a woman dressed head to foot in deepest purple, walking across the end of the newsroom as though leading a funeral procession. Her head was bowed, her movements slowed, as if weighted down by the sorrows of the world.

'Athene!' Judy called, but the mourner did not hear.

The reporter rose and nipped quickly over to the furthermost corner of the room, where there was a desk secreted behind a Chinese screen, draped with silk scarves and ostrich feathers. This was the lair of Athene Madrigale, the greatest astrologer the county of Devon had ever known, the person to whom every subscriber to the *Riviera Express* turned first on a Friday morning to discover what the week ahead held in store.

'Pisces: an event of great joy is about to occur – to you, or your loved ones!'

'Sagittarius: look around and see new things today! They are glorious!'

'Cancer: never forget how kind a friend can be to you. Do the same for them and you will be rewarded threefold!'

Athene was, in a county undoubtedly blessed with more sunlight hours than any other, the one ray of sunshine which never hid behind a cloud. People who read her words felt infinitely strengthened, while her page in the newspaper carried more weight than any sensational news from the town council or the magistrates' court.

Those few who were privileged to meet Athene – and there weren't many, for their day was her night – saw the astrologer as if through a glass prism infused by the colours of the rainbow. She might wear a lemon top, pink skirt, mauve trousers with plimsolls of differing hues on each foot. Her wispy grey-blonde hair would be pinned back by a blue paper rose, and the glasses suspended on the end of her nose radiated a delectable glow of Seville orange. She was remarkable.

Today, though, her clothing and countenance were the colour of death, and her voice sounded as though it came from beneath the grave.

'Athene, dear,' said Judy with concern as she sidled around the screen, 'what on earth is it?' She adored Miss Madrigale for all the good things she imparted, and would do anything to spare her even the slightest discomfort.

'It's impossible,' said Athene in a broken voice, 'I thought by doing this in daylight it might make things better, but it doesn't.' She picked up an ostrich feather and fanned the air as if to soothe it, or herself.

'What is it? Why are you dressed like this? Has someone died?'

'*I* have died, dearest. My soul has been thrown overboard.'

'What can you mean, Athene?'

'You were away last week. The editor came over to see me and said I had a wonderful new job, one that would bring me even more adoring letters.'

'Oh yes?' said Judy suspiciously, 'did he now.'

'I do so love an educated hand, don't you? Look at this lovely letter from Bedlington this morning – what a wonderful person this must be – and she takes the time to write! You should see the delightful things she…'

'Athene,' said Judy, 'what did Mr Rhys ask you to do?'

The astrologer laid her hands palm upwards on the desk and stared wretchedly into their empty wastes.

'He has made me an agony aunt. And now for the first time I understand the meaning of the phrase for, Judy, I am in *agony*. The sorrows of the world! All here! On this desk!'

'He didn't tell me he was going to do that.'

'He wanted it to be a secret. He said he had been keeping back letters from readers who had special problems. He said he knew that if anybody could solve their woes it would be me! But I can't, Judy, I can't!'

In an instant Miss Dimont had grasped the problem. Agony aunts dispense their wisdom with breezy disdain, exhibiting a dangerous lack of contact with human misery, safe in their comfy chair and with a loving husband in the kitchen making them a cup of tea. They are secure, emotionally and financially, and disengaged from the plights and problems of ordinary folk. It is these very qualities which allow them to issue lifesaving instructions to those pitched into life's ocean without a hope.

Athene possessed none of these attributes. Gentle, sensitive, the merest shadow of a being, she was too fragile to sustain a marriage, too unsure to issue instructions, too caring to dismiss the cries for help. Her great triumph was her personal joyousness, her upbeat message, told simply, carried from the stars, to every Sagittarian and Capricorn and Piscean in Temple Regis. To ask more of her was to ask too much.

'Don't worry, I'll talk to Mr Rhys,' said Judy decisively. 'I can't have you upset. And for heaven's sake, Athene, drop the purple – nobody died!'

'Only me, Judy. Only me.'

The editor was back from lunch and wrestling with his disgusting briar pipe. His wardrobe was particularly ambitious today – rumpled tweed suit, old brogues, grey shirt and woollen tie. The suit was ancient and its exposure to the elements over the years meant the trousers had shrunk and no longer reached his ankles.

Miss Dimont shut the door. An ominous sign, for Rudyard Rhys preferred it left open.

'Richard, a word about Athene.'

'Rr… rrr!' came from behind the briar pipe. The great man did not like to be reminded he'd been born with a less glamorous first name than the one he now bore.

'She can't do it. The agony column. It's making her unwell.'

'Rr… rrr.'

'Richard, why didn't you ask me? I could have told you she's not up to it – she's in despair.'

'We have to move with the times. Everybody's got an agony column these days. We have to keep up-to-date.'

Miss Dimont looked down at her wartime comrade and

wondered whether, in the thirteen years since peace was declared, he'd entertained a single 'up-to-date' thought.

'Well, Athene can't do it. You'll make her ill.'

'Somebody has to.'

'There's a crowded newsroom out there brimming with talent. Pick one of your reporters or sub-editors and let them have a go at the column. Any one of them would love to do it.'

Rhys looked out of the window at the circling gulls as if they were waiting for his corpse to be tossed on to the promenade.

'Betty then.'

Judy blinked. Rhys's capacity for making the wrong judgement knew no bounds.

'Well, she'd *love* it. But consider this – is a woman who's never been able to sustain a relationship with the opposite sex qualified to tell others how to sort out their love lives? Should someone who never knows what time of day it is tell people how to live a more orderly life? Is a person who wears a dead cat on her head qualified to hand out fashion advice?'

This last question briefly stirred the editor out of his post-prandial torpor. Friday lunch at the Con Club was the high point of the week, a moment when Rhys could sit as an equal with the city fathers while they discussed matters far too important ever to get an airing in next week's paper. The lunches were heavy and long.

'Rr… rrr, dead cat? What're you talking about?'

'A figure of speech, Richard.'

'You'd better write it this afternoon for next week's

paper. I'll get someone else on Monday.' His body language intimated there was not enough room in his spacious office for two.

'Another thing, Richard.'

'Rrrrrrrrrrrrrr.'

'The murder over at Buntorama. I doubt we'll be able to keep it to ourselves until next Thursday. You'd better prepare yourself for the usual Fleet Street hue and cry.'

Rhys looked desolate. If there was one thing he couldn't bear it was an invasion of the national press into Temple Regis – shouldering and bullying their way around, noisily filling up the Palm Court at the Grand Hotel, bribing people to tell half-truths which made his own printed version of events seem tame – inaccurate, even – when the versions delivered by the national and local press were compared by the readers.

'What have you got?'

'I saw Bobby Bunton this morning and that dreadful woman he tugs around – Fluffles.'

'The one who was thrown out of the Marine?'

'Yes. She's the latest sweetie-pie. That woman who was shot over at Buntorama was part of that incident. There was a dust-up in the Primrose Bar involving her and Bunton and Fluffles. Bunton spent the evening talking to her and ignoring Fluffles, and there was a fight. Then two days later, the woman was dead.'

'She was a holidaymaker at Buntorama but drinking in the Marine? That's unheard of. Two different classes of people altogether. The Marine doesn't allow Buntorama customers inside their doors if they can possibly avoid it.'

'She was a prostitute, according to Bunton.'

'A prostitute? And he spent the evening talking to her? We can't have that in the paper.'

'Why ever not?'

'Because,' said the editor wearily, 'first, he's an important employer in Temple Regis and we don't want the town thinking he's a wrong 'un. They may start questioning why he was allowed to start up the camp in the first place.'

'Ah, the *Express* backed those plans, of course.' The faintest drop of acid in her voice.

The editor ignored this. 'Second, I want no mention of prostitutes in Temple Regis. It will only encourage the others to flock back. Third, I'm really not keen on suggesting there's been a fight at the Marine, given its remarkable reputation, and fourth, I think the least said about the dead body in Buntorama the better. It'll soon go away.'

'Not if Fleet Street gets hold of it.'

Rudyard Rhys groaned horribly.

'Look, all I'm saying is – use the *soft pedal*, Miss Dimont.' He did not like to use her first name. 'The summer season's starting up, and there are those new attractions over in Paignton and Torquay. Heavens, people are even going to Totnes now – and *Salcombe*! Soon they'll have deserted Temple Regis altogether!'

If she could, Miss Dimont would have felt pity for her editor. But long experience told her this was a vacillating, fearful man who only made problems for himself by virtue of his nervousness. If there was an important decision to make between two choices, he'd always pick the wrong one.

'Here's the story, Richard. The Marine Hotel knowingly allows a prostitute to ply her trade in their bar. It allows its business rival, heaven knows why, to sit drinking in the same bar until his piece of stuff topples off her high heels and exposes herself to the world, then it kicks them both out.'

'Bunton's not a rival,' growled Rhys. 'Different ends of the business – carriage-trade versus knotted handkerchief brigade.'

'Precisely my point,' said Miss Dimont crisply. 'And do you think that when Fleet Steet gets down here that particular penny isn't going to drop? The battle between upstairs and downstairs? Class war on the coast?

'This is only Buntorama's second season. But already you can see the resentment and rivalry building up between these two establishments – side-by-side and away from the centre of town.

'Bobby Bunton's a maverick, and when it suits him he'll turn his guns on the Marine – accuse them of being snobs. Then we'll have an all-out battle in Temple Regis, and just when the local economy was picking up nicely.'

The editor picked up a box of matches and turned it over in his hand. The room smelt of old dogs, though it was probably his overcoat which hung on the coat-rack winter and summer. The sun's heat was coming through the window and Miss Dimont realised why in general it was better to leave the door open.

'Don't think I hadn't considered this,' he said weightily. 'It was a mistake letting Bobby Bunton into town and I'll be frank – but this must go no further – I saw Hugh Radipole at lunch today. He warned there were likely to be severe repercussions if Bunton steps out of line.

'He was telling me something of Bunton's past – d'you know he carries a cut-throat razor in his top pocket all the time? – and unless Bunton calms down and stays out of the Marine there'll be some howitzer-fire going over the fence. Radipole's not a man to take things lying down.'

'Good Lord, Richard,' said Judy happily, 'I think you've got yourself a scoop there!'

FIVE

Auriol Hedley sat waiting for her friend on the back deck of the *Princess Evening Tide*, an old but beautifully turned-out yacht whose sheets were white, whose brass was polished, and whose prow was sharply elegant.

Evening Tide occupied a space against the harbour wall from where Auriol could see all the way down the estuary to its mouth, while over her shoulder she could keep an eye on her place of business, the Seagull Café. It was her habit in summer to come down here for a gin and tonic, usually in the company of her dear friend, Judy Dimont, on a sunny evening.

'She's late,' said Auriol to the elegant gentleman sitting across the deck, shoes twinkling in the sunlight. His eyes were half-shut.

'Good Lord!' said the old boy, stirring from a half-slumber. It was hot. 'That the time?'

'Are you going to say something to her before you go?'

'Not if she doesn't hurry up. I've that train to catch.'

'It's been going on too long, Arthur, this campaign to keep her mother at arm's length. If Madame Dimont finally carries out her threat and pays a visit, we're all in the soup.'

'Not me,' said Arthur, chuckling. 'I'm off!'

Just then the sputtering and clacking which usually proclaimed the arrival of Herbert pierced the early evening air. Meandering gulls on their evening stroll scattered to make way for man and machine, lifting off into the gathering haze. Miss Dimont clambered aboard.

'Ginger beer, no ice,' said Auriol, shuddering as she proffered the customary glass. 'What kept you?'

'Tell you later,' replied Judy, offering a cheek to the old boy. 'Hello, Arthur, what a surprise, how lovely!'

'Just passing,' said her uncle lightly, though this could not conceivably be true. 'Auriol's gin fizzes – what a miracle!'

'Your glass is empty.'

'Just going.'

'But I've only just got here!'

'Taking the Pullman to London. Been here all afternoon. Hoped I'd see more of you before I went. Must dash, though.'

He was old but still had a schoolboy bounce about him. 'I say, Huguette, will you come up to town and have lunch with me at the club? Your mother's coming. You could help out.'

'Bit busy at the moment,' said Judy, guardedly. 'Been a murder over at Buntorama.'

At the mention of the word 'murder', the old man's face lengthened in a mixture of disbelief and resignation. There was a pause. 'I do not know,' he said, slowly, 'even after all these years I cannot *understand*, what brings one man to want to do away with another.'

Miss Dimont was hoping he might go on – he usually had something very useful to say after all those years of experience – but he was eager to disembark.

'Train to catch,' he said. 'If you won't come and have lunch with Grace and me, you know she'll come down here. I thought you wanted to avoid that.'

'When she comes, uncle, she straightens up my house. Goes through my drawers. Reads my correspondence. Looks down her nose at the neighbours. Dislikes intensely what I do for a living. But still she comes and sits in the *Express* front hall every lunchtime expecting to be taken out. She absolutely despises Terry and…'

'You often have a word or two to say about Terry yourself,' chipped in Auriol. 'And not always complimentary, Hugue.'

'She's your mother,' sighed the old man patiently. 'Be kind, Huguette.'

'If only she could be kind to me!'

All three stepped onto the quayside and Auriol wandered back to the café, leaving uncle and niece together by the waiting taxi.

'Auriol sent for you, Arthur.'

'I say, that sounds a bit accusatory!'

'To do her dirty work for her. She's been on at me for months to have Maman come and stay.'

'Wouldn't it be better? Get it over and done with?'

Miss Dimont shook her curls impatiently. 'She's your sister, uncle, can't you do something about it?'

'You know how odd she is. Running away to the Continent all those years ago, insisting even after your father died she should still be addressed as Madame Dimont. Talking in that affected Frenchified way.'

'Still you named your daughter after her.'

'She made me,' said the old boy with a conspiratorial

smile – they were in this together. 'Come to the Club. Get me out of a hole.'

'Oh – all right then.'

'Don't sound so dashed. It'll save her coming down here and rifling through your things.'

They embraced, and the taxi sped away up Bedlington hill towards the station. The reporter walked slowly back to the Seagull Café to rejoin her friend.

'A shame you missed him,' said Auriol, cracking eggs into a bowl. 'He was on wonderful form, telling me lots of things about the old days. Really, some of his adventures!'

'Permanent schoolboy,' said Judy.

'Your mother has him under her thumb.'

'Did you get him to come all the way down here just to tell me I must have Maman to stay? That seems a bit steep.'

'He was passing through on his way from Dartmouth. Bit of a reunion, by the sound of it.'

Auriol turned to face her friend. She was still gloriously attractive, thought Miss Dimont, almost unchanged since their days in the underground corridors of the Admiralty building all those years ago. Everyone from able seaman to Admiral of the Fleet had been stunned by Auriol's dark hair, coal-black eyes, perfect deportment and beautiful figure. Moreover, in a branch of the armed services almost completely peopled by men, she had the commanding presence to issue orders which they were happy to obey.

More than that, Auriol was the perfect sounding board – you could throw facts at her and she would size them up, turn them round, look at them upside-down and deliver them back to you in such an orderly fashion they were almost unrecognisable. Often when she was stuck with a problem, Miss Dimont would hand a bundle of information over to her friend and watch her go through it like a costermonger feeling up the apples and putting the best ones at the front of the stall.

'. . . so you see,' Miss Dimont was saying, 'Bobby, Fluffles, then this woman Rouchos.'

'That name sounds familiar.'

'Does it?' She was slicing up tomatoes to go in the omelette, their sharp sweet odour pricking her nostrils.

'Can't think why. Keep going, it'll come to me.'

'I just feel in my bones there's something very odd about this set-up. Why in the first place did Hugh Radipole allow Bobby Bunton to loll about in the Marine making trouble when, really, his presence was a pain in the proverbial?'

'His money is as good as anyone else's. And it sounds like that piece of stuff of his is a thirsty one.'

'And how! But the point is these two men were at each other's throats. There's Radipole on the one hand, urbane and sophisticated, who's had that end of the beach all to himself ever since he arrived here years ago. Builds up a reputation for his hotel as a rich man's hideaway – I mean, he doesn't even want the *Express* in there to publicise the place, I always get a nasty look when I go in. He's snooty, his guests are snooty!

'Then,' said Judy, laying out the knives and forks and freshly laundered napkins, 'there's the King of the Holiday Camps.' She uttered the words satirically. 'He's noisy, he's brash, he lacks polish and wears horrible clothes. And the way he talks!'

'Never had you for a snob, Hugue.'

'I don't mean that – he talks like a spiv, always slightly threatening in the way he says things. Smarmy one minute, would take a cut-throat razor to you the next. And that frightful woman!'

'The fancy piece? What did you call her – the courtesan?'

'I was being polite. She's the worst kind of advert for our gender you could ever imagine.'

'Men seem to like her,' said Auriol evenly, serving on to the plates, 'a lot. By that I mean, a lot of men like her a *lot*.'

'What I feel is that there's something toxic about her – you could see that men might kill over her, however worthless she may be. Goodness, even Terry…!'

Auriol often heard complaints about Terry. Judy didn't always mean what she said.

'What interests me is this other woman, Rouchos,' said Auriol, switching tack. 'Clearly not the kind of person you'd normally find in a Buntorama. Disguised herself with her choice of clothes, but the jewellery gave her away, didn't it? What the devil was she doing there? And more importantly, where was she when she wasn't in the camp?'

Miss Dimont thought about this. 'Bunton said she was a prostitute, but I don't believe it. The clothes she left behind, the make-up, the perfume – all wrong for a woman in that line of business.'

Auriol arched an eyebrow. 'And you'd know?'

'I would *assume*,' added Judy quickly. 'OK, she's sitting on her bed fully dressed, she might have been waiting for a client, but when you think about it she hadn't been seen around the place all week so she wasn't using the chalet as a place of work. Why would she suddenly change tack?'

'According to what you say, Bunton claimed she was going to the Marine Hotel to grab a client or two. Maybe she had a room there.'

'What, a room in Buntorama and one in the Marine? Why on earth would she do that?'

'I'd check,' said Auriol with that sliver of authority which once had junior naval officers scurrying to make her a pot of tea, no sugar, two digestives.

'I will. Now what about *Does the Team Think?* – it must almost be time.'

Auriol switched on the radio and they sat with a glass of wine listening to silly jokes from the mouths of Jimmy Edwards, Ted Ray and Arthur Askey, a world away from the sinister doings in Ruggleswick. Both were listening, both were laughing, but both were thinking at the same time.

However, as a rat-tat of audience applause signalled the end of the show, the conversation did not immediately return to murder but to another kind of death. On the wall above the bakelite wireless hung the same photograph each woman displayed in her home, a black-and-white portrait of a man they both had loved – Auriol as a sister, Miss Dimont as his fiancée.

'Not his kind of humour,' said Auriol, switching off the radio. 'Coffee?'

'I think he'd have enjoyed *The Goon Show* more.'

'Yes, madcap. Like Johnny Ramensky.'

It was always painful steering the conversation round to Eric Hedley, almost like picking at a scab, but most times they did. Both bitterly felt his loss, his heroic sacrifice in the last days of war when really he could have been spared.

Auriol and Judy were friends, but Eric was what made their friendship eternal.

'Johnny was a terror.'

'It's why Eric adored him so much. And, Hugue, you have to admit, the neatest safe-cracker you ever came across.'

'To be honest,' said Miss Dimont, 'I never knew that many men with a passion for gelignite.'

Back in the office Betty Featherstone was making up for time off prompted by the hair debacle. She was doing the early pages, her desk overflowing with scraps of paper sent in by correspondents with a greater passion for the minutiae of village life than Betty could ever muster.

But her mind was on the colossal sense of entitlement Dud Fensome seemed to have. What Dud wanted, Dud got. The green patches among the platinum were, after all, just the tip of the iceberg when it came to his demands.

She dithered for half-an-hour over the Ashburton Sheep Sale market report, with its complex, interwoven, arcane and utterly boring detail on greyface ewes, whiteface ewes, clun ewes, kerrys, hoggets, wether lambs and registered greyface lambs. To turn into readable prose the pencilled notes scribbled on the back of a sale bill – was that the poor sheep's last drop of blood tainting the dispatch? – required more concentration than she could cope with at the end of a long day. She lifted the paper to one side but it stuck to her fingers, the blood not quite dry.

'Ew!' Betty squeaked, as John Ross strolled by.

'Ay, lassie,' growled the Glaswegian. 'Ewes indeed – they got you on the early pages, eh? Try to *get it right this week*.'

‘I simply haven’t the energy,’ said Betty, thinking about cycling home to have another go at her hair.

The chief sub-editor leaned over and started shuffling through the confetti on her desk.

‘Good one here,’ he grunted, voice tinged with venom. ‘Women’s Institute announcing their new competition – “A SALAD FOR ONE.”

‘And look! The winner of last week’s lampshade-making contest! Gloooorious…’ he added bitterly. Once he’d been a football reporter on a Fleet Street newspaper, now he was reduced to inventing headlines for the pitiful scraps of information sent in from the far-flung extremities of the newspaper’s circulation area. Dispatches from places where reporters never trod.

‘Och!’ he said, shaking his ugly head at a missive written in block capitals, ‘WAR DECLARED ON THE RABBIT POPULATION.’

‘And this! “DRAMATIC RESCUE ON MUDFORD CLIFFS”,’ he intoned, adding with heavy irony, ‘“NOT MANY DEAD”.’

One more caught his jaded eye. ‘That old chestnut about no public lavs down at Bedlington. Again. Oh mother Mary, save me now!’

Once upon a time Ross would be consoling himself in the pub by this hour, but since he was sworn off the booze these days he took it out on anybody left in the office after opening-time.

‘You just don’t get the quality of local corr any more,’ he said, churning hopelessly through the paper mountain on Betty’s desk as if panning for gold. ‘The stupidity of the village correspondents. You ask them to give you a story and all they can come up with is – oh, *Christ*!'

Betty abruptly put down the hand-mirror. She'd given up typing and was inspecting her green and platinum stripes. 'What is it, Mr Ross?'

'Girrlie, girrlie, oh girrlie…' he whispered as if he had struck the mother lode, 'ye canna believe… look at this week's Umbrella!'

This was not an invitation to step out into the rain but to scrutinise the cage-droppings of a chum of the editor, a man who once made a half-funny speech at Rotary and was immediately snapped up to do a weekly column.

This half-wit called his column 'Between Ourselves' and signed himself 'Umbrella Man'. Nobody knew why.

'What's it about?' said Betty listlessly.

'Dog bowls in pubs,' replied Ross, his voice hoarser than an undertaker's.

'Well, look,' said Betty, trying to break the mood. 'Just think, next week I'm off to meet Moomie. We'll get something wonderful out of that!'

The chief sub looked at her suspiciously. 'Mommie?'

'No, Moomie – Moomie Etta-Shaw, the jazz singer. She's doing the summer season at the Marine.'

'Ay,' said Ross. 'I know who you mean now. She and Alma Cogan used to work together at the Blue Lagoon in Soho.'

'Didn't she start out as a cloakroom attendant?' asked Betty, who'd been doing her homework.

'Nah,' said Ross caustically, walking away. 'She only took people's coats.'

If this was supposed to be a joke it went over Betty's

head and she returned to the fuss over the building of a bus shelter in Exbridge – nobody wanted it outside their house yet everyone agreed it was vital in winter to stop villagers being splashed by passing traffic. Betty's fingers were flying, the copy-paper was emerging from the top of her machine, but you couldn't call it writing.

'Time for a quick one,' said Terry, who'd emerged from the darkroom and was looking for a drinking partner. Betty touched her hair – she wouldn't be seen dead in the Fort or the Jawbones in her present state.

Unless, of course, she put the dead cat on her head again.

'Won't be a moment,' she said, nippily pushing her typewriter away.

SIX

Frank Topham sat solidly in his chair at the head of the table while his detectives hunched over their notes, waiting uneasily for the inquisition ahead.

'So,' said the Inspector without the slightest hint of hope in his voice, 'what have we got?'

One of the grey-faced assistants cleared his throat. 'I checked on Bunton's movements at the time of the shooting and it couldn't have been him – he was at the Buntorama in Clacton, just like he said.'

'Well, you had to ask. But he's hardly likely to go round shooting his own customers, is he? Not good for business.'

'You never know, sir.'

'His piece of Fluff?'

The man managed a weary smile. 'She was with him when the woman was shot, she's always with him – she won't let him out of her sight. She's going to have that man for breakfast, lunch and dinner.'

'Bunton's under the impression she's just his latest piece of stuff,' said the other copper. 'He has no idea that she's his next wife who'll take him for every last farthing before she spits him out.'

'Splits him out,' said the first, referring to the regrettable incident in the Primrose Bar. They both laughed, in a tired sort of way.

Topham was not so amused. 'The victim? What new information do we have?'

'Address in Chelsea she gave to the reception people at Buntorama turned out to be false. It's a chemist's shop.'

'How did she pay?'

'Cash, they prefer it that way in holiday camps.'

'I daresay the Inland Revenue might have something to say about that,' said Topham, a decent man who believed in people paying their taxes. It would be a useful bargaining chip when trying to get more information out of the clam-like Bunton.

'And you didn't get any more from any of the punters over at the holiday camp?'

'One or two of them said they saw her. Posh, is what most of them say, in spite of her cheap clothes – the way she smiled but said nothing. Polite but condescending in that us-and-them sort of way.'

'But are you saying she spoke to nobody at Buntorama? Didn't go to the dances, sit in the bar? Wasn't she missed at mealtimes?'

'She was single so she was put on the long table where all the odds and sods end up. Everybody moves around – it's not like being given a table for four in a hotel or on a liner where you know everybody's business by the end of the fish course. She was on what you might call a moveable feast.'

If that was a joke it fell flat.

'So,' said Topham, 'she was noticeable enough to be noticed, as it were, but nobody's missed her.'

'One woman said she didn't smell right.'

'And you checked back on her possessions?'

'You saw yourself, sir, there was almost nothing in her suitcase. Cheap clothes, newly bought. Old suitcase. Two pairs of shoes in the wardrobe, make-up bag but no handbag. Clothes she was wearing when she was killed were the same make as the ones in the suitcase, no clues whatsoever. She was wearing expensive earrings, very yellow gold, no hallmark. Gold bracelet, also no hallmark. Very odd, that. Wedding ring on her third finger, right hand – old.'

'How old?'

'Older than her. Could have been her mother's. Could've been a hand-me-down from a marriage which failed.'

'She could be French,' hazarded the other detective, but this fell on stony ground. He didn't have a clue really.

'No question, then,' said Topham with conviction. 'A mystery woman with expensive jewellery and cheap clothes. If that isn't a disguise I'm a Chinaman's uncle.'

Not having heard of any oriental relations in the Topham tribe, his men nodded in affirmation.

'What next, sir?'

'I have absolutely no idea,' said the Detective Inspector with finality, gathering his papers and standing up. 'You just carry on.'

Dear Hermione,

I am known among my friends for having a generous nature but now I feel the milk of human kindness has drained away and may never return. Please help.

Every year I am fortunate enough to have a bumper crop of strawberries. Last year I gave some to my best friend to make jam. She has now won First Prize for her strawberry jam at the Mothers' Union and has been boasting to everyone how clever she is, without once mentioning that it was my strawberries that done it.

She has been my friend for years but now I feel I hate her. What can I do?

Miss Dimont looked again at the letter, took off her glasses, polished them, and replaced them on her deliciously curved nose. After a pause she got up to make a cup of tea. The letter was waiting when she got back, looking up pleadingly and urgently demanding Hermione's adjudication. Miss Dimont stared at her Remington Quiet-Riter for quite some time then decided its ribbon needed changing.

A sub-editor wandered by and for a good ten minutes they discussed the latest film starring Dirk Bogarde at the Picturedrome. It turned out neither had seen it, but both had heard good reports.

The letter remained. There was, in fact, no answer to the agonising dilemma it presented and yet the heartfelt plea to Hermione cried out for a response, and Miss Dimont's sense of duty told her she must answer, truthfully, and to the best of her ability.

She pushed the letter to one side and picked up another.

Dear Hermione,

I am in tears as I write this. I feel my son has been poisoned against me by my daughter-in-law and no longer wishes to see me. I am seventy next birthday and a widow.

I fail to understand why things should be this way when I have always gone out of my way to help my daughter-in-law with her children. I am always on hand to give good advice, even going to the trouble of writing her long letters advising her of better ways of managing things. I pop in at odd times to give the children a surprise – also it gives me a chance to help with the cleaning, going through the cupboards and so on.

I feel for some reason this annoys her, though why I can't…

Miss Dimont looked up at the big clock down the other end of the newsroom. Almost lunchtime!

Dear Hermione,

I have been happily married for five years, but recently my husband has been suggesting that we…

Instinctively Miss Dimont told herself to read no further. Some problems are best left unexplored, certainly in a family newspaper like the *Riviera Express*, and without further ado she let the letter float gently into the wicker wastepaper basket by her ankle.

Just then she spotted the ethereal figure of Athene Madrigale flitting through a door and she beckoned her over. Devon's most celebrated astrologer negotiated her way over to Judy's desk and sat down.

'Yes, dear?'

'I see what you mean,' said Judy.

'What's that?'

'This wretched agony column, Athene. Since I got you off writing it, I've become Hermione.'

Athene blushed. 'I never meant for that to happen, dear.'

You might have predicted it if you'd looked in your crystal ball, thought Judy unkindly, but aloud she said, 'It's impossible to answer these cries for help, isn't it? Impossible!'

'They made me quite upset,' said Athene. 'I had to go and lie down. There was one from a happily married woman whose husband had been suggesting…'

'Yes, I threw that one in the bin. But Athene, how tangled people's lives become! A woman who interferes in her daughter-in-law's child-rearing, two old friends falling out over a pot of jam…'

'You see why I couldn't do it,' said Athene. She was plaiting her hair into the bright blue paper rose which was her favourite adornment.

'Well, I can't do it either,' said Judy. 'And anyway what a rotten idea to have an agony column in the first place.'

'Mr Rhys. His idea. Only a heartless man could wish to expose other people's misery to the world.'

'It's called journalism, Athene,' sighed Miss Dimont. 'It's called journalism.'

SEVEN

It was never quite the same, doing a job with Betty. She was efficient, she asked the right questions, she had a good shorthand note and was usually charming enough to winkle that extra cup of tea out of the grieving widow, football pools winner, or someone whose young Einstein had just won a place at university.

Terry liked her, but that was it – she did not infuriate him like Judy did. She never told an interviewee what to think, which Judy sometimes did. She didn't make a nuisance of herself by challenging heavy-handed authority, which Judy *always* did.

She had a lovely smile but often it was spoilt by the wrong choice of lipstick, and the haphazard way it was applied at her desk without the benefit of a mirror did her no favours. And then her clothes! Lime green seemed to be the favourite of the moment, but teaming it with royal blue or pink, as she did, verged on the downright reckless.

Terry snatched a glimpse of her as they drove in the Minor out to the Marine Hotel, Betty looking out at the grey listless sands stretching for miles to the rainy horizon. Temple

Regis boasted the most sunshine hours anywhere in Britain, but just a mile or two down the road at Ruggleswick, there seemed to be a micro-climate which favoured grey over blue, wind over stillness, stratified clouds over a clear blue sky.

To the well-heeled patrons of the Marine, this was a bonus – their view of the sands and sea remained largely uncluttered by the human form. For the inmates of Buntorama it was proof, yet again, that British holidays were a washout. They dreamed instead of joining the exodus to Benidorm where they could drink cheap brandy and get a nice all-over sunburn.

'This makes a change,' Betty said half-heartedly, but she was not her usual chatty self. Terry didn't interest himself in her love life, but she'd brought him up to speed on the matter of Dud Fensome and his thing for platinum.

This morning she was wearing a silk scarf on her head, so it was difficult to see what had been achieved over the weekend by way of damage-control but Terry, with his photographer's instinct for the ways of women, guessed it had probably not been a great success. At least she wasn't wearing the ruddy cat.

'She's got an amazing voice,' Terry was saying. 'You could hear it all the way down in the lobby when we went to see Bobby Bunton last week.'

Betty wasn't listening. Instead she said, 'I wanted to ask her about – well, she's quite stout, isn't she? I thought our lady readers would be interested in what she wore, you know, underneath – to keep it all under control.'

Terry looked at her disbelievingly. 'Woman's angle, is it? Crikey, Betty, Moomie Etta-Shaw is one of the greatest jazz singers this country has ever been lucky enough to host.' He sounded a bit like the advertising handout he'd glanced at before leaving the office. 'She's had hit records! Been on the *Billy Cotton Band Show*! You must have heard her singing "Volare" on the radio!

'Stout! You don't know the meaning of the word!'

Betty did. Dud had used it quite recently.

'I prefer a dance band myself,' she said, quickly changing the subject, but Terry was ahead of her. Maybe she *had* put on a little weight.

'Almost there,' he said. 'Pictures first, Betty, then you can have as long as you like with her.'

Here was the perennial struggle between snappers and scribblers, as to who went first. Terry usually got his way, but with celebrity set-ups like this one he could take up to half an hour getting what he wanted, leaving little time for the reporter to get to grips with her subject. It was often a point of dispute between Terry and Judy, but Betty was more flexible and didn't mind much who did what – it was just a relief to be out of the office. And the great thing was that if it was a picture story, she could always get a ride in the photographer's car rather than catch the bus, which is what reporters were supposed to do.

Again this was something which could elicit a peppery remark or two from Miss Dimont, but Betty was more pliable. The photographer looked at her once more and realised that, whatever else happened over the weekend, she'd been let down again.

'Good weekend?' he asked, hoping to draw her out.

'We're here,' sighed Betty with just a touch of tragedy coating her voice. 'Don't take too long!'

It probably didn't improve things that Moomie was singing 'Lover Come Back To Me' as they entered the ballroom. Wrapped in a figure-hugging silk dress, she looked ready to entertain a thousand fans at the London Palladium, not rehearse a one-hour set for her debut tonight. Terry thrilled at the colour combination of her dark brown skin, dazzling white teeth and midnight blue wrapping – even though his newspaper still only printed in black and white.

'Wonderful,' he breathed, reaching into his bag for his Leica. Just for a moment he shared Betty's curiosity about the strength of Moomie's underpinnings – her figure was as huge as her voice – but at that moment the song finished and Betty stepped forward to make the introductions.

'You must know,' said Moomie with a serene smile and a wave of her arm, 'these lovely musicians it is my privilege to work with. Mike Manifold on guitar, Cornish Pete on bass, Sticks Karanikis, drums.'

The trio nodded, absently. Professional musicians rarely look up above their score-sheets and then only to talk to each other – there wasn't any point in wasting time getting to know them.

'Gorgeous, Moomie,' said Terry, seizing the initiative, 'you put a special dress on for me! You look a million dollars! Harrods, is it?'

He said it ''Arrods'.

'C&A, darling. Cost me five guineas.'

'Gorgeous,' burbled Terry. You couldn't tell whether he meant it, or whether it was the standard snapper-patter to create an early intimacy between lensman and subject. Betty had heard it a million times before and wandered off in search of a cup of coffee.

Terry launched into his routine – flattering, cajoling, instructing, begging – and Moomie happily went along with it, her queen-size laugh and roistering personality turning the event into a lively celebration.

'You're a bit gorgeous yourself, Terry,' she said, pouting her lips and leaning forward.

'Fantastic!' panted Terry, as he threw himself onto his back on the dance-floor to get the up-shot.

'Fabulous! Can you spare a couple of tickets for tonight, Moomie?'

'Have a dozen, darling!' she laughed, batting her eyelids. And so the courtly ritual continued for the next twenty minutes. The pair may never meet again, but for this short span they had been lovers in all but fact. Such is the compact between photographer and celebrity – a secret contract which no reporter could ever be part of, since photographers flattered and wooed while the scribblers just asked damned awkward questions.

'Contessa,' snapped Moomie in answer to Betty's first question. 'Strongest support in the business. I'll give you the name of my fitter if you want.'

Betty blushed – had her intention been quite so transparent? – and stumbled on into the interview. Meanwhile Terry wandered over to the musicians who were lighting cigarettes and drinking cups of tea.

'One word from me and she does what she likes,' said Mike Manifold, the band leader, nodding at Moomie.

'We don't normally do requests, unless we're asked,' added Cornish Pete.

'You must understand – our music is far better than it sounds,' said Karanikis.

Terry grasped that these were musicians' jokes, a polite way of telling him to shove off. The trio really only wanted to sit there moaning at each other – about the management, the accommodation, the number of encores they were expected to play before going into overtime, and the next recording session. So he dutifully strolled off, back out to the lavish entrance hall, with its wide sweeping staircase and important-looking sculpture. He paused for a moment, then went over to the receptionist.

'Will you tell the lady reporter I'll be back in a little while? She'll be half an hour or more with the band. I won't be long.'

He loaded his camera bag into the boot and drove off through the gates. It took no more than two minutes to arrive at the entrance to Buntorama where he left the Minor in the car park, and strolled away without any apparent purpose. Over in the distance he could hear the funfair going at full tilt, the screams from the helter-skelter cutting through the still morning air.

Terry had a pocket camera with him – he rarely went anywhere without it – and as if to justify his presence in the camp took a handful of snaps. There were a few pretty girls, a couple of irritable pensioners, and a lively group of teenagers. A man and woman got very cross and swiftly parted when he levelled the camera at them – moral trappitude, thought Terry, and moved on.

Soon he reached the management block and, led by instinct, he walked up the steps. There in a corner sat Bobby Bunton in his braces, and Bert Baggs with a tragic look on his face. He thought he'd wander over and have a word with the King, but His Majesty was too busy holding court. So

Terry sat down behind a potted fern and waited his moment, watching the dust particles slide through the bright sunlight in their gradual descent to earth. It would take an f1 at 1/24, he calculated, to capture that.

'. . . then he said to me, "She died on your property, how's that going to look?"' This was Bunton's voice, though since sitting down Terry could no longer see the two men.

'What we going to do, boss?'

'It's blackmail. Blackmail! And all because I...'

'It wasn't you, boss,' came Baggs' sycophantic tones, 'it was 'er.'

'Hardly matters now. This has never, ever, happened before. And just as I've got the Archbishop of York to come and do the Sunday service!'

''E won't know, boss. Not as if this is going to end up in the newspapers.'

'But it is, Bert, it is! We've only had the local rag round so far, but in another twenty-four hours the whole of Fleet Street will be here – soaking up our hospitality, writing innuendoes, behaving in that rotten two-faced way they do.'

'You'll win 'em round, you always do. Don't forget we've had dead 'uns before,' came Baggs' reply. 'Remember that couple up in Essex...'

'That was different! They shouldn't have tried that out!'

'Within the privacy of their own bedroom, boss!'

'Oh, shut up!' burst out Bunton. 'This is different, I tell you – this woman, dead in bed, bullet through the chest. We might get away with that but the fact that nobody knows who the devil she is suddenly turns it from routine into Page

One. Put mystery in a headline and things turn nasty. Trust me, I know.'

'Well, what are you going to say to – you know?' said Baggs.

'I wouldn't put it past him to go public. It'll ruin me – finish the business. The Archbishop of York, Bert, the Archbishop!'

'We can always cancel him.'

'How will *that* look when Fleet Street gets a hold of it?'

'If only I'd known,' said Baggs dolefully, 'I'd never have let her in in the place. She looked an odd 'un, sounded it too. I blame myself.'

'Go on doing that and you'll be out of a job. You've got to help me think of something – and quick!'

Things suddenly went silent and when Terry looked up, there was Bobby Bunton standing over Terry with a thunderous look on his face. 'What the fuffin' fuff are *you* doing here?' he demanded.

Eagleton, a cool hand in times of crisis, looked up with a relaxed smile on his face. 'You know, Mr Bunton, those pictures I took last week of you and Miss Janetti turned out so well I thought I'd drop some prints off. Might look nice in a frame on your desk.'

Bunton eyed him sideways. 'OK,' he said suspiciously. 'Thank you. Where are they?'

'Back in the car,' lied Terry with a smile. 'Just wanted to make sure you were here first.'

'Well, give them to Baggs. I'm going off for lunch.'

'I will, sir. And…'

'Yes?'

'Miss Janetti, sir. The editor asked if she would do a separate interview, talking about her life as a dancer. A few more nice photos. Wouldn't take up too much of her time, make a nice Women's Page feature.'

'Fix it up with Baggs,' said Bunton, still uneasy. 'Were you listening in just now? To our private chat?'

'Me? Certainly not!' said Terry. 'That would be rude, wouldn't it? My editor Mr Rhys doesn't like his staff being rude to people.' The vein of sarcasm in his tone was barely evident.

'Very well, then,' said Bunton and strode off.

Terry was in no hurry to leave. He wandered out of the management block into the sunshine and took a deep breath. Everywhere there were smartly blazered staff marching in earnest with fixed smiles on their faces. Given the stiff south-westerly wind which was blowing up, their apparent joy seemed misplaced – but obviously they'd all taken their happy pill with breakfast.

In robust denial of the elements the holidaymakers milled about the sports field, tennis courts and bowling greens dressed as if a tropical heatwave was only just around the corner. Their faces, however, puckered at each new gust of wind, and the ladies hugged their cardigans tighter. None looked as though their spirits would be raised by a visit from an archbishop.

Terry was wandering towards the funfair with no apparent purpose in mind when he felt the back of his jacket being tugged, hard. He turned to see the pink-cheeked Baggs.

'What're you doin'?' said the under-manager, his tone not friendly.

'Just taking a look around,' said Terry, 'it's a free country.'

'Not exactly. You have to have a pass. Otherwise we'd have every Tom, Dick and Harry from Temple Regis poking their noses in. People save all year to have their holiday here, you know, it's not a free show.

'You come with me,' said Baggs, and holding on to Terry's coat pulled him towards a low chalet with a sign hanging outside. It said 'The Sherwood Forest'.

'In 'ere,' ordered Baggs. Terry obliged.

'Usual,' said Baggs to the barman. 'And whatever 'e's 'avin'.'

'Now,' he said, 'what was you doin' earwiggin' my conversation with Mr Bunton? I saw you listenin' in.'

'Not me,' said Terry.

'Yes you was. I was watchin' you in the mirror.'

'I was waiting to give Mr Bunton the prints of him and Fluffles.'

'Oh, yes? Where are they, then?'

'In the car. I told him.'

Baggs leaned forward. His breath revealed this was not the first glass of usual he'd swallowed this morning.

'Listen. This is a very tricky time for Mr Bunton, what with this murder on his property and the Archbishop due any time. Business is good down here in Devon, but it can turn on a sixpence with just the wrong word in the Press. As it is, we're waiting for the Fleet Street mob to turn up and make a nuisance of theirselves, so we don't need any more grief from the likes of you.'

Terry just smiled. Baggs saw he was failing to make his point.

'Look,' he said aggressively. 'You've had your fun 'ere. You've got all the pictures you need. Mr Bunton has been very generous with his time, and now I want you to scarper, get it?'

'You're asking me to leave?' said Terry.

'Moochin' round 'ere, snoopin'.' A fresh glass of the usual had been put before the under-manager, though nothing for Terry. 'I want you to 'oppit, otherwise something nasty might occur.'

'Meaning?'

'You know what I mean.'

Terry did, but he didn't care. He was enjoying this. 'What about the Archbishop?' he teased. 'You'll be wanting me to take a picture of him when he turns up, won't you?'

'That's different,' said Baggs sulkily.

'Ah, right! So what you're saying is, you want the press to publicise all the nice things happening at Buntorama, but not mention anything nasty? Like the battle between your boss Bunton and the chap over the road at the Marine, old Radipole?'

Baggs went white. 'Sling yer 'ook,' he said, his face just inches away from Terry's. 'You don't want to end up like that woman over in Knightsbridge, do you? On a slab?'

'*What?*'

'You 'eard,' said Baggs.

EIGHT

Miss Dimont was in London lapping up the Chelsea sunshine. She'd just had lemonade and a bun in a coffee bar called Fantasie and was looking forward to a stroll up the King's Road to gather strength for her lunch-date. Nothing like a little light shopping to ease the torment of meeting Madame D again! At least Arthur would be there to deflect the worst.

She looked in the window of Bazaar, a smart new clothes shop, humming the tune of 'Freight Train' which the skiffle group in Fantasie had played several times while she was there. She meandered through streets filled with the artists, eccentrics, bohemians and stranded gentry which made up the bulk of Chelsea's populace, and again felt the thrill of the London life she had so long ago left behind.

It was 11 o'clock in the morning but it was as if this particular quarter of London had only just woken up. A few bedraggled souls made their way to breakfast in the Chelsea Potter pub while others wandered, as if in a daze, into Simeon's bakery. For some reason cars and buses made only occasional, almost apologetic, appearances on the streets – Chelsea was a village with its own rhythm and rules.

She'd spent the previous evening at the Arts Club, that noisy, rackety den of inspiration which seemed to have grown wilder and noisier since her last visit. She'd attracted the attention of one long-haired painter who demanded her presence in his studio next day – 'your profile – so noble, so bold, so... *rafinée*' – and was still debating whether to take up the offer.

For now, though, it was time to adopt a more conventional demeanour and travel west, to a different kind of clubland. She hopped aboard a 22 bus and spent the journey looking out at a cityscape still marred by the exigencies of war, many streets still with holes where houses and shops once stood.

She alighted in Piccadilly and wandered down to the leafy garden square which housed Uncle Arthur's gentleman's club.

He stood on the steps in the sunlight, old now but still ramrod straight, his blue eyes twinkling and with a boyish smile on his face.

'I say, guess what! She's not coming! Hooray!'

A wave of emotions hit the reporter – disappointment, relief, irritation, hurt – but to Arthur she simply said, 'Crikey!' in a jovial sort of way and allowed herself to be wafted by a club servant into the Ladies' Dining Room. The sunlight from the vast window overlooking the square illuminated the white table cloths and sparkling silver, and all was still.

'Dashed nuisance, of course,' Arthur was saying as they sat, 'because we'll only have to face up to it another time. But lovely to have you all to myself, Huguette. By the way, you're looking wonderful.'

'That's jolly nice of you, Arthur – two compliments within the space of twelve hours. Perhaps I should move back to London.'

'Were you with those artist friends of yours?'

'One of them wants to paint my portrait.'

'You be careful. You know where that sort of thing can lead.'

Miss Dimont did know. The thought did not perturb her at all.

As the club waiters hovered with menus and drinks and bread and murmurs, the talk was of Arthur's family and Judy's mother.

'She telephoned last night. Said she was taking the boat to Belgium this afternoon – something to do with the family estate, a bit complicated.'

'She does that,' said Judy irascibly. 'Makes appointments, breaks them at the last minute. She likes to keep people waiting. Shows you who's boss.'

'You don't need to tell me. She was always boss when we were growing up, even though I'm a year older. I must have told you about…'

Arthur fell into reminiscence, as old men do, about his family upbringing and about how Grace had fallen for a man in a shop. 'She was seventeen, hadn't even come out yet, was bowled over by him. Followed him down the street then raced ahead and dropped her handkerchief so he had to pick it up. I mean, have you ever heard anything so comical!'

It was probably less comical when he took her to the hotel, thought Miss Dimont, but despite the fifteen-year age gap they surprised everyone by announcing their engagement within days, and by the time she was eighteen years old Grace Dimont was in Belgium, the wife of a successful diamond trader and with a baby on the way.

'A glass of champagne, madam?'

Invigorated by its bubbles it was Judy's turn to reminisce. 'You know, Arthur, I was only six when we came to England but I remember our old house so well. Full of ghosts, of course, but magical.'

'My dear, it was a positive castle – a palace! Servants galore. Your father was a hugely successful man.'

'I remember the house better than I remember him. He only came home at weekends, and then the place would be filled with friends and business people. He was lovely, wonderful, to Maman but she always warned me, business comes first. I rarely saw him.'

'He expected Grace to be the chatelaine,' said Arthur, 'but she was still only in her early twenties. She'd always been bossy but I think all that responsibility – the acres, the staff – well, you can understand how she turned out, in a way.'

Judy sipped at her champagne. They'd chosen a later hour to meet, and the dining room was already emptying, causing her attention to shift from the people at other tables to the ancient portraits on the walls. 'Maman couldn't quite get over coming back to England. All the money locked up in Belgium, Papa in the army, then in the prison camp.'

They went slowly upstairs to the Waterloo Room for their coffee. Arthur moved quite slowly these days but his forward movement went unremarked in an establishment where nobody seemed to be under seventy-five.

'Still, you got a good schooling. And he taught you the diamond trade.'

'The war finished him, as you know, Arthur. By the time I was eighteen he was like an old man. He didn't want to go back to Antwerp – and so I became him, in a strange sort of way.'

'You were brilliant,' said Arthur proudly. You could see he loved his niece more than his own children.

'Well, that was then. This is now. I've been waiting till lunch was over but I wanted to know what you thought of this,' said Judy.

Arthur smiled benevolently. 'The old game, eh?' he chuckled, adopting a knowledgeable demeanour. 'Well go on, try me!'

Judy poured the coffee and told him the story of Patsy Rouchos. The murder, few clues, false name, no apparent motive…

'And then this absolute – well, I suppose you'd call it a turf war – between Bobby Bunton and Hugh Radipole, the owner of the Marine Hotel. You know, what I often think is…'

'Wait a minute!' snapped Arthur. He'd been looking out of the window down on to the garden square. Between the leaves of the great plane trees you could see lovers walking hand-in-hand around a statue of one of England's kings on a horse. He looked regal enough but a bit on the heavy side to be galloping into battle. Poor horse, thought Judy.

'Hugh Radipole, you say? Used to be in the motor trade?'

'I have no idea, Arthur.'

'If it is him the man's a rascal. Frightful fellow! Sold me a Lagonda, absolute death-trap. Refused to take it back – the man's a criminal, mark my words, Huguette, a criminal!'

'Criminal enough to murder a girl in a chalet in a holiday camp?'

'I'd believe anything of him!' expostulated Arthur, and

before she could stop him set off on a tirade about the iniquities of the motor trade, filled as it was with people claiming to have gone to schools whose tie, shockingly, they dared to wear in public.

'They're all the same,' said Arthur, shaking his head in disbelief, 'chaps who chat to you about the cricket score and Donald Bradman's century and all that. I mean to say…'

Judy smiled. Arthur had a bee in his bonnet about cars and about Lagondas in particular. 'He must have done very well out of the war, uncle. He came down to Temple Regis with pots of money, rebuilt the old Marine Hotel into a deluxe establishment, all steel and glass and chrome and modern art, and counts his well-heeled guests as his friends. Though they might not always feel the same about him.'

'A stinker. I bet he did it,' said Arthur, but Judy could see that his contempt for people who wore a phony tie was on a par with murder. It was pointless asking further advice, though she hadn't known about Radipole's days in the motor trade.

It was time to go. Judy was catching the 4.30 from Paddington and Arthur was ready for a snooze.

The club library had the deepest, softest leather armchairs in the whole of London.

'Just one thing, uncle. Can you remember – there was a to-do you were involved with, years ago – Auriol and I were talking about it the other day. Only after you'd gone did I remember that you'd once crossed swords with Johnny Ramensky.'

Arthur's features softened. 'Oh, yes!' he said, brightening, 'Gentleman Johnny! The best safecracker in the business! It took forever to run him to ground, he was a real pro, and actually a very likeable chap underneath all that Glaswegian bluster. I wonder whatever happened to him.'

'He's still around, not much older than me, actually. Had a very good war.'

'Not surprised,' said Arthur in lordly fashion, 'criminal types always do.'

'He taught Eric how to crack a safe. Just before he went off on that final job.'

'Oh,' said Arthur, 'I say. Well, good luck to him.'

'Walk me down the stairs, uncle, I want to ask you a couple of things about him.'

The old man and his still youthful niece slowly descended the club's grand staircase and walked out into the sunshine together.

Terry was waiting for Betty as she walked out of the hotel entrance.

'Get what you wanted?'

'She's a dish,' said Betty. 'A real character. She asked if I'd like to hear her sing a song to me – a special performance.'

'What!' said Terry, 'I wish I'd been there for that!'

'You could have been – where did you disappear to?'

'Tell you in a minute. What'd she sing for you?'

'"And Her Tears Flowed Like Wine" – a real swinger, and I don't even like that kind of music.'

'My favourite,' said Terry, bitterly. 'I hope she'll do it again tonight. Shall we take the pretty way back?'

They took the coast road out of Ruggleswick, a winding ribbon of highway, shut down during the war and rarely used now except by more adventurous locals, so close it was to the cliff edge. The grey weather over Nelson's Bay had evaporated and now thin white clouds like silk veils were all that separated them from the huge blue sky above.

Betty flipped down the sun visor to check the state of her hair. 'I had a chat with the drummer afterwards,' she said. 'He's very nice.'

And very married, thought Terry.

'He was telling me about the murder over at Buntorama, seemed to know quite a lot about it.'

'Forget that,' said Terry, 'tell me about Moomie. Isn't she adorable? What did she have to say? I think I'm in love!'

Oh Terry, thought Betty, what a fool you are about women. 'Just a singer,' she said artlessly. 'On the other hand, Sticks on the drums...'

Oh Betty, thought Terry, what a fool you are about men.

And so their journey continued, the blind leading the blind all the way back to St Dunstan's.

Terry told Betty about his encounter with Bobby Bunton and his under-manager, but she was only half-listening.

From high above Betty could look down onto the broad sands of the estuary, cloud-shadows chasing dog-walkers across the beach as if trying to swallow them up. Out on the water she could see the strong purposeful chugging of the fishing boats, while nearer the shore the lone ferryman plied his solitary trade. Betty knew this man, had seen him in the Old Jawbones with his prematurely aged face and his lonely pint, had realised that although everyone in Temple Regis knew his face and had taken his ferry, he was so busy collecting the threepenny fare from everyone and steering and docking his boat he never had time to exchange more than a please-and-thank you. From above, he looked even lonelier – and for a moment Betty abandoned her thoughts of the drummer to make way for a pang for the ferryman.

'But then,' said Terry, 'this was the strange thing, this man Baggs who seemed so straightforward when we met him the other night suddenly starts threatening me. Almost as if he was saying my life might be in danger if I carried on wandering around his blessed holiday camp.'

'People are like that, though, aren't they?' said Betty, who was only half-listening. She was thinking about the intro to her story on Moomie and whether she should do a separate Women's Page piece on how professional singers (of a certain size) can still look great on stage with the assistance of helpful corsetry, encouraging the readers to think likewise. Betty liked writing about clothes, which was strange when you thought about how wretched her personal choices always were.

'They're really worked up about this murder. I think it's because they've got the Archbishop of York coming, and some admiral as well.'

'Oh yes, Sticks was talking about that,' said Betty, still only half-concentrating. 'Said he knew the girl who was killed. Well, didn't know her, but knew who she was.'

Terry applied the brakes to the Minor very hard. They skidded to a halt so hard the contents of Betty's make-up bag scattered all over the floor.

'What was that for?' she squeaked. 'Look what you've done now!'

'Betty,' said Terry. 'Are you on this planet? Are you a journalist? Do you work for the *Riviera Express*?'

'No need to take that tone with me, Terry!'

'You do realise, don't you, the woman who was shot at Buntorama last week – that nobody knows who she is? That she gave a false name when she checked in to the camp and the police have failed completely to find out her real name or where she came from?'

'Then they should have asked the drummer. He knows.'

Terry gaped. 'Betty, you're a reporter, don't you realise this is a breakthrough?'

'Sorry, Terry,' she said sharply. 'I don't take orders from photographers. I don't need you to tell me. Of course I was going to mention it when I got back to the office.'

Both knew this was an untruth.

'Come on then,' said Terry, shifting into gear, 'tell me who the mystery woman is. Her name.'

'No idea,' snapped Betty, looking in her compact mirror to check all was well before they arrived back at the office. 'You'll have to get Judy to have a word with Sticks – it's her story, after all. But I don't think she'll get much, he was pretty vague about it.'

Terry shook his head. Not much good with men, and not much good at her job either. Thank heavens they'd got that wonderful Moomie picture story to bring back. What a gorgeous woman!

NINE

If it's Tuesday, it must be Magistrates' Court. Throughout the year, even in the holidaymaking season, justice was dished out from the redbrick building across the market square with a mixture of compassion, eccentricity and sometimes downright brutality. Colonel de Saumaurez, the chairman, was on the side of the angels and always had a softness for a hard-luck story, but some of the other townsfolk who'd wangled their way on to the bench as a means of social advancement were often less attractive than the people standing in the dock.

Betty was on duty this morning, her mind as usual half on the matter in hand and half on the events of last night when she'd accidentally bumped into Dud Fensome.

She was walking home past the Freemasons' Hall when he came down the steps, little brown attaché case in his hand. Instinctively Betty crossed to the other side of the road but he spotted her and called out.

'No, Dud, you got my telegram. That's it,' called back Betty quite firmly, and walked on. But then something caught her eye in the window of the Home & Colonial and she stopped.

That was the trouble with Betty – indecisive. Nobody else had come forward as a new beau since the hair-dye incident, and it was better to be chased by a Freemason than by nobody at all. The doorway of the Home & Colonial was privy to a sharp exchange of views and some special pleading by the Worshipful Master, together with the promise he would never mention her weight again. The fact that they walked on together to the pub spoke volumes.

This morning in court, as the grumpy magistrates' clerk Mr Thurleston adjusted his filthy wig and instructed those present to be upstanding for their worships, she realised her mistake in reheating the soufflé – if love with a square-headed insurance salesman could be dignified thus. Things never worked second time around, though heaven knows she'd tried often enough, and this morning in the sobering halls of justice she realised it had all been a mistake.

Now the drummer at the Marine – that was another thing altogether! And wasn't there something she was supposed to be telling Judy about…?

All thought processes ground to a halt as the familiar figure of Reg Urchward rose from the public benches. He was here to get a licence extension for a party at his pub, the Old Jawbones, normally an open-and-shut case, but things were not going well this morning.

'And then there's this letter from the Noise Abatement Society,' said Colonel de Saumaurez, peering down over his gilt-rimmed *pince-nez* at the rough-hewn publican. 'I'm sorry, Mr Urchward, but we do have to listen to the voice of reason.'

'Bloody buggerrrs,' growled Reg through his teeth. 'Ruddy killjoys! The whole point of this town is to have fun.'

Betty was taking notes. She had good shorthand, and while her antennae were not supersensitive to the possibilities of every story, she knew a good one when it was plonked in front of her. The measly little paragraph she'd fashioned out of a reader's letter from the Society could be built up into something much bigger – 'THE POINT OF TEMPLE REGIS IS TO HAVE FUN, COMPLAINS PUBLICAN WHO SLAMS TOWN'S "KILLJOYS".'

This was just the sort of thing to capture the imagination of Rudyard Rhys, who enjoyed lively debates on the forward progress of Temple Regis. And also the kind of story likely to find its way to Page One, rather than grisly details of mystery women being shot in the town's much-regretted holiday camp. Plus, happily, just the kind of tale to earn Betty an extra-large byline.

'Sorry, Mr Urchward, on this occasion I am going to say no,' said the colonel in the gentlest tones.

Reg was a good sort and raised money for the lifeboat.

'I'm blimmin'...' started Reg angrily, but then stopped. There was always next time for licence applications and it didn't do to upset the beak.

Betty quickly scanned down the list of charges being brought before their worships and saw there was nothing newsworthy immediately ahead. She followed Urchward out of court and in time-honoured tradition, stepped in front of him.

'Reg,' she said. 'A quick word.'

'Blimmin' noise-abaters,' he barked in reply. 'They 'ad their party in my back room a year ago lars Christmas. Made enough noise to blast down the walls of Jericho.'

Betty's pencil slid across her notebook. Soon she had assisted the publican in ordering his thoughts sufficiently to create a broadside against these johnny-come-latelys who wanted to tell everybody what to do.

'Bin 'ere all my life,' he raged obligingly. 'Done my time on the trawlers. Done my time on the lifeboat. Now I welcomes one and all into my nice little pub and these ruddy spoilsports want the town to – y'know what I mean!'

These were brilliant quotes, albeit helped along by Betty – 'Do you think the noise-abaters want the town to turn teetotal as well, Reg?'

'Ur.'

'Those spoilsports want the town to turn…' said Mr Urchward.

Regrettable, perhaps, but it's the way news is made.

'And just think,' said Betty, smiling sweetly but twisting the knife, 'only last week Mr Radipole got his licence for music and dancing and drinking until two in the morning for the whole of the summer season. I've heard that band, and their singer, Moomie Etta-Shaw – they make the dickens of a racket.'

'One rule for the posh, another for us lot,' said Urchward, watching with growing concern as Betty's pencil flew across her notebook. ''Ere, you're not going to print any of this, are yer?'

'Always up to the editor,' said Betty, pushing onwards quickly before a blanket withdrawal could be issued. She was ruthless when it came to that Page One byline.

And so the newsmaker and newsgatherer parted, one to wait in ignorance until his deeper prejudices about posh folk were given an airing in the local rag, the other to facilitate it.

Betty was feeling pleased with herself as she made her way towards the office, but not quite so delighted to find herself faced with Miss Dimont and Terry, champing at the bit, wanting to find out more about the identity of the dead woman.

'I told you last night, Terry, I don't know – Pat something – go and talk to the drummer. Better still, let me, he gets on well with me!'

'What are you on?' said Judy.

'Reg Urchward telling Colonel de Saumaurez where to get off. In court this morning.'

'Page One,' predicted Judy, 'better get on with it.'

So Betty did. She wasn't that keen on murders but she did love seeing her name on the front of the paper.

Over in Bedlington the Seagull Café had a 'Closed' sign swinging in the window, even though it was midday and people would soon be wanting a pasty and lemonade for their lunch. A couple pressed their noses against the window but there was nothing much to see and so walked on.

Inside Auriol Hedley was in conversation with an occasional visitor whose habit it was to drop in unannounced.

'I do have a telephone, you know,' she was saying in a tired voice, 'I've told you before.'

'Don't like too many people knowing what we're doing,' said the man smugly. 'Walls have ears, all that.'

'We used to say that in the war,' said Auriol, bringing an

old cardboard file over to the table and banging it down in irritation. 'War's over.'

'Not this one.'

'All right, what do you want to know?'

'Towards the end of 1943 you had your eye on one Cedric Minsell, a lieutenant-commander in submarines. You'll know of course that he is now Admiral Sir Cedric, in charge of a shore training establishment in Hampshire.'

'Over-promoted. Put out to grass.'

'Well, that's a pretty accurate summation. He hasn't got long before retirement and he's been making a nuisance of himself with Whitehall because he will insist on appearing on TV – *What's My Line?*, that sort of thing. Pushing himself to the fore when really...'

'... he ought to be keeping his trap shut,' said Auriol. She got up and brought two lemonades to the table.

'You remember him.'

'Very well. Very cocky, extraordinarily handsome.'

'Ah yes. The boys in the backroom did wonder whether you and he...'

Auriol looked pityingly at her guest. 'So typical. The boys in the backroom, given a similar task, would take great pleasure in – how shall I say – getting to know a suspect, especially if she was good-looking. When women apply the same technique it's a cause for a lot of blue jokes.'

The man took out a cigarette case but catching his hostess's eye, put it away again.

'Anyway,' said Auriol. 'The upshot was that we knew he had Russian sympathies before the war, and we were doing a routine check on him, given his sensitive position in submarines.'

'The result?'

'Just that – he had Russian sympathies. Nothing more.'

'They were, of course, our allies then.'

'Not really,' said Auriol with a world-weary smile. The sun through the window brought out secret red strands in her coal-black hair.

'Well,' said the man. 'You may be delighted to hear your boyfriend's coming your way.'

'Posted to Devon? I thought he was about to retire.' She took a sip of lemonade. It needed a little more sugar.

'Yes, he's Flag Officer, Hampshire, until the autumn. Somehow he secured that knighthood, heaven knows how, but now he's accepted a directorship of Buntorama, that nasty holiday camp you've got over the other side of the bay. Apparently he and Bobby Bunton were on some TV show together and they got on like a house on fire.'

'Something to keep him out of mischief, then.'

The man drew in his breath slowly. 'Not exactly,' he said. 'As you know, we've just laid the keel of the country's first nuclear submarine. Up in Barrow-in-Furness.'

'*Dreadnaught*.'

'I see you like to keep up. Yes. Well, donning his celebrity mantle Admiral Minsell managed to get himself invited up to the Vickers shipyard and was given a tour around the place. We're not terribly keen about that.'

'Those old Russian sympathies.'

'Worse than that. He's still in touch. With the other side.'

Auriol stood up. 'How long have you known?'

'Pretty well all along. Certainly since 1950.'

'And you let him rise to the rank of Rear Admiral? You didn't think, perhaps, of arresting him and charging him with treason?'

The man cleared his throat and shuffled his feet. 'Look, we're asking for your help, Auriol. You knew him – and he liked you a lot. Why, even you thought…'

'It was nearly twenty years ago. Are you telling me that in all that time, while he's been under suspicion, you've allowed him to be promoted to admiral when he should by rights be in jail?'

The man defied his hostess's unspoken rule and lit a cigarette. 'Standard practice,' he said after a pause. 'Promote him sideways, away from the sensitive stuff, make him feel that he's still on an upward career trajectory. Feed him harmless or false material to pass on to his brethren on the other side of the Iron Curtain and hope to catch the others in the chain.'

'So what do you want me to do – go and seduce him again? I'm nearly sixty, you know!'

'You're fifty-five. Just this – if he comes this way, cosy up to him. He's seen the plans of *Dreadnaught* as well as the keel, and no doubt the Muscovites are very, very pleased with him just at the moment. You're on the retired list, and have the perfect cover – a tea shop. D'you make any money out of this, by the way?'

'None of your business.' Auriol walked over to the window and pointedly turned the 'Closed' sign around.

'I rather fancy the look of your pasties.'

'You're not invited to luncheon, Commander. All ashore!'

The man picked up his briefcase. 'You're a very attractive woman still, Hedley. Go and use those wits of yours, and those looks, and bring us home some results.'

'I don't work for you any more.'

'In our branch of the service, there is no such thing as retirement. Do as you're told!'

TEN

Though Temple Regis recorded more sunshine hours than anywhere else in the country there was always one place where perpetual gloom featured on the weather-map, and that was the coroner's court.

Overcast, thundery and always with the chance of a stormy outbreak, it was never a healthy place to linger – a view eagerly promoted by its boss, Dr Rudkin. If possible the crotchety old boy would have reduced the number of inquiries into unforeseen death to zero, since they only ever brought unwelcome publicity. And if there was one allergy from which the doctor suffered, it was the Press.

Not long ago there'd been the messy business of Bengt Larsson, the celebrated inventor who brought such lustre to the town with his Rejuvenator. This device had introduced new vigour to many a flagging life, and visitors to the beauteous gardens at Ransome's Retreat, Ben's big pile up on the cliffs at the mouth of the estuary, used to come to pay homage.

But then the town's most famous citizen went and got himself – well, one never wants to say murdered, not in Temple Regis! – got himself done away with.

There'd been such a stink in the gutter press, such accusations of skulduggery – and then on top of it all, the *Daily Herald* had the cheek to suggest that the Rejuvenator didn't work, was a piece of outright chicanery, had in fact killed more people than it cured.

It put Dr Rudkin in a tight spot. In his lexicon there was no such word as murder, and to have to utter it in his own court – and to the serried ranks of bumpy-faced hacks who'd turned up from who knows where to hear his verdict – was more than he could bear. It had been a terrible business and one he had no intention of repeating.

All this was known to Frank Topham, who shared the coroner's resolve of keeping the reputation of Temple Regis clean and unsullied. But it slowed his regulation quick-march from the police station to a saunter while he thought about the conversation ahead. A bullet through the heart is murder, whichever way you look at it, there's no parlaying that into an accidental, and Rudkin would be forced to utter the hated M word. Meanwhile Topham would have to bear the brunt of the coroner's wrath for having allowed such a catastrophe to occur on his patch.

Rudkin's door was open and as Topham marched in, the coroner's officer, Bill Paddick, scooted away. He could smell trouble in just the way most sailors can smell a storm ahead, and he hopped off to the safety of the kitchen.

'Morning, doctor,' said Topham, affably enough. He was a strong man, had won his medals in the desert, was not easily cowed. 'The matter of this woman Rouchos.'

'Is that her name?' snapped Rudkin.

'So far as we know, sir.'

'Can't you do better than that?'

'The only name we have, sir. The one she booked in to Buntorama with. You'll see from the note I sent you that she left absolutely no identifying items in her room, and the clothes she possessed were all bought cheaply in chainstores. The items of jewellery on her body denote a different background, but if it was her purpose not to be identified she's done a very good job of it. At present, we don't know who she really is.'

'So we're going to have the Press baying at our heels again, are we, Detective Inspector? Woman shot dead, police have no clues, coroner forced to declare it murder?'

'No escaping that, sir, with a bullet through the heart.'

'The gun?'

'No gun remained, but it was a .45, probably a service revolver. That might indicate it could have been a former officer who did it – on the other hand there's a hefty black market in ex-service weapons so, equally, it could have been anybody. The only real clue we found in the room was a small photograph album, but it amounts to very little – there's no picture of the dead woman among the snaps and no names attached. They're anonymous people from nowhere.'

The two men eyed each other. Dr Rudkin – a highly educated medical man, after all – looked down on the dirty drear doings which make up the daily routine of a police detective. He was a man who wore starched collars and cuffs and who washed his hands regularly – all in his world was clean, disinfected, ordered. It had been many a year since as a junior clinician he'd had to cut open a body to explore the mysteries within.

Topham had seen many a corpse – in the desert, and now here in Temple Regis. Sailors seemed to top the list, they were always getting themselves dead, but farm workers and reckless drivers came a close second. There were suicides and a fair few manslaughters; in fact, there seemed to be no end of ways of bringing life prematurely to a close.

All of these sad departures had a place in Dr Rudkin's court – despite his pathological hatred of publicity, he had a fine way about him when delivering sympathy to the poor bereaved, those left behind to scrape up the remains of a broken life and try to piece together their own shattered existence. He knew instinctively how to combine soft words and firm judgements and many were touched by his air of condolence, leaving his court feeling as if they'd been personally blessed by a bishop.

Such was the way in Temple Regis. It was a little piece of paradise which had no place for murder, and sensational murder at that. So why then did newspapers send in their attack-dogs to disrupt the calm of the coroner's court, chewing over every juicy morsel which emerged, relishing the opportunity to tell the world that Temple Regis was not the serene idyll it claimed to be?

'Murder, I'm afraid, sir. No escape.'

The coroner's hand shook slightly as he picked up his fountain-pen to make a note. He sniffed and looked abruptly out of the window. The interview was over, the case would be heard this afternoon, and Topham wanted his lunch.

As he emerged blinking into the sunlight of the market square a small person in a hurry bumped into him.

'Inspector! The very man! A brief word, if you please!'

Topham had borne the anguish and ratchet-dry response of the coroner with relative ease. Encounters with Judy Dimont were somehow more unendurable.

'Ah, Miss Dimont.'

'Hope you've got a good potato crop this summer. It was awful last year, wasn't it? My leeks too, ruined, you know, with all that rain just at the wrong moment.'

Like all good reporters Judy squirrelled away personal information along with the professional when in conversation with her subjects, and cheerily deployed it as an icebreaker when necessary. She had a voluminous memory, her brain like the reference shelves of some ancient county library.

'You'll be trying for the cup again this year?' Mrs Topham had been runner-up in the Regis and Bedlington Flower Festival two summers ago and was known to be keen to bring home a trophy.

'I doubt it. Maud has developed a bad back. Now I know you want something, Miss Dimont, but I want my lunch. So be quick about it.'

The sun was hot and the pair moved to stand in the shade of a horse chestnut. Its shadow somehow had the effect of making their conversation more private.

'I know you're not a mean man, Inspector, but you're tight-fisted when it comes to information, you always have been. So let me tell you what you won't tell me.' She rolled out a beautiful smile but it could not disguise the determination in her voice.

'She's a woman of thirty. Probably came down from London – or possibly abroad. Certainly not local. She almost certainly knew the person who killed her and made no attempt to escape – unless she was asleep on the bed, which is always possible, though in the middle of the day? And sitting up?

'There was one shot, no commotion, the murderer just walked away. There's so much noise over at Buntorama – especially now they've got that new helter-skelter, it's the perfect place to commit a murder.

'In fact,' she said, flapping her notebook, 'you could commit half-a-dozen murders in that camp and nobody would turn a hair.'

The detective looked down at the reporter and wondered where she got it all from. So far she was spot on.

'What I want to know, Inspector, is this. We have the inquest this afternoon and I'm going to be writing a big piece about the mystery death in Temple's latest attraction. What else do you know that you can share with me? The clothes? The photo album, for example?'

'Oh,' said Topham, 'you know about that! D'you pay for information, is that how you get it? Well, I can tell you that the album is hopeless, no names in it, a group of people smiling at the camera, unidentifiable backgrounds, nothing to be had there. It's a clue but it's not a clue.'

'Tantalising,' said Judy, thinking. 'Maybe if the *Express* printed a couple of the photos, might that be of use?'

'Can't see how it would. She's not local. Your paper only sells locally, how's that to help?'

There followed a brisk conversation where the dread prospect of Fleet Street was raised. Miss D reminded the policeman of the vicious remarks cast by the crime reporters who'd come down for the murders of Gerald Hennessy and Bengt Larsson. Allow the *Express* sole right to photograph the album, and disseminate the pictures as the editor saw fit – that way, Fleet Street's finest would be kept away from the police station, but the pictures would appear in the national press and if anybody recognised the snaps, job done!

Topham paused only for a moment. On the one hand his complicity would bring down the wrath of Dr Rudkin, and probably that of the mayor, Sam Brough, as well – put all that together and it would ensure the next meeting with the Chief Constable would be a bumpy one. On the other hand, Fleet Street was sure to get involved sooner or later, given Bobby Bunton's thirst for publicity, so to that extent his options had narrowed decisively.

'Go on then,' he said in an exasperated voice. He felt somehow he'd been outmanoeuvred by Miss Dimont, not for the first time. 'Get Terry to come round this afternoon. He can take a nice picture of the roses Sergeant Gull has been rearing while he's at it. Now, those are going to get the cup this year or you can watch me eat my hat.'

Hugh Radipole swung elegantly round in his seat and looked out to sea. The morning's work was done, soon he would take his private lift down to the ground floor, wander out to the Primrose Bar, and accept the congratulations of all around for the joy his hotel brought them. Despite the ruinously high prices – from having your shoes cleaned to the ten-course dinner – people were indebted to him for having created this rare oasis of civilisation. They offered him drinks, clapped him on the back, whispered secrets to him they would not even tell their wives.

For Radipole, this was a necessary moment of calm. Since the war's end he had dedicated himself to creating a Mayfair-class hotel and resort in this unlikely spot at the unfashionable end of Temple Regis. A dozen years on and he had turned fashion on its head – the Rolls-Royces and Bentleys parked in the garage stood testament to that – and recouped his sizeable investment. While the oldsters in TR still laughed at the sudden fashion for Ruggleswick Sands, Londoners and people from the posher shires did not.

Perhaps it was the fact that he never drank or had married which gave him the room in his life to devote to this monument to good taste and style. The rooms he occupied at the top of the Marine Hotel were the reflection of a man of culture and refinement, draped in subdued colours and hung with pictures and drawings from the Bauhaus. The furniture was tubular steel, the carpets a zigzag of browns and buffs, the mirrors encased in chrome. The music which gently wafted from a walnut box at one end of the room was gypsy jazz played by Django Reinhardt, the books which lined the walls were Huxley, Kafka, Eliot and Wyndham Lewis.

On a side table next to his desk stood the only reference to his previous life – a shining heavy silver reproduction of a Bentley S3 racing car, enamelled in British racing green, whose patina was dulled by the constant caress of his fingers. For a man who spoke, and behaved, like an aristocrat, it would be hard to believe that he started out life covered in oil leaking from the undersides of such a beast, but so it was.

Deekins, his man, popped his head round the door. 'Someone to see you, sir.'

'I'll be down in a few minutes.'

'No, they'd like a private word.'

Radipole smoothed his sleek hair and stood up. 'Who?'

'Reporter, sir. From the local paper.'

'Who?

'Miss Dimont.' He pronounced it 'Dy-mont'.

'Dammit, I had to put up with that grizzled old bore Rudyard Rhys at lunch the other day – what more do they want?'

'Didn't say, sir.'

'OK, tell them five minutes only.' He wandered over and gazed into the mirror as Miss Dimont was ushered in.

'Only take *ten* minutes of your time,' said Judy by way of introduction. She wasn't going to allow a manservant to dictate the length of her visit.

'I saw your editor Rhys only the other day. I can't think there's anything…'

'Just a couple of questions, Mr Radipole – you may remember we met at the Rotary.'

'Mm.' But Radipole didn't remember people who weren't important to him. This woman – flowery dress, unkempt hair, glasses down the end of her nose – didn't look like the sort of person you'd come across in the Primrose Bar. He looked out to sea again.

'Mr Rhys asked me to write a piece about the, er, death across the road,' lied Miss D. He hadn't – if anything Mr Rhys had ordered the opposite. Ask him what business he was in and the right answer would not be Press, but suppress.

'Better get over there, then, there's nothing much I can help you with here. It really has nothing to do with the Marine.'

'I think there was a bit of a dust-up the other night involving Mr Bunton.'

'I wouldn't know about that.'

'He and his companion Miss, er, Janetti, were asked to leave after an incident. Told not to come back.'

'Well, that's not true, is it? I saw him in here last night.'

'But on the night he was thrown out...'

'Listen, Mrs... er... – we don't "throw out" people from the Marine. We're not that sort of place, we don't attract the sort who need to be "thrown out", as you put it.'

'But I'm told it was you who did it.'

The stately Radipole was unaccustomed to being challenged. 'I really don't think...!'

Miss Dimont pushed her spectacles up her nose. 'I'm not going to write anything derogatory about the Marine, Mr Radipole,' she said. 'It's the murdered woman I am interested in. Since the event took place somewhere else, I don't think there's any need to drag the Marine into it.' Without invitation, she had seated herself on a sofa. Radipole's long rangy body towered over her.

'I have no recollection,' he began.

'Then let me help. Mr Bunton and his companion Miss Janetti were in the Primrose Bar. It might not be unreasonable to suppose Miss J had participated liberally in the Marine's hospitality, indeed I gather the waiting staff were rushed off their feet looking after her.'

'They're not the sort of people I generally encourage.'

'But you let them in.'

'Better the devil you know.'

'Well, not quite. I gather that matters between you and Mr Bunton are not exactly tickety-boo.'

Radipole looked down at her. 'What do you want?' His eyes seemed to be focusing quite hard on the tip of her nose.

'Mr Bunton spent some time that evening, not with Miss Janetti, but up at the bar with a woman we only know as Patsy Rouchos – the woman who was murdered two days later. Mr Bunton told me she was a prostitute.'

Radipole went white. 'I've… never… heard… anything… so… ridiculous,' he hissed. 'She's – she was – that's to say, that man is a coarse, vulgar, self-opinionated oaf who would naturally assume that any woman standing alone in a bar was a…'

'Prossie is the word he used.'

'I'm appalled you should be talking such talk, and with such people,' said Radipole. 'I was led to believe that the *Express* was a respectable paper!'

'It's a newspaper, Mr Radipole. If you look in any newspaper, you'll find the good alongside the bad. If it isn't a terrible cliché, that's life. We at the *Express* concentrate on the good things people do, but we don't ignore the bad.'

'You should try harder.'

'It's not the way things work. Anyway, this lady, Miss Rouchos shall we call her, was in the Primrose Bar every night since she arrived in Temple Regis. For someone who was staying across the way at Buntorama, that seems – let's say, unusual.'

'We're not snobs, we welcome everybody – as long as they behave themselves.'

'Not what you said a minute ago – "not the sort of people who come here." And odd, don't you think, that she had the money to pay for your expensive drinks?'

'I think you'll find there's an outstanding bill.'

'I wonder why you would extend credit to someone staying at a holiday camp,' said Miss Dimont. Radipole did not seem unwilling to fence with her, but her epée had yet to find its target.

'Ask the barman.'

'I did. He told me to ask you.'

'Ah. Well there you are, then. I think it must be time for lunch, and I feel sure that Mr Rhys must keep you awfully busy. If you'll excuse me I really must be…'

'Don't you find the whole thing a trifle strange?' persisted Miss Dimont. 'The drinks. The fact she was in the bar so often. I don't know, it almost seems as if there was some connection between you.'

Radipole just looked at her.

'We've never really done a proper interview, have we, the *Express*, I mean?'

'You're always most generous with your publicity.' He didn't mean it.

'I was just wondering about your story – you know, how you managed to create this magnificent place. Against all the odds, you might almost say.'

'Mm.'

'The determination, the vision – the money. You were in the car trade, I believe?'

'My story begins and ends with the Marine,' said Radipole harshly. He was clearly on the back foot.

'It's just that my uncle knew you before the war. You sold him a Lagonda.'

'Which model?' The hotelier's fascination with man's automotive machine overcame his shyness about his background.

'The L3, I seem to remember. He wasn't awfully happy with it.'

'Tricky machines.' Radipole was gathering up his keys with rather too much display and heading towards the door. 'I really think it's time to…'

'A very successful business in Hampstead, uncle told me. Carriages for the gentry.'

'All so long ago. I look only to the future.'

Miss Dimont got up. 'It may seem rude to say this, Mr Radipole, but however successful you were, the money you made could never have bought this place and refashioned it in the enviable way you've done. Or kept it going until the rich and famous finally discovered it.

'So where did the money come from? And what's the dead woman's connection with it?'

ELEVEN

From the hills above you could see at a glance why people loved Temple Regis so much – why they resisted the new fad to holiday abroad, and kept returning to this idyllic corner of Devon's prettiest resort. The small bay at North Sands was perfectly situated to catch every last one of the sun's rays, its sands flat and wide, its rocks so climbable, and the whole thing flanked by hilly crags decorated with pine trees where the sun-weary could take sanctuary, and still view the clear blue water below.

It seemed a completely private spot, away from the hustle and bustle of the main beaches, and yet it was as if every primary-school age child had been told the secret. They played in their dozens with their buckets and spades, their puppies, and their kites. Joe, the one-armed ice-cream salesman, made them form an orderly queue up to his tricycle.

It was Sunday afternoon, the tide was out, and across the beach against the rocks stood a group of perhaps twenty or thirty people singing in unison to a small harmonium. The Church Mission for Christ's Resurrection saw no reason not to take advantage of God's sunshine, and whenever weather and tide permitted during the summer months, they transported their worship to the water's edge.

Stripped of the formal surroundings of a church building, the congregation looked overdressed, their movements too stiff, their expressions too serious when compared with the joyous holidaymakers further down the beach. But the music they made, funnelled up into the skies by the gentle onshore breeze, seemed wholly appropriate. It imposed nothing on the non-believers, but it was so beguiling that many a guilty parent promised themselves they would be in church next Sunday.

A figure of authority hoisted himself onto a small rock and waited for the final strains of 'Eternal Father, Strong To Save' to flutter away on the breeze.

'Today,' he began, opening his arms, 'we remind ourselves of the words of that great commission Jesus left us: "Go and make disciples of all nations..."'

Two figures unobtrusively detached themselves from the congregation and walked slowly away towards the waves. The casual observer might deduce they had heard these words too often, and preferred a short stroll before the hymn-singing began again in earnest. In fact their purpose was very different.

'So, Richard,' Auriol Hedley said to Rudyard Rhys as they scrunched through the drying sand, 'there it is. We never seem to escape the grip of Whitehall.'

'Speak for yourself,' said Rhys grumpily, fishing in his pocket for his pipe. 'Really, Auriol, it's Sunday afternoon, my day of rest, and I usually like to...'

'Spare me,' replied Auriol crisply. Her foot irritatedly kicked a small puddle.

'As for all this subterfuge – what's wrong with phoning me at home if you want to know something?'

'Walls have ears.' Apparently Miss Hedley had finally seen the light of day on this point.

'What d'you want to know?'

'Bobby Bunton. What's he about? What's he doing? Why are we seeing the Archbishop of York in his terrible little holiday camp? Why the sudden influx of dignitaries onto the board of directors?'

'What's it got to do with…?' Rhys was simultaneously trying to light his pipe and avoid the puddles. He wasn't particularly successful with either.

'I know you know Hugh Radipole – Judy told me.'

'He comes to our lunches at the Con Club on Fridays, yes.'

'She told me Radipole is gunning for Bobby Bunton.'

'That's right. You might say they're at each other's throats. Bunton thinks Radipole is snooty beyond belief, Radipole thinks Bunton is scum – and he may well be right. Did you know he keeps a cut-throat razor in his top pocket at all times?'

'From what I've heard of Radipole, he probably keeps his sewn into the lining of those Savile Row suits.'

'I wouldn't say that to anyone else,' said Rhys, a trifle importantly. 'Hugh's a gentleman.'

'Hm.'

'Of course, quite naturally he made strong objections to Bunton setting up a holiday camp next to his hotel. He's worked hard on the Marine for ten years and more – it's the jewel in the crown of Temple Regis.'

'Are you invited often?' quizzed Auriol, turning to face Rhys and halting him in his tracks.

'Well, I've dined there a few… he's a good fellow, Radipole.'

'Who tried to blow Bunton and his holiday camp out of the water, and no doubt offered hefty inducements to various councillors to get their veto.'

'If he did, it didn't succeed. Buntorama's here to stay,' came the reply. It didn't sound like a ringing endorsement.

'So it's all-out war, then. Bunton bringing in the funfair and planting it right beside the perimeter fence so as to cause maximum disruption. Fights in the Primrose Bar, Bunton being kicked out, turning up the loudspeakers on the dodgems – good Lord, Richard, I can hear them all the way over in Bedlington!'

'I thought nothing could disturb the expensive peace of that part of town.'

'Oh, shut up. Tell me about Bunton and his race for respectability.'

'Simple. There were too many stories about loose goings-on in his holiday camps – not so much here in Temple Regis, but those ones in Essex – according to Radipole, he has been fearing a police raid for some time now. He can't stop his punters from doing what comes naturally, and actually he doesn't want to. If it's an unspoken secret that illicit encounters go on on the premises, it makes his camps all the more attractive to certain kinds of people. The war's over, Auriol, everybody wants a bit of fun.'

'So he's got the Archbishop of York to come down and give his blessing to the fornicating hordes.'

'I believe His Grace's wife and children will be coming too, for a short stay. Bunton has one or two VIP chalets tucked away.'

'Well, I don't know whether it'll keep the police at bay but it might calm a few fevered brows – the man's a real old Bible-thumper.'

From above the whisper of the surf they could just hear the words of another such thumper: 'To know Christ and to make him known…' but the rest blew away in a small but welcome gust.

'Is that all?'

'What I'm telling you next goes no further, Richard, and is the reason why I got you out here. Among the new names on the board of Buntorama is that of Admiral Sir Cedric Minsell. Apparently they met on some television show and Bunton persuaded Minsell to join the board. He's retiring as Flag Officer, Hampshire, shortly and I expect we'll be seeing something of him down here soon.'

Rhys just looked at her.

'So what I want to know…'

The journalist started to walk away, very quickly. 'Don't want anything to do with it,' he called angrily over his shoulder. Auriol had to scamper to catch up. 'Just keep away from me and do what you have to do. I won't have anything to do with it!'

'You remember him, then.'

'Of course I remember him! I got put on his case after Judy left the Service. He has some very ugly friends and I really am not going to get involved.'

Auriol struggled to maintain her superiority, a difficult task when a man is walking away from you.

'I want you to invite him to lunch,' she called. 'Get to know him. Write something nice about his joining the Buntorama board! It's not beyond you, Richard – you used to do this sort of thing all the time.'

'Not on your life.'

'Richard!' she appealed to the journalist's disappearing back, 'Richard! I need your help!'

'Not on your life.'

'Help me!'

'Go away.'

Oh hell, thought Auriol furiously, coming to a halt in a chilly rockpool.

I suppose I'll have to go and seduce the ruddy Admiral after all.

For a cat of no known pedigree, Mulligatawny had lordly pretensions. Imperious in his shouts for food and love, he could just as easily walk away from both without so much as a backward glance.

In winter he could be gratifyingly cosy, snuggling up to Miss Dimont as they gazed at the fire together in her pretty cottage, listening to a concert on the radio, but come summer he did a disappearing act, preferring the company of his friends in the wild – whether they be delicious mice or voles or rabbits.

This evening, though, his lordship had decided to have an evening in, and had taken up residence in his mistress's favourite chair. Judy entered the room juggling a whisky glass, extra spectacles, a new novel and a magazine she'd been meaning to read for a fortnight, only to discover the usurper looking up at her with a smug look on his face.

This made her quite cross – it'd been a long day and with

little to show for it – and though Mulligatawny's presence was a bonus, his choice of seating was not.

The options were limited. Either she sat in the lumpy armchair which constantly needed the cushions adjusting, or else she'd have to move the pile of recipes she'd spread out on the sofa ready to be folded into her recipe book. There seemed little point in moving Mull from her favourite place – there was always a scramble to see who got there first – because if she did, he'd be off for a night out on the tiles. And she did love his company, the brute.

'Oh, Mull,' she sighed, plonking down into the lumpy seat. The whisky-and-water was a consolation at least and actually, when she looked, his lordship did look particularly handsome sitting there, since the evening light shone through the windows onto his big fat head and made him even lovelier than usual.

She was waiting for *Ray's A Laugh* on the wireless. Ted Ray and his stage wife Kitty Bluett made a huge comedy out of working on a newspaper, the *Daily Bugle*, which came as something of a consolation when you worked for Rudyard Rhys where there was no comedy at all. She laughed at Ray's ridiculousness and Mulligatawny stretched out his paws.

The telephone rang as the audience was still applauding Ted and Kitty. 'People do *not* ring after eight o'clock at night,' she huffed to Mull, but he was busy investigating a burr lodged in the fur of his leg. Apparently it was the devil of a job to shift it.

'Arthur here, Hugue. Sorry it's late.'

'Not at all, Arthur, lovely to hear your voice.'

'You were asking about that man Ramensky. You know, the safecracker.'

'The one who taught Eric.' Her eyes flickered for a moment to the photograph on the mantelpiece.

'Well,' said uncle Arthur, 'it's a very curious thing. You know you were talking the other day about the man Radipole – you know, the rotter who sold me that ghastly Lagonda – well, apparently he and Gentleman Johnny knew each other. I told you Radipole was a stinker!'

'I thought you said you liked Ramensky.'

'Well, he's an out-and-out criminal, you see. Easy to admire the type when you bump into them. No, it's cardsharps and double-flushers like Radipole you've got to watch out for. Why, the cylinder head gasket on that Lagonda...'

'Ramensky, uncle. Back to the point.'

'Mm? Ah, yes, well... I was talking to an old police contact in the club earlier and Johnny's name came up. Johnny's what you'd call a white-collar criminal – steals a lot of diamonds but nobody gets hurt. But one day he was involved in a burglary somewhere in north London where a chap got stabbed and died. Not his modus operandi – far from it – but he was the only suspect.'

Miss Dimont was polishing her glasses on the sleeve of her dress. 'Yes?'

'Police made a cat's-cradle of the case. They just couldn't prove Ramensky had killed the man, even though he'd gellied the safe. But it was a nasty job, apparently – many knife wounds to the throat, heart, even the wrists.'

'Who was the victim?'

'Mm? Oh, some Greek chap, Patrikis, I think he said. Very rich, can't remember what from, but a pillar of the Greek community in London. Widower, only had one child who was so distraught by his murder she ran away and has never been seen again. Ramensky got a spell in the cooler for the safebreak but there was no evidence offered at the trial as to the murder. I don't think he can have done it.'

'Well, very interesting, Arthur.'

'I say, old thing, is that a help?'

'Don't know yet, uncle. But as they say, knowledge is power.'

'I'm still at the club, actually. Chap I know has promised me a game of billiards.'

'Don't stay too late. Keep off the brandy.'

'Ha, ha. Bye bye, darling, I'll let you know about your mother.'

Miss Dimont sharply put down the phone wishing he hadn't said that last thing, and reached for the whisky decanter. A stiff drink always helped when the prospect of Madame Dimont loomed.

Mulligatawny had vacated his place of repose and was currently draped over the brass fender in front of the fire – no telling with cats – so Miss Dimont bagged her place back before he could change his mind, and put the whisky to her lips.

She peered at the photo of Eric, looking down with his mildly sardonic smile as if to say, 'why are you involving yourself in this murder game?'

'I don't know,' sighed Judy back at him. 'But nobody gets shot in Temple Regis – nobody! And here we have a woman who apparently welcomed in her murderer, sat on the bed quite comfortably, as if inviting him to kill her. No sign of a struggle, no sign of forced entry, no clue as to why someone would want to do that. And on top of it all a woman who has very deliberately, and very successfully concealed her identity. What can it mean?'

Eric looked down but said nothing.

'Then again,' she went on, 'this business about Johnny Ramensky – does that have anything to do with anything? We've got Radipole, who must have been a war profiteer to have made all that money to buy and do up the Marine. And we've got Bobby Bunton, a crook in a suit, peddling his questionable holiday camps – both men knew the woman, they've admitted as much. Did one of them kill her to somehow score off the other? They hate each other so much, I wouldn't put it past either of them.

'Come to that, was the reason Radipole threw Bunton out of the Marine not about that silly woman Fluffles – but about the dead woman Patsy Rouchos?' She took a swig of whisky. 'If that's what her name was – which it wasn't… I really must, tomorrow, look into that drummer chap Betty mentioned, see what he has to say. Not that you can ever trust a jazzer to tell the truth…'

The thought-processes were beginning to unravel, perhaps with the mention of her mother she'd poured too stiff a measure of whisky into her glass. She decided to stop talking to Eric and take up the conversation with Mulligatawny instead.

'Eric was such a fool,' she said. He closed his eyes as if in agreement. 'When that man Ramensky turned up to give a master-class on safebreaking and sabotage at Eric's commando establishment, it was as if all his birthdays had come at once. In no time at all he decided he wanted to *be*

Gentleman Johnny – buying him drinks, hanging on his every word. He even tried to copy his Scottish accent.

'But Eric couldn't possibly be him. Johnny had grown up the Gorbals, spent his time down the mines, lived and breathed the criminal life from childhood – that's what made him so brilliant at safecracking. Eric was a sweet and adventurous boy who'd had a sheltered upbringing but who so desperately wanted to break away from it.

'After that course he was ready for anything, and I suppose who could resist that man Ewen Montagu and his madcap ways of kicking the enemy? Parachuting him into Germany to blow open a safe when he'd only just learned the rudiments – really!

'Oh Mull,' said Judy, 'he was such a darling. But despite all that bravery, so innocent…'

Mulligatawny might, or might not, have agreed with this character analysis but it was late, and by now he was fast asleep, paws stretched out in front in an elegant salaam.

TWELVE

'And her tears flowed like wine
Yes, her tears flowed like wine
She's a real sad tomato
A busted Valentine
Knows her momma done told her
The man is darn unkind…'

Terry was in particularly infuriating form. He could never sing in key, his whistling was worse, the tunes he picked to murder had no merit in the first place. Why make things worse by torturing innocent bystanders?

They were in the Minor on their way to cover some routine announcement by the Chamber of Trade.

Light rain was falling, a grey mist crept like a ghost up the estuary, and Miss Dimont had stayed on for one more glass of whisky with Mulligatawny last night.

'Oh *do* shut up!'

'Thought you were a music fan.'

'That's not music, Terry, if you really want music switch

on the Third Programme. Look – there's the radio button – press it!'

'He'd spend it on the pony
He'd spend it on the girl
Buy his mother gin and roses
For her poor old henna'd curls
But when his wife said 'Hey now! What you got for me?'
He socked her in the chopper
Such a sweet, sweet guy was he…'

Terry was now deliberately singing off-key. 'You should have heard her last night, Judy, just sensational!' he yodelled. 'The way she fills the room with that voice – the way she fills that big blue dress…'

'Put a lid on it!'

They pulled up outside the Corn Exchange but neither felt the urge to rush in. The Chamber of Trade was the dreariest job in the diary, and why the *Express*'s chief reporter and chief photographer had been sent to cover its tedious, self-congratulatory annual announcement and not some brand-new junior, eager to please and ready to impress… it rankled.

''Oo put this in the diary?' asked Terry grumpily, voicing the thoughts of both.

'Mr Rhys. Either he's punishing us for something, or he wants us out of the office.'

''Ave you done somethin' wrong, Judy? Not another Conservative Ball disaster, I hope?' Terry could be quite nasty when he liked, which wasn't often, but Judy was in prickly form this morning and he wasn't having it.

‘Oh pipe down – that was ages ago and anyway, it wasn’t the disaster people always make it out to be.’

‘Everybody seems to remember it, though,’ said Terry. ‘Especially the bit where you…’

‘Pipe down!’

Terry went back to humming the Ella Fitzgerald tune but the rain was drumming down on the car roof so hard it did a good job of drowning him out. They both watched a lone holidaymaker make a dash for cover with a newspaper covering her perm – who said the *Riviera Express* wasn’t a useful purchase? – while Miss D thought the best way to stop the awful racket was to engage her snapper in conversation, though she didn’t particularly want to. Her head!

‘So Moomie gave a good performance last night?’

‘Blimmin’ marvellous. She gave Betty and me front-row seats,’ said Terry, and she looked sideways at him at the mention of her fellow-reporter. He had a habit of looking up to the heavens when relating some enjoyable occurrence which really got on her nerves.

‘Betty? What was Betty doing there?’ Hard to tell, with the rain lashing down, whether the note in her voice was laced with anger, contempt or jealousy, but it certainly didn’t sound very sweet.

‘Well,’ said Terry in lordly fashion, ‘she was the reporter who did the story, you know. I was given two tickets and Betty’s name was on one of them. Simple.’

‘She doesn’t know anything about jazz!’

‘Neither do you. You’re always going on about Mozart and… people… you never listen to anything modern.’

‘I do! I love Michael Holliday!’

'That old square? Listen, Judy, if you'd just get away for once from your choir practice and those ruddy concerts at the Guildhall, I could take you somewhere where you might hear something worth listening to.' Usually, Terry was immune to his reporter's snits but the rain was making his knee ache.

Miss D was in no better shape. 'I don't know, Terry, are you walking out with Betty or something?'

The photographer turned his head and held her in a steady gaze. 'You know,' he said, slowly, 'it really was a surprise when you came to join us at the *Express*. We'd never had anybody like you. But for all you're such a smartypants, sometimes you just don't get it, do you…?' His sentence trailed off in exasperation and he reached over to the back seat for his camera-bag.

Whatever his problem was, Miss Dimont flew straight past it. 'You promised to tell me about the drummer chap. Dick somebody.'

'Sticks,' said Terry sharply. 'Sticks Karanikis. They call him Sticks because of his drumsticks, in case you don't get it. You want to talk about music? I thought you were only interested in this murder!'

'Of course I am!' If only the headache would go away!

'Well, here it is. Sticks is a jobbing percussionist, does the West End, small shows, longer gigs like this Moomie Etta-Shaw season, and private parties which pay well. Because he's a London Greek boy he gets invited to lots of functions among the richer set – the shipping people, the petrol people, restaurant owners, that kind of thing. Those Greeks love a party.

'After Moomie's set was over last night – three encores,

Judy, think of it! – we sat in the bar with Sticks and he told us he used to see the dead woman at those London parties. Obviously, most of the time he's playing drums so he can't hear much, and he never learns her name, but he says until about four years ago she was a regular on the circuit.'

'Go on.'

'Only he says he barely recognised her the night he clocked her in the Primrose Bar. Said she'd changed her hair, was wearing very frumpy clothes, cheap shoes – he thought she was down on her luck or that something had gone wrong in her life – in the old days she used to wear a load of jewellery, had expensive hair-dos and looked as though she'd stepped out of the pages of *Vogue*.

'He couldn't understand what she was doing with a twerp like Bobby Bunton. Rich he may be, Judy – but the wrong sort, a real creep. And obviously pretty nasty with it too – I've yet to tell you what his man Baggs said to me. Threatened me, he did! They're a dirty lot!'

'So what actually happened that night?' said Judy, her mind finally clearing. 'I'm beginning to get the feeling, I don't know why, that Radipole probably chucked Bunton out – not because of Fluffles' drunken behaviour – but could it be because he and Bobs were arguing over this woman?'

Terry looked at her with a mixture of disbelief and annoyance. 'One minute you can't remember your umbrella, even when it's raining,' he said, 'next minute you're ahead of me. Seeing round corners! I tell you, it's infuria…'

'Get on with it,' urged Judy, her headache speaking for her.

'Well, you're right in a manner of speaking,' he conceded. 'Sticks and the boys came into the Primrose Bar for a quick one after their rehearsal and saw it all. Fluffles was three sheets to the wind and had obviously been knocking it back for some time – summoning the waiter to light her cigarette, fetch her fresh napkins, and so on – anything to draw attention to herself. Bunton was at the bar with this Rouchos woman for a very long time, heads together kind of thing, and then Radipole comes in. The two have a row, the Rouchos woman backs off and disappears, then Fluffles gets up to have her say and falls over. Apparently quite a sight to see – most of it came out on display. Shame I couldn't have got a bit more of that in close-up when I was taking her pic the other day, because…'

'Yes, yes,' said Miss Dimont impatiently. Men – and bosoms!

'She took over the row because Bunton was pie-eyed by this stage. He kept on saying, "We've got to sort this problem out," but nobody was listening. Fluffles laid into Radipole, called him a snob, a crook – all sorts of things – then turned it on the woman – even though she'd hopped it – and started discussing her morals. Bobs had been chatting her up something rotten but Fluffles thought it was the other way round.

'It was getting out of hand, so Radipole called the head waiter and had them slung out. Clever man – he went round every table, apologising, ordering them drinks, explaining that Mr Bunton had had too much sun and that he, Radipole, was concerned about Miss Janetti's ankle which he thought she'd sprained, so he'd called them a taxi. She was still only half-clothed as she left the bar – that satin dress of hers had split wide open and Sticks told me…'

'Yes, yes,' said Miss Dimont, urging him forward,

'concentrate, Terry, on what's important! The row between these two men – who everyone thinks are at loggerheads over a perimeter fence and who appear to be on the brink of triggering a class war in Temple Regis – I'm right, aren't I? It wasn't about their respective businesses, but about the woman?'

'Prob'ly.'

'Probably! Huh! You know, Terry, you really ought to…'

But the driver's door of the Minor had already slammed. If he had any manners the snapper would have offered to see Judy across the road, but long ago she'd resigned herself to this kind of behaviour after views had been exchanged. She scrambled into her Pacamac and hurried across to the Corn Exchange.

She and Terry never quite made it. As they turned the corner into Temple Street, the main thoroughfare through town, a hooting, shouting, seething mass of people waving flags and placards suddenly appeared and headed towards them, exhibiting all the signs of that finely judged level of controlled anger at which the British excel. It was a march, a protest march. The crowd ranged from scruffy youths to ladies in hats, from clergymen in dog-collars to mothers with prams. They moved slowly but with purpose, and the thin line of townsfolk who stopped to witness this surprise disruption seemed to be nodding their quiet approval.

'That's Jacquetta Hawkes!' said Miss Dimont, elbowing Terry, who was struggling with the catch on his camera-bag. 'Quick – get her against the crowd and I'll do the interview!'

The hat the woman wore, pulled down as a shield from the rain, obscured most of her face but the moment Judy heard the roars of' 'Ban the Bomb', she knew it must be her. Nobody had given advance warning of the march, but since the early spring such demonstrations had been cropping up everywhere – 'a good way of getting the young out for a nice long walk' she'd remarked jauntily at the photos of the first Aldermaston march.

But now she could see for herself the earnestness in the marchers' faces. Even as they joked and skipped along to the music from a steel band, there could be no denying they meant what they said on their boards and banners.

Let our Earth
Be A
Nuclear-Free
Zone

Youth
Against The
Bomb

Nuclear War
=
Suicide

The Ban the Bomb movement had hit a particular nerve. For the older generation, the threat so soon after the end of the war of a further, far more calamitous conflict was enough to win their sympathy. Among the younger generation the future of mankind – or the lack of it – was enough to drive them onto the streets.

At the head of the procession was an earnest-looking chap in a dog-collar and one or two individuals who might be very distinguished indeed had not the summer rain made them look like drowned rats.

'Come on!' said Judy, summing up the situation in an instant, 'let's get her now!'

She joined the head of the march and introduced herself to Miss Hawkes, the celebrated author of *Dawn of the Gods* and married to somebody terribly famous.

'This is wonderful!' Judy, her face lighting up, shouted at her. 'So unexpected! But why here – why Temple Regis? You've done these marches in Aldermaston and Manchester and places, but a seaside resort in Devon?'

'Look for yourself,' called back Miss Hawkes with an impressive sweep of her hand. 'These people watching us have come from all over the country to have a pleasant holiday. They'll take home with them to the many places they come from the message we bring.

'Look at their reaction!' she went on. Terry obligingly swung his lens around. 'They're pleased to see us – their conscience is speaking to them, and even if they're not joining in the march you can see what's going through their minds.'

'Erm, look, can you stop for a minute? Just over here by the bus shelter?' called Judy. 'It's important I get the best out of this story – and I must say, Miss Hawkes, you could have let us know you were coming! Just a few words.'

'Just for a moment,' conceded the lady, rather grandly. 'Then we're off to Exeter.'

They edged into the bus shelter, already full to overflowing with people escaping the summer's ravages, and Judy dug out her notebook. Terry had disappeared into the crowd.

'Please,' she repeated. 'Why the protest here, why the protest now? What do you hope to achieve?'

The great woman pushed back the brim of her soaking felt hat to reveal a noble face. 'It's time for women to make their voices heard,' she declared. 'London is full of politicians, and they're all men. But we are more than half the population, and we're entitled to have our voices heard.

'I don't like to segregate women from men, that's not what I want to do. But this is different – men have gone beyond killing each other – they're now preparing to kill us and our children. We have to do what we can to stop it!

'We women are nurturers, we give birth. We have a responsibility to see that this madness comes to an end. Look over there,' she said, pointing back at the march, now trailing away towards the railway station, 'more than half of them women. We have to make our voices heard!'

Well, thought Miss Dimont, I'll drink to that. I must get back to the office to write this up quick – and *ohdearoh-dearohdear* – that means goodbye to the Cat Rescue Coffee Morning and the Austerity Lunch!

She turned to thank her interviewee but Miss Hawkes had already gone, striding back towards the head of the march, hips swaying slightly to the tune ringing out from the oil-drums of the steel band.

She looked round for Terry. The march had cut a swathe through the holiday crowds but now things were returning to normal and they mingled as before, bringing back the more measured pace of life in Temple Regis. The rain had stopped, the plastic hoods were taken off precious perms, and hunched backs returned to their former upright posture.

She got back to the Minor but there was still no sign of Terry. They had an arrangement that if ever they got parted on a story, whoever had the keys (it was usually Terry) would drive back to the office while the other took the bus. Miss Dimont made a beeline for the bus-stop which a green-and-cream single-decker was approaching.

As she reached for her purse a hand touched her sleeve.

'Excuse me… sorry to interrupt… hope you don't mind my asking – I noticed you talking to the woman at the head of the procession. Are you a reporter, by any chance?'

Just my luck, thought Judy with an inward groan. She seemed pleasant enough but this really wasn't the time to be discussing what a wonderful life I must have, meeting famous people and all that.

'Well, yes,' she said in a guarded but perfectly polite tone whose timbre carried the message, I am charmed that you've noted my job but I hope you can see I am a busy person in a bit of a hurry to get back to the office to write this story up. 'Judy Dimont, *Riviera Express*.'

'I do so love Athene's column,' said the woman but got no further. It infuriated Miss Dimont because people always said that. Not, what a glorious front-page exclusive you had last week on the bust-up between contestants in the Glamorous Grannies competition down at the Lido. Or, I remember the wonderful exposé you did on the ruinous cost of the new flower-baskets outside the Town Hall. No, it always had to be Athene!

'She's a lovely person, very sincere.' The bus mercifully was nearing the stop, her escape just moments away.

'There's something I think you should write,' said the woman. Her hand was still on Judy's sleeve.

'Oh yes?' So often people's idea of what constituted a story was infuriatingly wide of the mark.

Had this woman suddenly discovered a new way of growing prizewinning azaleas? Did she think the Mothers' Union ought to get more coverage in the *Express*? Perhaps her daughter was a child prodigy…

'Erm – bus is here,' said Judy. 'Look, can I give you…' and out of her purse, mangled by the heavy copper coins with which she was going to pay the fare, she dragged a small business card. 'We always welcome readers' ideas,' she said, churning out the usual old response. 'Perhaps you'd like to write in?'

The woman's grip tightened. 'No, listen,' she hissed. 'This is something you must expose. It's gone on too long, it's tearing people apart, it's ruining people's lives! Something must be done!'

Judy looked at her as if for the first time. The woman seemed very ordinary, far too ordinary to be in the possession of a scoop. Yet beneath her soft exterior she could sense an inner fire, a determination to see this thing through.

Dammit, she was going to miss the bus! 'Let's sit down on the bench over there,' she said, gently taking the woman's hand off her sleeve. 'We'll have a nice chat about it.'

THIRTEEN

'You have no idea,' the woman was saying, the words fizzling out like an electric current, 'I've waited years to say this! I've hoped others would say it for me, but nobody seems to have the courage to break the magic circle.'

'I can see you're really quite upset,' said Judy, focusing properly for the first time – so much seemed to have happened this morning, and starting the day in a whisky-induced fog was no help – 'please tell me, though, who you are.'

'I will tell you, but not my name.' The woman's urgency seemed at odds with her dress – middle-class, anonymous, hiding the shape of a pitifully thin body. Her face was worn and anxious. 'It really can't go on!'

She half-turned towards Judy. 'For ten years I've been dying. No, I'm not ill – I'm dying because of a mad, misguided belief which has driven a stake through the heart of my marriage. I need your help!'

'I don't think...' said Judy, shifting uncomfortably on the bench, 'I'm afraid however distressing, the *Express* doesn't write about personal domestic troubles... it wouldn't be...'

'It's not me,' interrupted the woman. 'Or, not just me – it's the many women in Temple Regis! And if it's the many here, then think how many more up and down the land, families put to shame by the wretched Freemasons.'

'The Freemasons?'

'They're supposed to be the most wonderful organisation, aren't they? We hear only about the good they do, the charity they distribute round the world. The determination to follow a—' and here she paused before almost spitting out the word, '*Christian* path.

'Well, I know it sounds a cliché, Miss, er, but don't you think charity should begin at home? And if not there, then where? What's the point?'

'Dimont. Judy Dimont.' The rainclouds had disappeared and the holiday crowds were milling happily around again, but even with the hot sun the woman's forceful words made the air seem chilly.

'The bailiffs came round today. They came into my home, and they marked pieces of furniture and other things which they say will provide some money when they sell them. It broke my heart when they said my grandmother's portrait might make ten shillings.'

She looked bitterly towards Judy.

'We have no money, for ten years we've had no money. After university my husband found a respectable job, but then he went and joined the Freemasons. From that moment on, it seems he was prepared to give away not only his money, but his independence and the capacity to think for himself. He – and the Freemasons – have ruined our family life!'

Miss Dimont was thinking of Dud Fensome. Were his rulings on Betty's hair and weight – issued with total disregard to her own wishes and feelings – born of this misanthropic culture? It sounded very much as though they were.

'Where does it all go?' the woman was saying, shaking her head. 'The money, I mean – that's the question I keep asking myself. There's all the stupid paraphernalia they have to buy – aprons made out of kid leather, gilded medals, fancy gloves – you should see the stuff he's shelled out on over the years as he's worked his way up through the – what do they call it? The Craft.' The woman spat out the word. 'You can't begin to believe the expense!'

'I do see what you mean,' began Miss Dimont, tentatively. 'But I don't see what I can…'

'I heard you talking to that woman, Miss Hawkes, isn't it? She was saying it's time women got up and did something about the Bomb. Well, what I say is that before you start trying to do things about a calamity that may never happen, let's see if something can't be done about this wholesale extortion of family funds.'

The woman was well-spoken and clearly well-educated. Her clothes were chosen because they were hardwearing and likely to last, and had evidently been bought many years ago.

'The children's school uniforms – I have to buy them on the never-never,' she was saying. 'We have margarine instead of butter. My husband has a gin when he comes home in the evening but to make the bottle last, I don't. I walk and don't take the bus. I choose the cheapest cuts of meat at the butcher and look away in shame as he glances at me sideways as if to say, "what's a lady like you doing eating so poorly?"'

'Haven't you discussed this with him?' said Judy. 'Asked him to stop spending so much?'

'Of course I have! But he takes the view, like most men, that if he earns the money it's his to be spent as he sees fit. And he talks of all the good around the world the Freemasons do, and how we contribute to that.'

'Well, it's true,' replied Miss Dimont. 'They *do* do good.'

'What a shame, then,' said the woman sharply, 'that I don't get a visit from a man knocking on my door saying, "Hello, I'm a Freemason – do you need any help?" Because my answer would be yes, yes, yes! "Come in and help me balance the housekeeping, for a start!"'

'I see. It's a terrible...'

'It's not just that.' She looked down at the crumpled paste-board card in her hand. 'Miss Dimont, that's an unusual name. It's worse than that, Miss Dimont. It's a secret society for men, run by men, to advance men, to gratify men, designed to exclude women and keep them in ignorance and at their feet.'

The reporter nodded in sombre agreement but the note-book remained in her raffia bag.

'My husband works for the civil service – I won't tell you what he does but he has a responsible job. He's clever but he's stupid at the same time. We should be able to afford holidays but he says we live by the seaside, why go anywhere else?

'Once a year there's a Ladies' Night when we're expected to put on the finery we no longer possess, so we can do our husbands proud. Then – back in your box! – we're surplus to requirement. I tell you, Freemasonry may have done great things around the world but it's destroyed the love for my husband – and I'm not alone. My grandmother's portrait – ten bob!' She turned away, and her shoulders started to shake up and down.

'I wonder what you would like me to do,' said Miss Dimont, kindly. Certainly, there was a story here – why were the bailiffs knocking at her door? Was there, perhaps another story hidden behind this apparent tragedy?

'Does your husband gamble?'

'No, and he doesn't drink either, apart from the gin. And before you ask, he doesn't look at other women. I can see what you're thinking – how can this nice middle-class family find themselves washed up on the rocks when everything should be going right for them?'

'I must say I'm finding it quite hard to grasp,' admitted Miss Dimont. 'I can see that some might feel Freemasonry's cloaked in secrecy and mumbo-jumbo, but there can be no denying it does good.'

The woman looked at her. Her blue eyes, which had seemed so dull at the start of this encounter, were now sharp, piercing. 'Who told you that?' she said.

'Well… ' started Miss D, not sure how to answer, 'it's a commonly held belief, isn't it?' She didn't like to confess that her newspaper's proprietor and, worse, her editor, were both high-ups in the Craft. Or that a story which challenged their fundamental beliefs and prejudices was never likely to get into the *Riviera Express*.

'Well, can you write something about it?'

'I'd love to. But' – oh dear, here comes the evasion! – 'without adding your full name to the story – without mentioning your husband, his job, his rank in the worshipful brethren – there's not much to write.'

The woman stood up. Her shoes needed repairing and the handle on her handbag was threadbare, but she had a nobility and grace which made Miss Dimont feel ashamed of what she'd just said.

'The bailiffs...' she said, looking away towards the sea. 'When Graham was born I thought he might go to Cambridge, like his father. Now I see that will never happen. I live in crushing, awful, middle-class poverty. All too soon we will have to leave beautiful Temple Regis which I adore more than anything, and find somewhere horrible and cheap to live.

'And all because my husband has this deep-seated yearning for ceremonial, and mystery, and clannishness, just like all the other so-called worshipful brothers.

'And we, the wives, let them go on and do it. Now why, do you suppose, do we allow that to happen?'

The back end of Temple Regis was not quite the same as the glorious scenes you saw on the postcards. The city fathers had done their best but Mount Regis Square, its name a forelock's tug to the local squire, was no more than a collection of irregular bungalows sandwiched between shops which had long since given up the ghost.

Terry mooched along the broken pavement past the Temple Rock Shop (closed), This 'n' Hat (no titfers today), and Sand & Sea Shoes & Beachwear (too far from the beach) in search of the police station's outpost in Lydford Lane.

Sir Robert Peel House, a shed behind the square, was where the Temple Regis police force kept their excess baggage. Sergeant Gull was waiting for him with an eager smile on his face.

'We're just a couple of streets away,' he said brightly. 'The missus'll have the kettle on.'

Terry blinked, then remembered the sweetener mentioned by Miss Dimont – 'you get an exclusive on the album as long as you do some snaps of Gladys Gull and her wretched flowers'. This was the curse of being a photographer – everyone wanted their picture taken, but nobody wanted to pay. The *Riviera Express* ran on a tight budget and explaining away half a roll of film and a few sheets of 10 × 8 was no easy matter, even when you were chief photographer.

When it was taken out of its box it seemed so small, so pitiful – a leather folder with maybe half-a-dozen photos pasted within. All were black-and-white, most with a fancy scalloped edge which showed they'd been printed up by a professional outfit, not by the photographer.

At a glance Terry could tell they were not recent – it wasn't so much the clothes, more the quality of the reproduction. The pictures themselves consisted of a group of individuals who looked related to each other – both by their looks but also the way they posed together. On the other hand they could just have been close friends, it was hard to tell.

'Look foreign to me,' said Terry to Gull, but the sergeant had his nose in a gardening magazine and not really listening.

'Ur.'

Committing the album to film took a matter of minutes – once he'd set up the lighting, which needed to be powerful, he just turned the pages and clicked the shutter. The fact there were so few photographs in an album which had quite obviously contained many more was a puzzle, but when he came to the last page he stopped. The print in front of him had been torn into four pieces, then reassembled and roughly glued back onto the page.

He leaned closer and asked himself what could have prompted someone to do such a thing, photo albums being such an important part of family history. The empty pages offered no response.

Finally Terry took a shot of the torn picture, and as an afterthought carefully lifted the four separate parts away from the page to photograph each one separately before replacing them carefully, pressing down hard so that the adhesive would work. He kept his back to Gull as he did this – tampering with evidence, especially in a murder case, could get your collar felt.

The job done, he had time to consider what he'd just committed to film: there were no obvious answers to the woman's background here – no names, no indications of anybody's identity. He scratched his head and thought about the ridiculousness of the situation.

'We wouldn't have to go to any of this ruddy trouble if we just took a picture of the dead woman's face and published that,' he said to Sergeant Gull.

Gull lifted his head from the magazine and shook it from side to side. 'Chief Constable won't have it. He's up for a knighthood. You wouldn't want it yourself – the expression on her face.'

'What sort of expression?'

'I got a quick shufty of the official snaps o' course, but she looked horrible – sort of shock, sort of pleading, sort of resigned. Quite put me off my dinner.'

'Death's never lovely.'

'They'm gorgeous blooms this yar, though,' Gull said, energetically motioning the photographer towards the door. Gladys would be getting impatient.

But it was Terry's turn not to be listening. The images he'd taken were burning themselves into his brain, fixing themselves there, gradually developing.

FOURTEEN

Betty hopped into the office through the side door. She'd noticed Perce, the Post Office lad, hovering around the front entrance and though he was a sweet fellow the tidings he brought – especially to Betty – were not always of the best. Boyfriends had developed the habit of using the telegram system as a means of saying goodbye, a less confrontational way of slipping Betty's manacle grasp.

Up till now she'd been feeling quite perky. Though the green hadn't quite disappeared she had discovered a new way of doing her hair so it didn't show, except if you looked at her from the back.

Furthermore, unless Perce had brought greetings from Dud (fingers crossed) things were back on again with a promise to take her to the pictures on Friday.

She still hadn't finished the early pages, and then there were the wedding reports to wade through, so that was her morning taken care of. She dropped her bag on Judy's desk and with relief picked up the dead cat and stuffed it in her bottom drawer.

Yesterday's teacups hadn't been washed up but surely Judy

would be in soon – her turn to make the tea! She pulled the hefty old Imperial Standard towards her, folded a sandwich of copy-paper and…

Then she took out her make-up bag and got to work beautifying her countenance, a lengthy and mysterious process.

'Early's late,' barked John Ross, cryptically; his convex belly sliding into view in her hand-mirror.

'Ye don' need lipstick to tell the worrld what's new in Temple Regis, girrly, just get on with it! Need it finished by ten o'clock!'

Betty winced and turned to the task in hand. First, joy of joys, was to sort out the winners of the sandcastle competition. Temple Regis' annual regatta was always a headache because so many people expected to see their names in the paper – woe betide if one went missing! But the way the results came in, scribbled on bits of paper, was haphazard and confusing. She found she'd muddled the crab-catching competition (needs the tide in) with the Mud Race (needs tide out) and had to tear the copy-paper from the Imperial and start again.

She'd allowed herself a moment of purple prose – *the flotilla of rowing boats progressed through the estuary with lit lanterns, creating an outstanding display of twinkling lights slowly disappearing into the night* – and was just getting to grips with the Swimming Gala when the phone rang.

'Betty?' It was Joyce, the new girl on reception who never seemed to get her clothes wrong and irritated Betty, especially because her hair always looked effortless.

'Mm,' said Betty offhandedly.

'Chap down here wanting to see you. Name of...' Joyce was hopeless with names and Betty could hear her asking whoever it was to repeat it. 'Karra Knickers sounds like.'

With her free hand Betty quickly grabbed the make-up mirror. 'Down in a jiffy!'

Even though it only took seconds to reach the front hall, Joyce was already hard at work on the drummer. Short he may have been, with a receding hairline and, to be frank, not half so attractive when he wasn't beating all hell out of his tomtoms, but nonetheless he had trousers. And a way about him to which a more worldly woman would have warned 'Beware – *musician*!' But this was Temple Regis, and jazzers were a cultural rarity.

Despite the fact he was here to see Betty, Sticks seemed in no hurry to tear himself away from present company. Joyce may be obliged to wear glasses, but the way she took them off and put them on again – well, it didn't leave much to the imagination.

'Why, St – i – i – cks!' yodelled Betty to grab his attention while at the same time signalling to Joyce they'd known each other for months if not years or a lifetime, whichever was longer. The drummer turned to the reporter, then back to the receptionist, while a foolish grin slowly spread over his face. Musicians!

'Betty,' he said, finally. 'You said to get in touch if I heard anything.'

'Yes, yes, yes,' said Betty proprietorially, 'a cup of coffee! Come along!' The vanquished Joyce put her specs back on with a sad movement which acknowledged defeat.

'Are you working? Should I come back at lunchtime?'

Betty thought of the paragraph she'd left behind, about the Orbridge Mothers' Union's visit to Exeter Cathedral, *After climbing a hundred and seventy-two narrow turret stone steps, they were able to feast their eyes on the glorious views of the city and its surrounds…* and decided John Ross would have to wait a bit longer for his late early pages.

She steered Sticks into the steamy comforts of the Signal Box café, having learned on the way there that he'd played on thirty-seven records, was divorced, lived in a converted Methodist chapel under the flight-path to London Airport, and had had a childhood ambition to join the circus. Soon she was able to add to this store of knowledge the fact he drank his coffee black with no sugar, and had no qualms about puffing cigarette smoke into a lady's face.

'So, does everyone call you Sticks?'

'Nah, but the name's a mouthful.'

'Try me.' Betty leaned forward.

'Theoclymenus. It's a pain having to repeat it, then spell it. Stick to Sticks.'

'OK. So what can you tell me about the murdered woman?' This was a breakthrough moment for Betty – so far Fleet Street hadn't done more than report a line or two about the shooting, simply because without a name the story remained without focus. If only she could identify the murder victim! What a scoop!

Betty Featherstone – of the *Daily Mail*! Featherstone of the *Herald*! The *Sunday Pictorial*! It only takes one big story – how many times had she been told this? – to make it into Fleet Street, to get away at last from boring old Temple Regis. And one name, one identity would do it!

'So who was she?'

'Dunno,' said Sticks.

'But you've brought me all this way to…!'

'What I found out,' said Sticks, stubbornly, 'is that she went missing from the party circuit about three or four years ago – disappeared completely. I talked to my cousin. He's a caterer for those parties I told you about and he remembered her, too. A strange woman, she was, liked older and very rich men. Mind you, she was one of the rich lot herself – I only ever saw her at the big houses in Kensington and north London and my cousin says the same.

'He thinks she could be a woman called –' and there the drummer paused a beat –'can't remember.'

Betty could have screamed. He was hopeless. However there was more to come.

'If it's her, the one I think it is, it's a terrible story. My cousin says her father was murdered a few years ago – stabbed to death – and now here she is, shot through the heart. I mean, she wasn't the nicest person out – I never spoke to her, but you see an awful lot when you're playing drums at a party. You can tell what a person's like, especially one with a face like that. With her, it was always about me, me, me. She was just that type.

'But then again,' he added unhelpfully, 'it mayn't be who my cousin thinks it is. But it's a start, isn't it?'

Betty had her notebook in her lap, but so far he'd given her very little to jot down – and certainly not the name he'd more or less promised.

'If it is her, might someone have got it in for the family?'

This was worth a try. 'Murdered both of them? Father and daughter?'

'Dunno. The Greeks can be a bit hot-tempered, like – I should know! But my cousin, he thinks the story is that the father died after a burglary went wrong.'

Betty was torn. Sticks was a very attractive man, and she'd love to linger in his company. On the other hand there were the late early pages to complete and this thin scraping of information didn't really take the story forward very much.

'Sticks, er, Theocl… Got to get back to the office now.'

'I was thinking – come up to London with me at the weekend. Moomie's taking a couple of days off for a funeral so we won't be playing till Tuesday – Cornish and the Manifold and me are driving up. Why don't you come and see what you can dig out, I'll introduce you to my cousin.'

'Well, that would be…'

'You can always come and stay at my place.' Sticks smiled a slow smile.

'Oh!' Betty was shocked. 'Um… er, I have a date! I mean,' she stammered, because despite his lack of height Sticks did have a certain something, perhaps something too precious to let go, 'I mean, I'd love to, but…

'Might make your name, if you crack this case,' said Sticks, easily. He'd listened at their previous meeting at the Marine to Betty's oft-repeated ambition to make the big time, to be in London.

'Ohh!' said Betty. He was ten times better-looking than Dud.

'Come on, then,' urged Sticks, 'come up with us to the old Smoke. Get yourself a – what do they call it? – a scoop?'

'Ohhhh!!' said Betty.

When she got back to the office, there was Judy hammering away at the Remington Quiet-Riter. As a machine it did not live up to its name, clanging loudly as she reached the end of each line, making noises as if from a mediaeval torture chamber each time the return lever was operated. The space bar sounded like the thundering of hooves.

Judy was in full flow, writing up her report of the Ban the Bomb rally, notebook by her side but so far unconsulted – when you return from a gripping story, people's words are fixed in your brain, no need to be reminded by the squiggles on a page. Old professionals always say, let the story tell itself, and so it does – if you write it straight away. Try to recreate the mood a couple of hours later, or next day, and the magic has gone.

Miss Dimont had seized the moment and was pouring in the quotes from Jacquetta Hawkes before they evaporated. Her head was down, her fingers drumming away, puffs of smoke as if from an Indian reservation coming from a rare cigarette jammed between her lips.

Betty knew better than to interrupt the flow and sat down quietly at the desk opposite. Of course, what she should really be doing was consulting her chief reporter on the murder story, informing her of the tentative progress made in her meeting with Sticks, but newspapers don't work like that.

Journalists guard their information and their sources with an almost pathological jealousy. Betty might tell a clergyman her wonderful discovery, or the lady on the cheese counter at Lipton's, or even Athene, but not another journalist. And certainly not Judy Dimont!

She sat and weighed the options, which had only partially to do with the story. Should she go to London for the weekend with Sticks and dump Dud, or play safe and keep her date at the Picturedrome? It was difficult to concentrate with Judy rattling away – always so irritating when someone else is in full flood on a story – so she got up and wandered off with her unfinished early page copy to John Ross.

The chief sub was sitting with a sardonic look on his face as he watched his underlings rummage their way through the interminable cricket results it was the *Express*'s duty to publish.

'Earlies all done,' Betty lied.

'Aboot time too,' growled Ross. 'We've got an extra advert on the page now, so you can chuck half of that lot away.'

Phew, thought Betty, they'll never know I didn't finish them. 'Got a few more items written up in case things change,' she said, her smile as false as the colour of her hair.

'Spike 'em,' snapped Ross, and Betty wandered away again. He really wasn't that short, she argued with herself, and the way he did those rim-shots in *My Melancholy Baby* was really very stimulating.

On the other hand, Sticks, Cornish and the Manifold were here for a six-week season only – the moment Moomie beat it back to London, they'd fly as well – and with caution born of long experience Betty felt things with Sticks were unlikely to last beyond the summer. Better to hang on to Dud.

'Your turn to make the tea,' called Judy from a brief lull in her cannonade. It wasn't.

Yet again, if she made some excuse to Dud she could have the weekend away *and* get her scoop – Sticks had promised an introduction to his cousin – and anyway she needed some fresh air. The furthest she'd been from Temple Regis recently was Newton Abbot, and that was no party.

The editor's door opened – now was her moment! She waved at Mr Rhys and skipped up the office, teamaking duties casually abandoned.

Terry came over to Judy's desk and sat in Betty's chair. The thundering ceased and Judy pulled the paper from the roller.

'What happened to you?' she said, stiffly, 'I had to get the bus back.'

'Went off to copy that photo album you borrowed from Topham,' said Terry with a note of self-importance. 'The dead woman. Didn't want to hang around listening to that old bat from Ban the Bomb and her crackpot ideas.'

Judy bit her lip. If Terry had no care for the future of the planet, if he couldn't see that it only took a finger on a button to see us all in smithereens, this was hardly the time to re-educate him.

'What have you got?'

'There were only seven photos left in the album, some more had been stuck in at some stage but then taken out again. Quite a few blank pages.'

'Did you take a picture of the album itself?'

Terry tipped up his head and looked down his nose. 'Whaddya think?'

'And the pictures show what, exactly?' They weren't getting on terribly well this morning. Was it the way he slammed the car door just before they came across the protest march?

No, it was before that – that silly tune he was singing, 'He Socked Her In the Chopper'. Deliberately out of tune, just to set her teeth on edge.

No, it was... it was... Betty. He'd taken Betty to see Moomie Etta-Shaw when really if anybody should have been poking their noses in the Marine Hotel last night, it should have been... the train of thought petered out as she watched Betty follow Rudyard into his office and close the door.

Or... maybe it was the whisky last night. Like most people who had supposedly reached maturity Judy didn't want to admit to self-inflicted wounds. It must be Betty or Terry that made her feel so grumpy.

'I've printed them up if you want to have a look,' said Terry. It sounded like he didn't care whether she did or she didn't.

'Oh well, I suppose...' said Judy, sounding just the same. 'Just let me hand this copy in. Did you get something decent from the protest march?'

'Jumped on a wall and got a top-shot.'

'Show how many people were in the march?'

'Whaddya think!' Things really *weren't* going well between them. 'Come on!'

The print room next to the darkroom was an oasis of calm in the noisy *Express* office. Few people came here and it would be a welcome retreat were it not for the overpowering smell of developing fluid which seeped from next door.

''Ere we are,' said Terry, drawing up two chairs to the print table.

Before them lay more than a dozen 10 × 8 prints, already curling slightly at the edges from the heat of the low overhead light. The first five showed the picture album, a small leatherbound pocket-size book of indeterminate origin but of some age.

'Front, back, spine, front inside, back inside,' said Terry. He was nothing if not efficient.

'When you picked it up,' said Judy, 'did you get any kind of feeling about it?'

'Foreign,' said Terry. 'It smelt foreign. Like…' he searched for a description, 'like when I was in Spain.'

'Anything else?'

'It had thirty pages, most of them not used. First couple of pages had whatever prints had been there removed, then a couple of pages with more blanks. Seven images remaining. I was able to take some of them off the page, just to see if someone had written on the back, like they do – but no dice. A couple of them had a pencilled initial – I reckon that was the shop that developed them leaving their mark. You'll see when we get to it.'

The print table was quite small and they had to sit close to each other in order to look at the images.

Terry switched off the overhead lights and all that remained were the print lights beaming down on his photographs, otherwise the room was a pool of darkness. He smelt rather nice.

'OK,' said Miss Dimont, 'fire away, Terry. Tell me what you see. Are these pictures going to solve the murder for us?'

FIFTEEN

'Who knows?' he said. 'They should tell some kind of story, but they don't.'

Miss Dimont drew the prints towards her, one by one. The first confirmed Terry's 'foreign' description – it was a picture of a large house overshadowed by olive trees, taken in bright sunlight. A lunch-party is in progress with maybe eight or nine figures around the table. A young woman stands in the foreground, behind her two men, their arms around each other's shoulders.

The next featured one of the two men, holding in his arms a girl of maybe six or seven. It was followed by a picture of a small group of people outside a restaurant, but the feel, the lighting, and the clothes were all different.

Miss Dimont was trying to weigh up what she saw. 'This looks like one family, they have strong facial similarities, at least the men do. Mediterranean – Spanish, Italian, Greek.

'This woman here,' she pointed. 'I think it's the same woman in each picture – I think the little girl is her too. The whole thing looks more complicated than it actually is because her hair's different in each shot. But take away the hair and – don't you agree?'

'Dunno,' said Terry. The light was bouncing off the table and when she turned her head, she could see a small area on his chin where the razor had missed its target this morning.

Terry pulled the next picture towards her – this time a rear view of a woman in her twenties sitting on the edge of a diving board, looking back towards the house – a very different kind of house – behind her. It was followed by a street scene with the unknown woman – it could be her, but then again might not be – wearing dark glasses and with a much older man by her side, also with dark glasses. Neither looked happy.

'Then this,' said Terry. The last shot was dark, muzzy, an interior. The room it depicted belonged to someone of wealth but not especially good taste. There didn't seem to be any particular point to the photo, which in any case was marred by a thick score across its middle. 'This one had been torn in half, and half again, and then put back together and the pieces glued back into the album,' said Terry. 'And that's it.'

They sat in the pool of light, neither moving or speaking. The print room was cold but Terry's wiry frame gave off a measure of heat. Shoulder to shoulder, neither seemed in a hurry to move.

'Well, there's a link, obviously,' said Judy finally. 'Let's try and assemble a storyline – I sometimes did this sort of thing in the war. Doesn't always work but it helps collect our thoughts.'

Terry was looking at the prints, proud that he'd got them so sharp. Picture narratives weren't particularly his thing, but he was pleased his work was receiving so much detailed attention – more than it did out on the editorial floor, where week after week they banged his stuff in the paper without comment.

'The common factor, quite clearly, is the girl. We see her as a child in the arms of what I take to be her father – or her uncle, maybe. The house behind shows this is a well-off family – the people at the side are servants from the way they group together and stand back from the camera as if in deference. It's a very big house, so we can assume they're rich.'

'There's one more.'

'I saw it, it's just an old car.'

'Not just a car, an Alvis. A TA-14. You don't see too many of those around these days.'

'Well, you can't see its registration number, so no clues there.'

'It's gorgeous,' sighed Terry. 'Alvis started making them just after the war. Based on the pre-war 12/70, you know – they were really were…'

Judy turned and gave him a look. Their noses were only inches apart. 'Honestly, Terry, the boxes of useless knowledge you keep up there in that attic of yours!'

It was water off the proverbial. Terry had grabbed a magnifying glass and was busy admiring the stately lines of the limousine. 'Looks new – you can tell by the sheen on the paintwork. If we can work out the sequence of these photos, we might just be able to put a date on it. They only made this model for a short while. And look, Judy, this one's painted white or cream or some very light colour – that's got to reduce the number of possibilities. Then, if we've got the date, and the model, and a rough guide to the colour we can ask around a few dealers, and maybe we…'

'Take a month of Sundays, Terry. Do you have any idea how many cars Alvis actually sell?'

Terry was cross. He tossed the photo to one side and picked up the others. 'OK, Miss Clogs,' he said, 'take these photos and tell me a story with them.'

Judy gave him a smile. In the half-light cast by the print lamps she looked particularly beautiful, even though her hair was, as usual, all over the place. Terry looked away.

'First thing,' she said, 'is to re-arrange the order they came out of the album. People don't always put pictures in chronological order – they don't always fit the page, or they paste them in randomly or sometimes they forget they've left the roll of film for developing at the chemist's and it doesn't come back till after they've put other pictures in. So you have to discount the order in which you found them.

'Looking at these, we might take it that the girl and woman who features in them, though she looks different sometimes, is the same person throughout. So we start with the first one, which is her at, let's guess, seven years old. She's being held by two men who look very similar, they could be much older brothers, or it could be that one of them is her father and the other his brother.'

'That's just guesswork!' said Terry. It didn't sound very scientific to him.

'Hear me out. Look at the light. And though this is a close-up, you can see trees in the background – olive trees. So it's fair to assume we're not in England but, let's say, somewhere Mediterranean. The next picture – the lunch party – then bears that out. Large house in the sunshine, olive trees – so similar.

'The girl is older now, maybe seventeen? If you look, you can see one of the two men from the first picture – he's standing close to her, the others in the party keep their distance. So, could be that this is the man who owns the house, and this is his daughter.'

'Where's the mother, then?' said Terry.

'If you look there's nobody here who looks like they belong to this man and his daughter – no woman of the right age claiming ownership of the girl – so she's probably the one holding the camera and taking the picture.'

'What next?'

'Well, that's when it gets difficult. It's either the restaurant scene, or the one of her sitting on the diving board.'

'The light's different.'

'So is the architecture, Terry. The house behind the swimming-pool is mainly obscured by trees, but you can see it has a slated roof, not terracotta tiles. The windows are really quite big – they need to let in a lot of light. And the trees, they're not olives but oaks and elms – we're now in England!'

'And the restaurant?'

'Well, they're standing outside because they want a photo to mark an occasion – it'd be too dark inside without a flash-gun, and anyway it's only people like you who have that sort of equipment. No, if you look closely you can see our woman – she looks different because she's older, her hair's been cut differently and she's much paler. There in the background is someone who looks like her father – but it might not be. Looks like London, could be Soho. They are, I'd say, ten years older than the lunch-party in the sunshine. She doesn't look happy.'

'Maybe it's somebody else's birthday, not hers,' said Terry.

Judy looked at him. 'You know, from you, that's quite a startling piece of observation.' It started her thinking.

'Get on with it, I've got to get the Leica fixed. It's causing me no end of problems.'

'Then there's this. She's standing against a lamp post with her father, they're both wearing sunglasses – why?'

'You can tell there's no sun, they're not lit by sunlight but daylight,' said Terry.

'Precisely. So why the sunglasses? Why the strained expressions on their faces?'

'Just a minute,' said Terry, who'd been inspecting the prints with his magnifying glass while Miss D had been pontificating, 'this isn't England. Though it's blurry – must be winter – you can just see the corner of a car. That's a Citroen Deux Chevaux. They're in France!'

Cars again. It was all men thought about. Apart from beer and the obvious. 'OK,' said Judy, 'I'll buy that for the moment. Then we have these other two pics – the room in the house, and the car.'

'No clues as to the room,' said Terry. 'It's a duff shot, taken by mistake, I reckon. You know how you do sometimes – press the shutter release while you're still lining the shot up. You do it all the time – I've seen your snaps.' From the mouth of a professional photographer the word was nothing less than an insult but Judy had to agree, there was no point in her ever picking up a camera.

'And the car – well, despite what you say, Judy, it shouldn't be impossible to narrow down its ownership.'

'Only if it was still in the possession of the person who first bought it.'

'True.'

Terry could tell he'd perhaps overstepped the mark with his snaps comment.

'Pub?'

'Pub.'

As they gathered up the prints and wandered out through the editorial floor they stepped around a tired-looking school party docked alongside the chief sub-editor's desk. John Ross was wearily instructing his audience in the rudiments of journalism.

'. . . the five Ws,' he was saying, his foot pushing his desk drawer to and fro so they could glimpse the Vat 69 bottle rolling around below. 'If ye have the five Ws, ye have yer story. So easy to remembairr – it's who, what, why, when, where. Tell me,' he said, bringing his gaze down from the ceiling where it had been resting for some minutes, 'who can repeat back what I just told you? Maybe we can find a journalist among the bunch of you.'

Alas that particular day, there was no future Hannen Swaffer to be found. The girls' eyes were soaking up the myriad sights and sounds of a great newspaper in production while the boys had homed in on Joyce, energetically doing her errands in a tight sweater.

Judy and Terry's onward journey past the editor's open

door might have offered them the sight of Rudyard Rhys and Betty Featherstone in heated debate, but neither bothered to look – both were too preoccupied with the photographs to pay any attention.

Inside the inner sanctum, however, editor and reporter were feverishly arguing the toss about the weekend ahead. Betty had laid before Rhys her London plans, hoping the chance of identifying the murder victim would find favour not only in his eyes but incidentally those of Fleet Street's talent-scouts, too.

'No.'

'But it could be the breakthrough! Old Inspector Topham sounds like he hasn't got a clue!'

'No, Betty, no! I have a special assignment for you on Saturday – no time to be running up to London. And I suppose you'd be expecting to put it on expenses, too.'

'Well…'

'Rrr-rr,' growled Rhys, fishing for his pipe, 'just an excuse for a shopping trip! No, I want you over at Buntorama on Saturday and just be thankful it'll get you out of doing the wedding reports.'

'Buntorama? But…'

'No more about the murder, Betty, I've had enough – in fact I'm sick of hearing about it. No, new things are happening with Bunton and his crew and I want a comprehensive report back from you my desk on Monday morning.'

Betty looked desolate. She still hadn't made up her mind whether she would actually stand Dud up on their cinema date, but she wanted the freedom to make the choice herself. If Mr Rhys insisted on her working on Saturday, she wouldn't be able to get to London in time to meet up with Sticks and his cousin.

On the other hand, she couldn't be sure about the drummer's invitation, and in some ways it was a relief. But the choice should have been hers alone, not Mr Rhys's! She tried to catch up with what he was saying, but he did drone on so.

'. . . Archbishop of York. But really what I want you to pay attention to is...'

'. . . have you got a piece of paper, Mr Rhys? Left my notebook on my desk.'

'Rr-rrr! Reporters should have their notebooks with them at all times.'

'And a pencil?'

'Rr-*rrr*!'

'You were saying about the Archbishop?'

'No, this is really the reason why I want you there – just make a few notes of what the Archbishop says, only a couple of pars, mind! Damned if I'm going to do Bunton's publicity for him! No, the real reason for your visit is to find out about a new member of the board, Admiral Sir Cedric Minsell.'

'The one who's on telly?'

'Ah, you've seen him. I haven't. He's joining the Bunton board and I gather will be there to greet the Archbishop on his arrival. I want you to engage him in polite conversation, say you want to write something nice about him, and look, here's a list of questions I want you to put to him. Only not in an obvious way, just sort of chatting as it were.'

Betty thought this odd. 'Should I mention that you were in the Royal Navy, Mr Rhys? He might know your name, that might help if I'm asking him off-the-record questions.'

'Rr-rrrr-*rrrrr*! *Don't* do that, Betty!' thundered the editor. 'Just wear a nice dress and hang around him till he's told you what you want to know.'

'What *you* want to know, Mr Rhys.'

'Yes, well. Off you go. And don't tell anybody about this conversation.' For heaven's sake, thought the editor, since I left the Royal Navy I have been a novelist, a reporter, and an editor. My life has moved far away from the carpetless underground corridors of the Admiralty, yet still I can't escape. They have me in their grip and that dreadful Auriol Hedley with her superior manner – telling me what to do. Spying on a spy! When I came to the *Riviera Express* I'd hoped that the thorniest problem I'd ever have to face was whether to get rid of the crossword!

He picked up his disgusting briar pipe and started jabbing at it with an old pencil-stub.

Over at Buntorama they were having trouble getting a huge steam tractor through the gates. It carried on a low-loader a vast piece of machinery which towered over the surrounding buildings. Inch by inch, the driver manoeuvred his gargantuan payload through the narrow gap until he could make a steady forward progress.

'Where ja wannit?' he bawled down through the steam and smoke.

'Over there, by the fence,' shouted back Mr Baggs, who was directing operations.

'What? Over by yon hotel? You sure?'

'Oh yes,' called Baggs, 'nearer the better!'

The great leviathan clanked and huffed its way forward. Behind it came several lesser vehicles carrying the ancillaries.

'Got it through?' asked Bobby Bunton, newly arrived in his Rolls-Royce.

'Went in a treat,' said Baggs.

'How long do they say to set it up?'

'Be done by nightfall, they reckon.'

'So we can get the Devil's Dodgems started first thing tomorrow, then.'

'Sure can, boss.'

'Get it going at breakfast-time, then. And make sure the volume's turned up to maximum.'

Baggs gave him a wintry smile. 'So it's war, is it, boss?'

Bobby Bunton took out a cigar and stuck it importantly into his lips. 'Nobody threatens me,' he said, squaring his shoulders inside his ugly suit. 'The snob!'

''E can't prove anything,' said Baggs. 'Nothing to prove!'

'He can go to the press.'

'What, that tinpot rag with the fortune teller and the reporter in specs? I warned their photographer to stay away.'

'No, no,' said Bunton. 'If he wants to dent my reputation he'll go to the nationals. "MYSTERY BOBBY BUNTON BABE SHOT THROUGH THE HEART" – that'll be the headline.'

'They can't write that sort of thing. There's such a thing as libel laws.'

'Yeah,' said Bunton. 'But those Sunday papers. They manage to tell a story with nods and winks so you know what's being said without them actually printing it.'

'Well, so what?' said Baggs. 'Not as if you made a habit of it.'

'It was enough to get Radipole at my throat, though, wasn't it?' laughed Bunton. 'His girl – and me? Ha, ha, ha!'

'What about Fluffles?'

'Well, that's it. If she finds out about it I'm a dead man. But I can't control what Radipole says to the press and so the only thing to do is fight fire with fire.'

'The Devil's Dodgems.'

'I can ruin his business in a week with the racket that ride makes,' sneered Bunton. 'He'll get a taste of it with his ruddy Oxford marmalade tomorrow morning.' He pronounced it 'Orxford'.

'You don't think he'll try any funny business? You know…?' Baggs lifted his hand with two fingers thrust forward and pulled an imaginary trigger.

'I think we are more than capable of withstanding any such threat, don't you, Bert?' said Bobby and patted his top pocket.

His henchman offered a twisted smile at the thought.

SIXTEEN

Betty was on strike. She sat at an awkward angle to her desk with a pile of magazines beside her, pushing from view the lost opportunity with Sticks, and the increasingly dismal prospect of a night at the Picturedrome with Dud. She took refuge in reading 'How To Dress To Please Your Man' by Enid Chandler in *Everywoman*.

Enid was something of a heroine to Betty, who dreamed of making the switch from local newspapers to being a columnist on such a vibrant magazine. Anything – anything! – to get away from Temple Regis!

'This week, a special emphasis on personal grooming,' whispered Enid. 'He likes you to be soft and silky!'

She was more forthright when it came to instructing her readers on how to hook, net, and land their man: 'A girl won't get far without polishing up her good points and disguising her bad ones so that he's completely befogged by glamour!' she commanded, to which Betty nodded vigorously in agreement. 'It's at this stage that the romantic compliments are paid and the diamond engagement rings are shopped for!'

The redoubtable Miss Chandler had further strong words of advice once those engagement and wedding rings were safely slipped on: 'Don't try to be the boss, don't be the slightly abnormal woman who wants to have her cake and eat it.'

Betty could see some point to this, but then she thought about Dud and his devotion to the Freemasons, and couldn't altogether go along with Enid. The fellow spent all his spare time, when he wasn't instructing Betty about the shade of her hair-colouring or the size of her waist, with his nose pressed into books which all had to be learned word-perfect.

So, thought Betty, looking again at the advice page, what would it be like married to Dud? Who'd be the boss? Would I ever see him, or would he be out masoning with his chums every night?

Would he expect dinner and slippers when he got home? She was beginning to realise what a mistake she'd made in reheating this particular soufflé.

Just then the telephone rang.

'You coming?' It was Sticks, his voice no more than an inviting drawl. 'London's calling!'

'I can't, I'm working,' wailed Betty. She felt wretched.

'Thought you wanted to solve this murder.'

'Well, of course! It goes without…'

'So I'll see you Friday night.' He sounded quite determined.

How, thought Betty, would Enid react in the circs? Her watchwords for the modern Fifties woman were 'sincerity, humour, understanding, reliability and tact'. Which of these to choose?

'Bye, Sticks, have a lovely life.'

As Betty replaced the receiver she felt a surge of rage at the male of the species – whether it be Dud with his stone-age attitude, or the iron-faced and compassion-free Rudyard Rhys, or that beastly Sticks with his pesky paradiddles – all messing up her life!

She went in search of Athene and a cup of her special tea.

They didn't go to the pub. Terry was feeling – well, he'd never admit it – but he was surprised by Judy's outburst over taking Betty to see Moomie Etta-Shaw. It made complete sense to invite her, after all she'd written the story up for the paper – and anyway, Judy didn't like jazz. For heaven's sake, what was it all about? Women!

On the other hand he knew something wasn't quite right – the way she was sniping at him, the way she looked down that nose of hers. Something had to be done.

'Not going to the pub,' he said firmly as they got in the Minor, 'I'm taking you to lunch. The Marine does a budget menu on Thursdays.'

'Oh,' said Judy, looking at him. This wasn't like Terry at all.

'We've got to get on to Riverbridge after,' he reminded her, 'see what's happening there. Otherwise nothing in the diary. And the view from the dining room is wonderful.'

Well, you'd know all about that, thought Judy, having splayed your elbows all over the table last night while you were paying court to Betty Featherstone. But she bit her lip – it was clear Terry intended to pay. Just as well she'd finished the Townswomen's Guild article before leaving the office!

There had been one of those outbursts of meteorological

bad temper this morning – a sudden influx of grumpy-looking clouds which raced in and hovered over Temple Regis in a particularly threatening manner. Holidaymakers who'd dressed for a glorious day ahead were forced to scamper back to their hotels and boarding houses for jumpers, umbrellas and Pacamacs.

But just as unexpectedly the clouds moved on to upset somebody else's day further up the coast, and as the Minor came over the hill towards the Marine a shaft of sunlight lit up the Ruggleswick shoreline. The long empty sands had a mere handful of people dotted across their wide expanse, and the waves came in with a satisfying clumping sound, signalling a turn in the tide. A few idle rooks patrolled about and in the distance a sand-yacht made a few experimental curves, waiting for the tide to recede before racing off to who knows where.

Through the windscreen you could see the stark but imposing lines of the hotel and from this angle its bulk obscured the more proletarian profile of Buntorama's wooden huts. But the moment Terry and Judy opened the car doors they knew Bobby Bunton's famous creation was alive and kicking.

The Devil's Dodgems were doing their work, and furiously. The clashing and banging as the cars careered into each other was overlaid by a veneer of screams, shouts and whoops from the campers who'd awoken this morning to a new addition to the splay of fairground attractions. A cannonade of sound aimed like heavy artillery at the snobs who lived next door.

'Crikey,' said Terry, 'what a racket!'

'Isn't that, er, Lord Rockingham's XI playing through

the loudspeakers?' asked Judy with barely disguised joy. A brazen saxophonist was bellowing his rocked-up version of a Scottish melody, interspersing his rude parps with raucous shouts of:

'Hoots mon –
There's a moose
Loose
Aboot this hoose!'

. . . which the holidaymakers seemed to enjoy bellowing out at full volume. Again and again.

'Let's get inside,' said Terry, shaking his head in disgust.

'I thought you liked jazz,' smiled Miss D, with only the merest hint of sarcasm. It was bedlam out here all right and unsurprisingly the Marine's terrace, the lawns, and the poolside cocktail bar were bereft of custom this late morning.

Inside the hotel's marbled reception, guests were stamping about in sulky fashion while a long queue had formed at the check-out desk, looking like a better-dressed version of the evacuation of Dunkirk. Just as they came in Cornish Pete and Mike Manifold made an appearance, and Terry went over to them.

'What's going on?'

'Those buggers next door,' said Pete, who despite his name spoke with a pronounced south London accent. 'Been like this since eight o'clock this morning! If somebody doesn't do something soon the hotel'll be empty.'

'Moomie's right upset,' added the Manifold. 'This is her first gig outside London and she was promised peace and quiet – she's writing songs, you know.

'But don't write that,' he added urgently to Judy, 'we're

recording an LP in a few weeks' time, all Moomie's songs! Top secret!'

He shared this information like a Hatton Garden jeweller shows you his loose diamonds – one eye on you, the other on the door – but Judy wasn't about to scarper with the earth-shattering news. She was more interested in the Devil's Dodgems.

Over at the other end of reception she could see the tall figure of Hugh Radipole surrounded by a group of elegant but very angry people. He gently waved his arms as if their soft breeze could blow away the racket from next door, but there was a crease in his forehead – for these were people demanding their money back. Important people, rich people, the sort of people he'd come to live among and who last night were calling him by his first name and offering him drinks in the Primrose Bar.

''E ought to get those Noise Abatement Society people round 'ere at the double,' said Terry, straight to the point. 'It's just as bad in 'ere as outside.'

'Might be difficult,' said Miss Dimont. 'Chairman of the Society is Patrick Marchbank and he supported Bobby Bunton putting his holiday camp here – he believes in equality. As a result, Mr Radipole cut his name out of the invitations to the Marine – shouldn't think Patrick could give a hoot, but it would make it difficult for Radipole to beg a favour of him now.'

'You're sweet on him,' said Terry accusingly. He hadn't been listening to her explanation but he suddenly came to when she mentioned Marchbank's name.

Miss Dimont smiled.

'Even though his wife did those dreadful things.'

They quite often discussed the case of the Hon. Adelaide Marchbank and her mad desire to put people away.[1]

'What d'you think,' said Terry, 'do you still want to have lunch here? It's chaos – all these people with their suitcases all over the place, that din going on out there.'

'I think it's fun.'

'OK, then – we shouldn't have any difficulty getting a table.'

As the couple mounted the broad sweep of the staircase, the walls hanging with pictures which could have been painted by Mondrian, a slight figure scampered down the stairs towards them. As they paused on the half-landing to let him past, the man spotted Terry and stopped in his tracks.

'You were here the other night,' he said. 'Photographer.'

Terry nodded encouragingly.

'I'm Sticks, the drummer. That reporter you brought along is useless!'

Miss Dimont's ears pricked up; he must be talking about Betty. Judy was of the old school that would not allow an outsider to criticise her family and near ones, but then on the other hand…

'Hello, Sticks,' she said beguilingly, 'I'm Judy. Are you talking about Betty?'

'Just a bit,' said Sticks, but when he answered he still looked at Terry. Some men were that way with Miss Dimont – they just did not see her. She couldn't care less.

---

1 See *The Riviera Express*.

'Not useless, surely? She wrote a very nice piece about your being here at the Marine, I read it.'

'Not that,' said Sticks, looking over the banisters now. He seemed unconcerned about bringing his eyes to rest on the person he was talking to. 'The murder. That dead woman.'

'Oh?' said Judy, and the way she said it finally caught the drummer's attention.

'She was supposed to be coming up to London this weekend – my cousin thinks he knows who the murder victim was.'

'Really?' said Judy, looking over Sticks' shoulder at Terry and nodding hard, 'we're just having a spot of lunch. Won't you come and join us?'

The whole story was out before they were halfway through the first course – Sticks' recognising the dead woman in the bar downstairs, his recollection of her at fancy London parties a few years before, the cousin who catered the parties remembering something odd – the eagerness of Betty to get to London to gather the information, then the last-minute turndown with no explanation offered.

Judy poured Sticks a glass of wine. Terry and she had some in the bottom of their glasses but it was just to keep the drummer company, they weren't drinking.

'Why didn't you tell the police this?' asked Judy.

'I don't talk to police,' said Sticks forcefully. 'Every time I do, it always ends up the same – "turn out your pockets, let's see if you've got any Mary Jane". So no.'

Miss Dimont wasn't sure what Mary Jane was but assumed it to be illegal – musicians live by a different set of rules, poor lambs. 'Well, tell you what,' she said with a smile, 'why don't I come in Betty's place?'

The drummer looked at her oddly. Perhaps in his explanation he'd failed to make clear there was more to the weekend invitation than the mere solving of a murder. He looked across the table at the lady of a certain age, in an ordinary dress with no make-up, sensible shoes, and wayward hair, and did not see her beauty.

'No thanks.'

'No, really, it would be a pleasure.'

'I don't think so,' said Sticks more urgently.

'No, I insist!' pressed Judy. 'I have somewhere to stay, it would be no trouble at all.'

The penny finally dropped. 'Oh!' laughed Sticks in relief. 'Yes! Ha, ha! Yes, you come along and I'll introduce you to Constantinos, he's sure to have the answer! Will *you* be coming?' he added to Terry, just to be on the safe side.

Terry shook his head. 'I expect you'll be busy polishing your Leica,' said Judy with just a hint of acid.

Terry looked at her, then wandered off to collect the car, the surly set of his broad shoulders speaking volumes in a way no words could.

The door to the branch office of the *Riviera Express* opened with a lively ting.

'Hello, Peggy, just passing, thought we'd drop in and say hello,' trilled Judy as she stepped into the relic of newspaper history with its Dickensian counter, all brass and mahogany, and ancient hand-printing press filling the front window. Here the paper was called the *Riverbridge Advertiser* to satisfy the vanity of the local populace but it carried just the same news, with only the occasional variation to justify its title.

'No, you didn't, dear,' came the crisp reply from Mrs Walthorp, the office manager. 'You've come for him and I can tell you, it's a relief – you can take him away. He's no use here!'

'No, no… it's just that Mr Rhys is concerned. He hasn't heard from Mr Charles for three weeks, and when he rings up he's never in the office.'

'He's always in the office. Never leaves. Sleeps under the desk, I shouldn't wonder.' Peggy nodded sharply towards the closed door of the inner office. 'The man's a hermit.'

'Well,' said Judy, 'we're always warned to remember he was on the beaches on D-Day and…'

'I wish you'd take him to the beach in Temple Regis and do something with him,' said Peggy, sharply. 'It's like having a dead body around the place. You expect a nasty smell every time you open the office door.'

'Well, obviously I'll have a word,' said Judy. She looked out of the window to see Terry taking a picture of a pretty girl sheltering from the rain in the bus shelter. 'What's the problem, Peggy?'

'He's letting the side down!'

'What d'you mean?'

'He hasn't written a single story for a month. He's the *editor*!'

'What does he do with his time?'

'Sits in there all day. Does the crossword, plays chess with himself, re-files the files in the filing cabinet. Sings songs.

Can't look at me when I take him in his tea. He's not well, Judy. But more important, there's no news about Riverbridge in the *Riverbridge Advertiser*! The pages get filled up with all the news from Temple Regis and around, and people are stopping me in the street and asking – why are we paying thruppence and getting nothing for our money?'

'OK, let me go and talk to him.' Terry was still snapping away at the girl in the bus shelter – his photo sessions always took longer when there was a woman at the other end of the lens.

Judy walked across the bare floorboards of the ancient office and knocked on the door. There was no reply, so she opened the door gently.

'Hello, Greville,' she said sweetly, 'just passing. Terry Eagleton's here too. Fancy coming out for a cup of tea?'

Greville Charles had changed considerably since she'd seen him at Christmas. Though still not forty, it was as if all life had gone out of him. His floppy blonde hair had turned grey, the suit he wore, though smart, belonged to a larger, stronger, man, his eyes had taken on a penetrating stare when he lifted them from the book on his desk.

'Lovely to see you.' He still had his perfect manners, but looked away as soon as their eyes made contact. 'How's Terry?'

'Same as always. Photographing some girl in the rain.'

A slight noise came from the man's throat but you could hardly call it laughter. He turned a page in the book and bent his head over it.

'Can I help, Greville?'

'Nothing to be done, Judy, nothing to be done. I just think there's nothing to be done.'

On the wall behind his desk was a photograph of Greville which can only have been a year old, yet could have been taken twenty years before. Judy sat down opposite him and looked into his once-handsome face.

'What's that you're reading?'

'*Parade's End*. There's some salvation here.'

'How so?'

'Everything comes out right in the end. Well, no it doesn't. But there's a way of looking at it which can be a help. It's best to look at it that way.' His eyes slithered across the desk as if he was searching for something.

'Peggy tells me you never go out of the office.'

'Mm.'

'Greville, you're a *reporter*. It's what you're supposed to do. Go out, meet people, get stories, write them. There can't be a more rewarding job in the world.'

He did not move.

'Mr Rhys is worried about you. And then he's worried about the *Advertiser* too – we can't go on filling up your space with stories which have no bearing on Riverbridge.'

'I'm stuck.'

'Sorry?'

'I'm stuck, I can't leave. I can't go anywhere, see anybody. Stuck!'

'Look at me, Greville.' He did not. 'I know what you're suffering, I've seen it in others – old friends, old colleagues. Shell shock is a terrible...'

'*Shell shock!*' Greville repeated, reaching for a packet of cigarettes. 'You haven't a clue. You just don't know…'

'I do know. I think what you should…'

'It's all very well for you, Judy – you had a brilliant war, now you're a brilliant reporter, you have everything I could wish for. You have…' he searched for the word, 'poise. The poise which comes with confidence in your abilities, the belief that your brain's well-stocked with ideas and experiences which can be put to use in your job, whether it's reporting or… whatever it was you did before.' He looked for matches. 'You cannot possibly know what it's like.

'I'm supposed to be a reporter. I'm supposed to wander up to people, ask them a few cheeky questions, sidle away and write up the story in a way which doesn't upset anybody but still appears newsworthy. Can't do it any more.'

'Yes, you can, Greville. You're a good reporter.'

'Not any more. I ask myself, what right do I have to go poking into other people's lives? Do they like what I've written when it appears in the paper? At what point does a genuine interest in a story become personal prurience? What's the whole thing about journalism, anyway? Why do we do it, and is it justified? Why not leave people alone, let them just get on with their lives without putting them on the front page?' His hand was shaking and he gave up the attempt to light his cigarette.

'These are very good questions, Greville, I ask them myself. All the time.'

'No, you don't. You get out your notebook and pencil, you do your impeccable shorthand, you sit in front of the typewriter and ten minutes later – job done! You don't ask whether you're ruining people's lives!'

Judy looked at him steadily. 'What you're saying is, you can't bring yourself to talk to people any more.'

'Yes.'

'And you don't want to go out – leave the office.'

'Yes.'

'Do you know the word agoraphobia?'

'Yes.'

'Is that what you're suffering?'

'No, it's not. I have come to a point in my life where I feel it is impolite – no, more than that, far more – to question people about aspects of their lives. We should leave them in peace.'

'Think of all those people who come into the office with their reports from the flower shows – they want to see their name in the paper.'

'Then why don't they just pay for an advert and have it printed that way?' He suddenly looked tragic in the way he sat there.

'Come out and have a cup of tea.'

'I don't want to. I'll sit here with my book.' The tears were rolling down his cheeks and he wiped them away with the end of his tie.

Judy got up. 'Are you saying that all journalism is bad, Greville? That we should shut down this newspaper and the *Express* and the rest?'

'Prying into people's lives.'

'I'm going to tell Mr Rhys that you are to have a holiday. You are in a deep dark hole and you need help in getting out of it. Coming into the office every day and yet repudiating the business which pays your wages is illogical.'

'I haven't spent the money! It's in the Post Office savings account. When they fire me I'll pay it all back!'

Judy came round the desk and put her arm round his shoulders. She could feel the bones through his suit jacket, moving up and down as he tried to stifle his sobs.

'They're not going to fire you, Greville. You're unwell, they will look after you. They love you.'

'*Zither*,' he said, suddenly.

'What?'

'Such a remarkable word, don't you think? *Zitherzitherzither*...' as the word trailed away his eyes went frighteningly blank.

Peggy put her head round the door.

'Dr Henderson has come,' she said. It was hard to tell whether her tone was one of disapproval, or relief.

SEVENTEEN

The journey up from Regis Junction was all Miss Dimont hoped it would be – soothing, charming, restoring. She had the cardboard ticket inside her glove and valise by her side long before the Riviera Express – never to be confused with the newspaper of the same name – clanked and shouted itself to a shuddering halt.

It being the holiday season, nobody much was leaving Temple Regis on a Friday afternoon and as the train slid to a halt she was pleased to see it was almost empty. She found a corner in the compartment nearest the restaurant-car and settled comfortably in as the Express shunted and puffed its way out of the station. There were two quick stops, Newton Abbot and Exeter, and then the steam train would begin its long leisurely voyage to the capital city, gliding on ribbons of steel, juddering occasionally as it crossed the points, yawing as it took the curves.

Her favourite waiter Owd Bert was on duty, and after Exeter came to knock politely on the compartment door to beckon her towards his domain.

'See you wuz on,' he said. His white bumfreezer jacket

looked jolly with its gilt buttons and the array of medal-ribbons over his breast pocket. 'You come up only the other day, din yer, Miss?'

'A sudden invitation,' said Judy, smiling. 'Nice to be back on board. I'll come with you now but just a cup of tea, Owd Bert, no cake, thank you.'

He looked disappointed. 'That's no good for business,' he chided, genially waving his arm towards the empty restaurant car. In the early evening light it was at its prettiest, with gleaming silver on starched white tablecloths, flowers bobbing in their silver vases, and the sun colouring the car with an almost mystical glow. Perhaps those few passengers aboard the Riviera Express had brought sandwiches, or maybe they were waiting for the dinner hour, but not a seat was taken.

'It looks so lovely,' said Judy to Owd Bert, and though perhaps his critical gaze focused more on the sheen of the wine-glasses and the polish on the wooden seats and bulkheads, he too could see and sense a beauty in his carriage. He marched off, every bit the soldier, to order Judy's tea from a backstage underling.

She looked out of the window at the racing fields and took comfort in her flight from Devon. Seeing Greville Charles in such a terrible state had unsettled her, for she was very fond of him. Before this illness he'd always displayed such a sweet nature, shy and retiring but playful and good at his job. Though ten years separated them each, armed with the knowledge that comes from half-spoken conversations about war work, viewed the other with considerable respect. Neither would talk about what the war had asked from them, or what they had given, yet both knew that the person opposite had given their all. Instinctively she knew Greville had been a hero on the D-Day beaches; just as easily he could tell Judy had excelled in the very secret game she played in the corridors below Whitehall. Neither needed to say more.

Owd Bert brought the tea and a plate of Lincoln biscuits, 'Don't spoil yer dinner!', and wandered off to draw others into his lair. Judy looked at the sharp bright polish on the shiny teapot, felt its heat, and things suddenly seemed better.

Greville had been a joyous member of staff, dropping into the *Express* offices with whimsical tales of Baskerville-like hounds eating the population of Riverbridge, of two-headed postmen and three-legged clergymen, the pockets of his tweed coat bulging with books of poetry. True, he had never married which was remarkable, given his charm and good looks, and for all the world you would think the war was behind him. But it constantly lurked in the shadows, and not only for Greville.

'Taunton! Taunton next stop!'

Perhaps he shouldn't have chosen a career in newspapers, but what else would he do? Or the rest of us, come to that? Who are we, thought Miss Dimont, this ragged bunch of mongrels and misfits who end up in local newspapers – why are we here? Why do we do it? Then again, who else would have us?

She thought of the bulbous John Ross, whistling his tunes of glory up and down the office, with the bottle of whisky he could never touch rolling around in the dark of his desk drawer. Of Betty, good at her job but terribly bad at life. Of Rudyard Rhys, the crouching tiger ready to spring on the failings of others rather than confront his own. Of Athene, a spiritual being cast down to dreary earth by a vengeful deity who knew perfectly well her place was up there in the clouds. Peter Pomeroy, who had to hide his sandwiches in his desk and peck at them like a heron, too embarrassed to be seen eating. And Ray Bennett, well into his dotage but still hoping the theatre would claim him back and whisk him away from this lowlier calling.

Come to that, what about herself? Heart broken in war, moral compass jiggered by peacetime espionage, her Devon sanctuary constantly threatened by the prospect of maternal invasion – was she any better than the others? Who was to say that Greville Charles was any worse?

She got out her novel and tried to think about other things, but as the miles rolled by and Owd Bert's tea gently permeated her veins, the words of Edith Wharton became less absorbing. She was going to London on a whim, at the behest of a journeyman musician she barely knew, with no clear idea of what might be achieved. The shock of someone being so brutally shot in cold blood spurred her forward and yet, with a gunman on the loose, she could easily be putting herself in danger.

Arthur had promised to pick her up at Paddington so at least she had a henchman to hand – even if he was, oh, seventy-two or three! But Arthur was still active, and his past experiences ideally suited him to the job – though it was true he did occasionally got hold of the wrong end of the stick.

Miss Dimont freshened the teapot from the hot-water jug and broke a biscuit in pieces. The lulling movement of the Pullman train, the orderly rows of tables and napkins and silver and glass, the occasional mournful cry of the engine's whistle, allowed her to review what she knew of the case, and prepare herself for what might come in the days ahead.

Patricia Rouchos, which wasn't her real name, came from a Mediterranean country but – it would seem from her reading of the album photographs – had settled in London long ago. That meant she could be a refugee of war.

Well-off, decidedly, but wearing cheap clothes when she was found. Choosing a cheap room at Buntorama, rather than one where she might enjoy Temple Regis' delights more comfortably – why did she do that? And why was she in Temple Regis in the first place?

'*Westbury – Westbury!*'

She stayed at Buntorama, but spent all her time – as far as one could tell – in the Marine Hotel. In the Primrose Bar she had spent a very long time in discussion with Bobby Bunton. Did she try to pick him up, or was it the other way round? What were they talking about? Bunton described her as a prostitute, but given the apparent affluence in which she was raised, was that really likely?

And when Judy mentioned this to Hugh Radipole, why did he take such angry exception to the idea? It had really quite upset him, which had left Miss Dimont to wonder whether it was just that the hotelier hated the thought of call-girls on his premises – or was there was something between him and the murdered woman? Did he know her better – far better – than he let on?

Certainly there was something between Radipole and Bunton, and not just the upstairs-downstairs battle which was going on between them – the holiday camp with its funfair pitched against the sophisticated hotel with the Chicago jazz singer. Radipole was urbane, smooth and worldly while Bunton was an upstart ruffian in an ill-fitting suit – and yet their actions seemed to stem from a common origin. Miss Dimont couldn't put her finger on it, but there was definitely something there.

And what about Bunton and Miss Rouchos – was there something there? Surely he had his hands full with Fluffles Janetti and the various Mrs Buntons he still had in tow? On the other hand...

'Tickets please!' Another familiar face leaned over the table-cloth and broke her thought pattern.

Great Western Railways employed the politest, longest-serving staff – men and women who took pride in their jobs and befriended the regulars – and here was Mr Brass. Miss Dimont could never remember his real name – something obscurely Cornish – and so she concentrated on his waistcoat buttons, which were always beautifully polished.

'Plenty of seats in First Class,' Mr Brass offered genially. 'It's almost empty, go on and make yourself comfortable!'

'That's so kind – but I've got my book here. And I may have a drink before we arrive. And,' she added, smiling, 'to be honest I just love sitting in the restaurant car, so comfortable, so elegant.'

Mr Brass said something indecipherable in Cornish, perhaps, as he clipped her ticket, and moved forward up the car. Another country, thought Miss Dimont, who though born in Belgium counted herself a full-blooded Devonian, and looked with wonderment at those who chose to live in the wrong county.

She cudgelled her brains over the nature of the killing – coldblooded, no-nonsense, leaving behind not a single clue. Some of the men she'd worked with in the war had those skills, and maybe she would have time to drop in to the Special Forces Club, hidden away in a small street behind Knightsbridge, and see who was hanging around the bar. The club was a gathering-place for all those who had a hand in wartime undercover work, a building filled with heroes every day of the week and she was a welcome guest. But Miss Dimont generally preferred the Chelsea Arts, where dangerous behaviour meant something completely different.

'*Pewsey! Watch your step when alighting the train, please!*'

The gin-and-tonic Owd Bert brought as the great steam locomotive forged its way onwards to Newbury fizzled in her brain and helped her concentrate. Her thoughts turned to what Uncle Arthur said about the safebreaker Ramensky – that he could have been working for Hugh Radipole when Radipole was still in the car-trade. It was pretty clear the hotel-owner had been involved in something underhand during the war – despite his lordly air there was a bit of a stench about him – and the obvious conclusion was war profiteering. It just wasn't possible for him to have amassed enough cash selling cars, however smart they were, to be able to buy and refit such a huge hotel as the Marine. It led her to think that maybe Radipole had come to Temple Regis in an attempt to re-invent himself, leave his past behind. No more selling dubious Lagondas to old chumps like Arthur!

'*Paddington! Paddington! All change please, all change!*'

The old chump himself was there when she alighted the train on Platform Four.

'Huguette, dear girl! Got the flivver waiting for you over there!'

'Not the old Lagonda, Arthur? With the cylinder head gasket?'

'No, I had it turned into corned-beef tins. Got a Jag now – whooo, you should see it go!'

Miss Dimont had to smile as they approached Arthur's new toy, a sleek and sinuous piece of engineering designed with the younger playboy in mind. He found it painfully difficult to fold his tall frame into it.

'Touch of gout these days,' he explained, as he pressed a button and the engine roared. 'Where to?'

'Well, we're meeting Sticks, ah, Mr Karanikis, in Soho – he's bringing along his cousin. A Greek restaurant called The Acropolis.'

'Oh, I've heard of that!' said Arthur with glee. 'The waiters dance on the tables and throw plates against the walls!' His eyes lit up in boyish delight as they whizzed up the Euston Road.

'Not so lucky, uncle. This one's rather more cultured than that.' Arthur indicated his disappointment with a showy and entirely unnecessary double-declutch.

The drummer and another man who looked remarkably similar were waiting for them at the table.

'Arthur, this is Theoclymenus Karanikis,' pronounced Judy flawlessly, 'known as Sticks. Sticks, my uncle Arthur – he adores Greek food!'

Arthur gave his niece a sidelong glance.

'This is my cousin Petros,' said Sticks, 'come and sit down and have some retsina.'

As waiters – with not a broken plate in sight – hovered, Judy got down to business. 'Sticks tells me you may know the murdered woman, Petros.'

'If it's who I think it is, I...'

'Would this be of help?' And out of her raffia bag she brought the 10 × 8 photos Terry had printed up. 'Do you recognise this girl?'

'That's her,' said Petros instantly. 'Definitely. A terrible person, a really horrible woman. Is she dead?'

'Yes.'

'Well, in that case I must try to find something nice to say about her, then. She had a beautiful smile.' Clearly this was a sentimental man who didn't believe in speaking ill of those no longer with us.

'No need to be so polite, Petros. She can't hear you.'

The man pulled at his bushy moustache and considered the prints.

'I used to see her all the time. The Greek community here in London – we have a lot of parties, family get-togethers, that sort of thing – I cater them, as well as running my own small restaurant in Notting Hill.' He sipped his wine thoughtfully.

'She's a member of the Patrikis family, can't remember her first name. They came here during the war – they're rich, shipping or oil or something like that. I once did a party at the family home in Hampstead – hah! Never again! She was a terrible woman – rude to me, rude to my staff, even to her own guests. With her it was all me, me, me.'

'Good Lord!' said uncle Arthur. He was peering quizzically into his glass.

'To be honest I think there was something the matter with her,' continued Petros, shaking his head.

'What exactly?'

'Hot and cold. I mean, we all know people like that, don't we, but with her it was extreme – smarming round some old geezer one minute, making life hell for everyone the next. She was out of control and it wasn't drink – I never saw her touch a drop.'

'Did you see her often?'

'I only got into the catering side of things a few years ago, and I suppose for about a year I would see her very regularly – always Greek parties, usually in north London but also in the smart houses around Hyde Park. I remember there was one house with its own ballroom and she stopped the band and cleared the dance-floor – grabbed the microphone and went into a tirade about – oh, I can't even recall. Just drawing attention to herself.'

'Did she have boyfriends, a husband? I don't know, but I reckon she must have been around thirty so there must have been someone.'

'That would be about right.' Petros and Sticks were enjoying the retsina and called for another bottle, but when they waved it in his direction Arthur said, 'I think I'll have a cup of coffee.' The expression on his face when he'd taken the first sip was a picture – what a shame Terry wasn't here to capture it! Now it was the old boy's turn to study the prints on the table. 'That's a Deux Chevaux!' he said, looking at the picture with the car.

'Top marks,' said Judy drily. 'Right first time, Arthur.'

'One of the miracles of modern automotive engineering. D'you know, I once had the opportunity…'

Judy didn't even wait for him to finish – if you got him onto cars he'd never stop, the family name for him was the Motor Drone – so she cut in: 'Petros, are there any members of the family still around?'

'I was just coming to that. Her father was murdered – did you know? Stavros Patrikis. Only a couple of months after they had the party at their house. They were devoted, I will say that, she may have hated everybody else but she adored him. Then he was murdered by a burglar who broke in and ransacked the safe.'

'I don't think that's quite how it was…' started Arthur, thinking of his friend Johnny Ramensky, but Petros was ploughing on. 'Then a few months after the murder the daughter just disappeared. She never went to any more parties after his death but I suppose that's understandable. Then one day – gone. She was heartbroken by the loss – there was only her and the father, no mother or brothers and sisters. Maybe she went back to Greece, nobody knows. That's what I heard, anyway.'

'Well, not if your identification is right, Petros. She only got as far as Temple Regis.'

Sticks had been paying more attention to the label on the wine bottle than to the conversation – that's drummers for you – but now spoke up. 'You don't think there's some vendetta against the family? That the guys who did the father in done her as well?'

'Sounds a bit far-fetched to me,' said Arthur with a certain authority. 'After all, more than four years separates the two deaths. They happened a couple of hundred miles apart, and the modus operandi just isn't sufficiently similar to say that one hand was responsible for both deaths.'

He spoke slowly, but with the command of one whose life had been littered with unusual occurrences. Petros and Sticks looked at him in surprise.

'Who else is there in the family?' asked Judy.

'Well,' said Petros, 'I was building my business up and so I didn't see much of the family after the murder – they weren't giving parties any more. There was no mother – I'm certain of that – it was just Mr Patrikis and his daughter. There was a brother, I think.'

'Address?' said Judy brightly.

Just then there was a crash of breaking crockery and Arthur, who had been visibly subdued ever since he tasted the vile retsina, cheered up in an instant.

'Ah, the smashing of the plates!' he beamed with satisfaction. 'Shouldn't we clear these photos away so they can get up and dance on the table?'

'They don't do that sort of thing here,' said Petros, shaking his head in disapproval. 'Somebody just had an accident in the kitchen.'

EIGHTEEN

'I meant to ask – how's Elizabeth?' They were sitting in the window of Arthur's mansion flat, high over London. The plane trees in the square were still, the taxis honked their horns far beneath, and in the distance could be heard the slow growl of a trolley-bus. 'Do you see her?'

'She moved to Bournemouth last winter. Too noisy in London, she said. We occasionally talk on the blower.'

'I always thought…'

'*Everybody* always thought,' said Arthur, crossly, 'except me. One wife's enough in a lifetime for any man! I got used to living on my own long ago – and then I have occasional treats like you coming to stay. If I get restless I go to the club.'

'Play billiards and drink brandy.'

'They were invented for each other.'

They hadn't stayed for supper in Soho – Arthur said the retsina made him lose his appetite, and since all the crockery seemed determined to remain intact there didn't seem much point in staying on – they'd got what they came for. Now they sat with cheese and biscuits and a bottle of old Burgundy, looking out of the window at the black-and-white humbug stripes of the night sky, backlit by a huge moon poking through streaky clouds.

'You've been saving it up all evening, Arthur. Now tell me about Johnny Ramensky.'

'Well, he's in hot water again, poor fellow. You know, a nice enough chap but a fool to himself. The moment he gets out he goes and does it again – can't help himself.'

'What happened this time?'

'Oh, he hopped it from jail. I think he got bored sitting around doing nothing all day.'

'I thought that was the point.'

'Well, Johnny likes a bit of excitement, but not too much. They gave him ten years for doing what he does best, which by anybody's standards is a bit steep, and after sitting it out a bit he decided to go over the wall. Trouble with Johnny, he always gets caught.'

'Always?'

'This must be the fifth time he's gone on the lam. Usually gets caught the next day but this time it was nearly a fortnight. He fancied a taste of London nightlife, I expect. Or maybe just needed a cuddle.'

'You sound as though you rather approve of our Mr Ramensky.'

'Takes all sorts. He's a whizz with explosives.'

'Ah yes. Eric caught the fever too. An hour in Johnny's company and he wanted to be a safecracker for the rest of his days.'

'And still you would have married him? Good Lord!' said Arthur, shaking his head.

'Oh, I daresay come peacetime I could have talked him out

of it. He had other plans too – an expedition to the Falkland Islands, some mad scheme of his.'

'He was very handsome,' said Arthur, 'but not exactly the reliable type, Huguette. What your mother would have said…'

His niece shuddered slightly at the thought and changed the subject. 'Go on about Gentleman Johnny, do.'

'Well, my dear, I tracked him down and I'm going to see him. Tomorrow! Chap at the club I told you about went and spoke to a friend, who spoke to a friend – it's all fixed up. He's on remand in Brixton Prison, they'll be sending him back to Scotland next week. Found him in the nick of time.'

'Well, that's brilliant, Arthur – you're back on your old form!'

'D'you know, I miss all *that* – the adventures we used to have in the old days. I and the old man, we'd sit next door in the office and work these problems out – it was always a bit of a thrill when something new came along.'

'You had some remarkable successes.'

'Well, you know, I'd put forward a theory, he'd put forward a theory. He was sometimes quite dismissive, but we got results.'

'How wonderful that he left this place to you in his will.'

'He was an extraordinarily generous man.'

'And terribly, terribly fond of you – even if he could never say it out loud.'

'Let's talk about Johnny,' said Arthur abruptly, tugging out a handkerchief. There must have been a speck of dust in his eye.

'Well, I can't believe you found him. If he's as willing to

oblige as you say he is, maybe he can solve this case at a stroke. You remember he burgled that house and was held on suspicion of murder.'

'Wouldn't hurt a fly. *Gentleman* Johnny, they call him.'

'Anyway. Now we know that the murder victim was Stavros Patrikis, and maybe Johnny might have a clue as to what his daughter was called – then, at last, we can name the second murder victim.'

'That should be easy enough,' said the old boy. 'D'you like this Burgundy? The '47 was a better year, but I think this '55 is pretty distinguished, don't you agree?'

Miss Dimont didn't like to disappoint. 'Absolutely marvellous, Arthur!'

'Finally got rid of the taste of that filthy Greek muck. Honestly, it clings to your palate like a limpet to a rock!'

'The retsina? Made a nice change, I thought.'

Arthur looked scandalised. 'Wouldn't wash my car with it!'

'Speaking of which, uncle, you will be asking Ramensky about Hugh Radipole? If it turns out he was working for Radipole, can't he give us some clue as to what Radipole was really making his money from before he came to Temple Regis?'

'Well, the man's an absolute stinker, that's for sure. That Lagonda, I mean to say! Wouldn't put it past him to have the Patrikis chap killed, and a dozen others for good measure too – he's that sort of type. Though it couldn't have been Johnny who did it.'

'I don't know, Arthur,' said Miss Dimont. 'Just because Ramensky never killed anybody before doesn't mean to say. If he was caught blowing the safe, what's he going to do – hold his hands up and surrender? We've got to face the fact Ramensky may have killed him.'

'I just don't see it,' said Arthur, shaking his head. 'Remember I know him, I've had a chance to size the chap up.'

'All right,' she said, 'but look here – Stavros Patrikis is murdered, and quite brutally. It wasn't necessary to stick the knife in quite so many times.

'Then, four years later, his daughter – whom we call Patsy till we know her real name – is the subject of an equally cold-blooded murder. Despite what you say, I think there has to be a single person at the back of this.'

'Well,' said Arthur, lifting the bottle, 'I say, Huguette, you've barely touched your glass! But look, it can't have been Johnny – he's been on remand for the past six weeks. You can't go swanning off to Temple Regis with a pistol and shoot a hole in someone's heart while you're detained at Her Majesty's pleasure. Her Majesty doesn't allow it.'

'Point taken. But two murders – father and daughter – is too much of a coincidence for us to ignore. Supposing it was Radipole who wanted to get rid of them – though I can't think why – if he was determined to see them both off, he could have used two murderers. Come to that, he could have done it himself!' The thought started to take flight in Miss Dimont's imagination.

'Yes!' she exclaimed. 'Radipole could have been in London when Patrikis was killed, and he certainly was in Temple Regis – just yards away, in fact – when Patsy was killed. We just need to find his motive.'

'Well, I certainly agree with that,' said Arthur. 'And, you

know, Huguette, if the man is a killer and he dispatched two members of the Patrikis family because they crossed him – who next? What about that man Bobby Bunton? Don't you think he might be next?'

'Because he's cocking a snook at Radipole with those Devil's Dodgems? You've got a point, Arthur, and when I get back home I'll go and see him. But you might get more of a clue when you've spoken to Ramensky tomorrow. When are you going?'

'Ten o'clock. Catch him after his morning exercise in the yard.'

'Can I come?'

'What? To Brixton Prison? My dear, you were too gently brought up to want to see inside a place like that.'

'You forget the war, uncle. I've seen worse.'

'Ah yes,' sighed Arthur. 'But no. This is a favour from a friend of a friend, chaps only. It's dashed irregular, but they slipped Gentleman Johnny a note asking him to request a visit from me. Neat, eh?'

'What's in it for him?'

'I'll see him right,' said Arthur, tapping his nose.

'Well, what shall I do while you're gone? I shall be pacing up and down waiting to hear what you find out!'

'May I suggest you pop over and see your mother, darling? It's only an hour on the train. Now you've come this far, why not go the extra mile, get the punishment over with? If you go early enough we can meet for lunch. There's a rather nice little place in Marylebone I know.'

Miss Dimont downed the glass of Burgundy in front of her.

'All right,' she said, 'all right! I'll go and see her! But you'd better bring me something wonderful back from Brixton, Arthur, or I'll never forgive you.'

'Sorry I can't be with you,' lied Arthur, a rapturous smile on his face. 'Send her my love, won't you?'

In a most unladylike manner, Miss Huguette Dimont blew a raspberry.

When it comes to covert meetings, the tradecraft rules are quite strict – never rendezvous twice in the same place. Which is why the two ex-spycatchers, Auriol Hedley and Rudyard Rhys, were to be found next day at the back of the Lilian Bailey Spiritualist Church down near the Temple Regis railway station.

Two unfamiliar faces, in most churches, would cause a flutter of interest among the regular congregation, especially since these newcomers were so clearly ill-matched – Rhys in his rumpled tweed suit while Auriol surreptitiously glowed in her Sunday best.

But that day, the faithful had crowded into church to hear Mrs Bailey's close friend Maud Prentice, a medium of high renown, deliver a message from their glorious leader before getting down to the exciting business of communicating with the other world.

Mrs Prentice stood on a raised dais and smiled down on the upturned faces. 'Among the great forces of Spiritualism is the power to heal the sick, either by personal contact, known as laying on of hands, or through absent healing,' she intoned. Most people there had heard this a dozen times, but nodded eagerly as though it were news.

'Patients can be treated from great distances away, using healing thoughts and prayers,' said the spiritual guide. 'Many incurable diseases have been successfully treated, although no healer can provide a guarantee. However, it is reassuring for the healer to alleviate suffering or ease a passing.'

The small crowd inched closer to the podium and an excited buzz passed through them as Maud prepared to communicate with the spirit world. Nobody had time to pay attention to the ill-matched couple at the back of the church with their heads bent together as if in search of their own dear lost ones.

'So, the Admiral,' whispered Auriol. 'What do we have?'

'I sent my reporter, Miss Featherstone, over to Buntorama and she got on very well with "Sir Bobs", as the staff call him,' said Rhys. Despite his initial reluctance, he had obviously caught the spirit of the chase.

'He's clearly dug himself into a hole. He's at loggerheads with Hugh Radipole over at the Marine Hotel and if it came to a fight, Radipole would have the edge – and Bunton knows that. He lacks Radipole's subtlety. Plus I think he's in trouble with the police – not local but Scotland Yard – because of the goings-on in there. An awful lot of high jinks between people who shouldn't, but also out-of-hours drinking and I have no doubt, some pills being exchanged for favours.' He wrinkled his nose in disgust.

Auriol nodded and picked up a Spiritualist leaflet, which encouraged her to get in touch with loved ones through a medium. She thought about giving it to Judy for her mother – they'd never have to see each other in the flesh! 'And?'

'Then there's this business of the dead woman. Bunton

spent a large part of the evening with her at the bar in the Marine a couple of days before she was shot. He claims she was a prostitute, but Judy thinks not. Either way, this episode adds to his vulnerability – the police are after him and with it being Scotland Yard, Fleet Street can't be very far behind. That's why he's suddenly packing his board of directors with the great and the good, getting the Archbishop to come and say prayers.'

'Anything that gives us a clue as to what's going on there?'

'Betty's good, you know. I told her to stick close to the Admiral at that party and so she did – he took quite a fancy to her.'

'Oh yes,' drawled Auriol, thinking, the man's just an old goat.

'He'd had a glass or two and he told her he'd just come back from Germany. Berlin. He's supposed to be still on duty – he doesn't retire for another month – but apparently he can find the time to go wandering around where he shouldn't and, no doubt, meeting who he shouldn't. The communists are all over Berlin and I can't think he went all the way there just to sit with a cup of coffee in Unter den Linden and look at the leaves on the trees.'

'I can check whether he was followed,' said Auriol. 'Looks like his guard is dropping.'

'I'd say he's a sucker for the young ladies,' said Rhys. 'With a glass or two inside him, a reporter from the local newspaper who hasn't even got her notebook out, where's the danger?'

'Even so. It's lax. I'm surprised at him.'

'You say lax – I call it pretty damn lax he hasn't been stopped before now!'

'I told you, they want the wider circle, not just the Admiral.'

'Well, are you going to hook him then, Auriol? With those special charms of yours?'

'Keep to the point, Richard,' Auriol swiped back. She knew how much he hated being reminded of his birth-name.

A bit of a kerfuffle was going on up at the other end of the church. Maud Prentice was shaking and gagging and staggering about as if ready to fall, and congregation members were anxiously reaching up to catch her. Clearly whoever she was drawing forth from the spirit world was giving her a very hard time.

'Looks interesting,' said Auriol. 'You should get some of this in your paper.'

'Certainly not,' said Rhys gruffly. 'They're absolutely batty. Don't want to encourage them.'

'You don't believe in supporting minority religions? They seem very committed to me – not a shred of malice in them.'

'Rr-rrr,' growled Rhys, who didn't like being told how to do his job.

'Quite refreshing in their way,' added Auriol mischievously, as Maud fell to the floor with a clatter and started mouthing the words sent to her from the spirit world. 'Mincemeat!' she was crying, her head whipping from side to side, and one of her audience was shrilling, 'Yes! Yes! Yes! It's my Reggie! It was always mincemeat on a Thursday!'

It was quite a performance, and Auriol put sixpence in the collection box as they walked out.

They stood for a moment under a tree, shielded from public gaze by a heavy shadow.

'Remarkable, don't you think, how many admirals let their country down?'

'You're thinking of Domvile,' said Rhys, a glint in his eye. 'One of our more successful nabs.'

'You're not all bad, Richard. You did a very efficient job in tracking down that mistress of his – what was her name?'

'Olive Baker. We had to give her to MI5 because she was a civilian. She got five years, though.'

'But the mistress of Admiral Domvile, and it was her evidence gave us the Admiral on a plate. You know he was going round telling ex-servicemen that when Hitler finally landed on the mainland, they could have Edward VIII as their king once again. He deserved more than that jail sentence.'

'Scum,' said Rhys, tugging out his old briar pipe.

'Yes, but Cedric Minsell is three times the scum that Sir Barry Domvile was. If he's handed over those nuclear submarine plans to the Russians, he's effectively given them the gun to shoot us all dead with. We have to get him, Richard, we really do.'

'I really don't think if he's the arch-traitor they think he is, they'd be leaving it to us, Auriol,' said Rhys, shaking his head. 'Think about it for a moment – you left the service ten years ago, I left after the war. We're no longer masters of the dark arts – there's a whole new generation with a lot more sophisticated tricks up their sleeve for catching people like Minsell. They're the ones that'll catch him – we're small fry, we're out to grass! Past it! Finished!'

Auriol stopped him in his tracks. 'You may be, Richard, I am not. I've been asked to do something which they've tried and failed to do – to get Minsell to confess – and I'll do it if

I can. The top brass at Admiralty have buried their heads in the sand – terrified what'll happen to their authority if this comes out. They really don't want to admit to knowing about Minsell and his treachery. Not on their watch anyway – let their successors clear up the mess!'

'Why not let sleeping dogs lie, then?'

'There's been a lot of talk in Westminster recently about combining the Navy with the Army and the RAF – think of the loss of face at the Admiralty if that happened! We're supposed to be the Senior Service – think of Nelson!

'It's the next generation – the admirals of tomorrow, if you like – who want Minsell's head on a plate. There's a struggle going on as to how the problem is handled, but until somebody gets a firm grip on it they're trying every avenue – including the small fry and the out-to-grassers – to get something firm on Minsell. He knows they're after him and he's enjoying every minute.'

'Because he thinks he's smarter.'

'Exactly, Richard, exactly.'

The editor turned and looked back at the church. 'I'm sorry,' he said, 'I'm just a bit too old for these games. Why on earth don't you get Miss Dim on the case?'

'Don't call her that!' said Auriol sharply. 'And anyway, she's got her hands full. You've got her doing the Rural District Council on Monday, she's trying to do something about the Buntorama murder and…'

'I don't want her anywhere near that!' barked Rudyard Rhys. 'She's a reporter, not a detective! She's paid to work for me, not for the police!'

'And there you are saying she should take time off to do some naval intelligence work.'

'That's different.'

'Trouble with you, Richard, is you pick on the small stuff. You've got Minsell on your patch but your main concern is that nobody says anything nasty about Temple Regis. A woman gets shot and you'd rather they carted the body off to Somerset than have her discovered there. I'm no journalist, but I'd say a cold-blooded killing on your patch is the very thing your newspaper was made for.'

'You would, would you?' said Rhys. His beard moved like a hedgehog getting up to walk after a long snooze. Auriol guessed that beneath the undergrowth a sneer had puckered his lips.

'You were quite brave during the war, Richard. What happened?'

'You don't know anything about newspapers, about preserving the town's reputation, about protecting its trade – not losing it to places like... *Torquay*.' He spat out the opposition's name.

'Anyway, it's you who's helping me on this,' said Auriol with authority. 'Room 39 says so. You did very well with Admiral Domvile. And here we have, not twenty years later, another traitor covered in gold braid.'

'Don't know what more I can do.'

'Nothing for the moment. I'm going to go and see him.'

The hedgehog wriggled once again. This time it could have been a leer.

'Put on your best dress, Auriol, if you want to nab him! You're not getting any younger!'

He's right, thought Auriol. What on earth am I doing smarming around a traitor who's never going to tell me a thing? The whole thing's quite absurd.

'Neither, Richard, are you. How's that novel of yours coming along? How long's it been, thirteen years? Think you'll get it finished before you shuffle off this mortal coil?'

That took care of it all right. The editor stumped off back to his office.

NINETEEN

Miss Dimont was waiting impatiently at the table in Belcanto's. The bread roll she'd been offered lay in crumbs on the tablecloth which she absently swirled around with her forefinger.

'Huguette! Sorry I'm late!'

Arthur was wearing a blazer and looking pretty pleased with himself. His niece soon put a stop to that.

'Didn't know you served in the Royal Navy, Arthur?'

'What? Oh!' he laughed, slightly self-consciously. 'You mean the blazer! Everybody wears them nowadays, it goes well with the old flannels.'

'Your tweed jacket would look nicer. Stop you looking like a chap who'd just walked off the poop deck. Is that a telescope in your pocket?'

'Good Lord,' said Arthur, 'I can see your mother's put you in a mood. How is she, Madame Dimont?' He said this with a chortle for despite her accent, her manner, and her style of dress Grace Dimont was as British as a bulldog.

'Talk about it later,' said Judy, grimly. 'Before you order anything, Arthur, I want to hear about Ramensky – you know that I must get back to Temple Regis tomorrow, there's not a lot of time.'

'Old Johnny?' said Arthur, stretching his legs under the table and giving her a genial smile. 'We got on like a house on fire – it was almost as if we'd been at school together.'

Men, thought Judy. It all goes back to their schooldays.

'Spill the beans?'

'Oh yes! What is it the Americans say? He gobbed a bibful.'

'That's disgusting. Tell me what he said.'

'Very simple, really. That sewer Radipole was involved, of course.'

'He ordered the murders?' Judy pushed the crumbs excitedly to one side and leaned forward.

'Not so fast,' said Arthur, enjoying the moment. 'It wasn't Radipole, it was his girlfriend. Only, no, it wasn't the girlfriend either… it was…' For a moment a cloud passed across the old boy's face. 'I mean to say, it was like this.

'Ramensky did a job for Radipole in Scotland. He burgled the safe of someone who'd crossed Radipole – this is while he was still running his motor business – and brought the loot down to London. When Johnny went round to the showroom he found him locked in an embrace with a young woman. Young enough to be his daughter.'

'Yes?'

'D'you know when you're on remand in Brixton they allow you to wear your own clothes? Johnny's a very snappy dresser, I got him to give me the name of his tailor.'

'Well, maybe he could persuade you to get rid of that abomination,' said Judy snootily. Evidently she had an aversion to men in blazers.

'Yes, well. This almost certainly was the murdered woman. Her name's not Patsy Rouchos, it's Helen Patrikis.'

'Well *done*, Arthur! That really is a major breakthrough!'

Looking smug, her uncle beckoned a waiter – evidently he felt he'd done enough to reward himself with a snifter. 'You know,' he said, 'when I started you out on this detecting lark, I...'

'Rubbish, Arthur! If you consult that failing memory of yours you'll recall I fell into it after being recruited by the Admiralty. And why did they recruit me? Because I knew most of the capital cities of Europe and was able to get by in several languages. Because before the war Papa had sent me as his emissary to all the diamond dealers in Paris and Berlin and Rome. The sleuthing didn't start because you were doing it – I barely knew about your activities because we didn't see very much of each other at that time.'

'Your mother's always been difficult.'

'We're straying from the point, Arthur. Dead girl was Helen Patrikis, she was Radipole's mistress, she was young enough to be his daughter. That it?'

'Haven't come to the best bit. It was Helen Patrikis who hired Gentleman Johnny to burgle her father's house.'

'And kill him?'

'No! Johnny didn't do it! The police tried to pin it on him, but they know their man – not an ounce of violence in him. No, what happened was Stavros, the father, kept his daughter on short rations. They were a very rich family, but the mother had died in childbirth and there wasn't anybody else – just father and daughter. He adored her, worshipped her, but he was a very controlling figure and decided the only way he could keep her close was to provide her with all the good things in life – but never let her have any cash.

'It meant she didn't have a car, couldn't take holidays, had to wait for him to stump up for her wardrobe. For a girl who'd been brought up among the rich of Hampstead it was pretty humiliating.'

'Your Johnny seems to know an awful lot about her.'

'I'll come to that in a minute.' He could see the waiter bringing the wine bottle and nodded energetically, as if to hurry him up.

'So what happened?'

'Well, remember this was four or five years ago. By that stage this Helen must have been in her mid-twenties – stranded at home with a father who was overpowering and very controlling.'

'Why didn't she go out and get a job, like everybody else?'

'That's just it – she tried. But apparently she had a most unfortunate manner – comes from being the apple of her father's eye, I suppose – a real madam. Expected everything her own way and very controlling too. She tried a couple of jobs but people couldn't put up with her. She was beautiful, but a pain in the posterior. If you'll excuse the expression.'

Belcanto's was noisily filling up with the Saturday luncheon crowd and now she had to lean forward to catch what Arthur was saying.

'In a nutshell, she wanted money. She told Johnny she wanted lots of money. She knew her father kept huge amounts of cash in a safe in his study, but despite her best efforts she'd never been able to find the combination. She fell on Johnny's neck – quite literally – when he came down to London with the loot from his Scottish job. She knew where the money was – all she needed was a safecracker to do the work.'

'Sounds like your Ramensky isn't too choosy about the jobs he picks. Burgling someone's house on the say-so of a young girl?'

'Ah,' said Arthur. 'I was coming to that. She seduced him. Johnny told me he'd never been to bed with anyone so posh.'

'But she was *Radipole*'s mistress!'

'Not by choice. Radipole had some hold over her, don't know what. He's a dreadful man, Huguette, dreadful! He sold Helen's father a Bentley just after the war – and seduced the daughter at the same time. She could barely have been seventeen, and him touching fifty!

'Radipole and Helen remained lovers over the next six or seven years, even though he had other affairs. Radipole was obsessed by her and, just like her father, she couldn't escape his clutches. I wonder if perhaps the father… ah, well… people are not always as we wish them to be, dear girl, let's draw a veil over that. She jumped on Johnny when he came along and got him to do her bidding.'

'Very manipulative.'

'Johnny said that. He said it was suffocating being with her because she was so self-obsessed, but he couldn't help himself. Couldn't keep away.'

'So she persuaded him to burgle her house.'

'Yes. He said the job was a walk through the park. She'd told him how to disable the burglar alarm, then she hopped off to stay with an old schoolfriend in Wales. He got in, cracked the safe in no time, then skedaddled.'

‘Leaving a bloody corpse behind him.’

‘I told you, Huguette, Johnny didn’t do it! It’s not his style, and when the police charged him with murder they told him not to worry, they just had to put someone’s name on the charge sheet.’

‘So who did it, and why?’

‘Well, naturally Johnny was keen to find out! He didn’t want to swing for a murder he hadn’t committed. They’re a powerful lot, that Patrikis family – managed to get out of Greece before the invasion in 1940. Being in the shipping business they had offices and money in Britain, and of course did pretty well out of the war – though in an honourable way, unlike our friend Radipole.’

‘We don’t know that.’

‘We suspect it,’ nodded Arthur. ‘Anyway, Johnny said he made a mistake when he did the petering job. When he shot out of the house he left a side door open – obviously that’s how the murderer got in. But he was confused by what happened because Helen had told him her father wasn’t in the house that day. Yet hey presto, pretty soon after Johnny had hopped it, in came the knifeman and did the deed.’

‘Almost too much of a coincidence, don’t you think Arthur?’

‘Oh, I don’t know,’ came the airy reply. ‘If someone was watching the house, they discovered their moment and pounced.’

A waiter came to take their orders; Miss Dimont pointed with her finger at something on the menu without even taking in what it was, so keen was she to hear the rest of the burglar’s tale.

'Anyway, old Johnny got the boodle and delivered it to Helen. He was amazed when she said she'd give him half, far more than they'd agreed – there must have been five thousand! He said she didn't even look at it when he handed it over, just told him to take half. I suppose that's what happens when you grow up with so much money.'

'Hardly, Arthur. She'd been starved of cash, remember?'

'Be that as it may, Johnny went away with a pocketful – and a broken heart. The moment the job was done she didn't want any more to do with him. "I was used," he said to me. He was very upset to hear she was dead, I think he made the fatal mistake of falling in love with her.'

'She seems a pretty cold fish, I must say.'

'And that's it, really. We chatted about old times and said goodbye. I promised to put in a good word for him when he gets back to Scotland.'

'You're all heart, Arthur. Did he tell you, by the way, the address of the house where the Patrikis family lived?'

'Yes, it's a big old place off the Finchley Road, up towards Hampstead Heath. We could drive over there after lunch if you like.'

'Who needs lunch?' said Miss Dimont, reaching for her raffia bag.

One thing you could say about Betty, she was a trier. She never liked to let people down, especially when they were nice enough to ask her out. Which is why she was sipping gin fizzes with the Admiral in the Yacht Club bar.

'Never been here before,' she said admiringly, dazzled by the high polish on trophies and tankards, monuments to many glorious feats under sail, which littered the place. 'Do they allow women in here?'

'When they're as pretty as you,' said Sir Cedric, looking over his glass and waggling his weatherbeaten brow.

'I expect you'll be bringing Lady Minsell here, then, when you get your cottage.'

'Invalid,' said Sir Cedric sadly, shaking his head. 'She rarely comes out these days. I travel a great deal by myself.'

He's sixty-five if he's a day, thought Betty. Beautiful clothes but a body like a sack of flour. Married. And more in love with himself than any man has the right to be.

'Did you see me on *What's My Line?* last Tuesday?'

'I don't have a television, Admiral.'

'Cedric.' He pronounced it 'Seedric'.

Oh Lord, thought Betty. Here we go again.

TWENTY

'I'm just going to knock on the door. You stay in the car.'

Arthur looked uncomfortable at this decidedly forward approach. 'Don't you think we should telephone first?'

'Do *you* have a number, uncle?'

'Well, no, actually.'

'Do we even know who lives here now? Mr Patrikis died nearly five years ago.'

'Hadn't thought of that.' Arthur was struggling with his stringbacked driving gloves. 'Go on then. Give me a call if you need anything.'

Miss Dimont shouldered her raffia bag and marched up the wide drive to the front door of The Glen, a curiously Scottish name for a house which backed on to Hampstead Heath. It was vast, imposing, set in impressive grounds and with a colossal front door.

A beautiful young woman answered her knock.

'Do forgive me. I'm a friend of Helen Patrikis, who used to live here. I was rather hoping you might be able to tell me if you know the whereabouts of any family members – I'm so sorry, I hope you don't mind…'

'I do.'

'You do mind. Well, many apologies, I'll be...'

'No,' said the young woman, 'I do. I do know the whereabouts of family members. I'm one myself – Elektra Patrikis. What did you want?'

'Oh!' stuttered Miss Dimont. Accustomed to knocking on people's doors in her other guise as a reporter, she was momentarily thrown to so easily find what she was looking for – detection's supposed to be more difficult than that. She played for time.

'May I come in?'

The woman looked at her suspiciously, but after a moment's appraisal decided this middle-aged and apparently uncharismatic spinster posed no particular threat, and stood aside.

The Glen's hall was huge, its panelled walls covered in oil-paintings of ships – ugly, utilitarian vessels in anonymous colours plying their trade through seas which lacked charm or identity. A housekeeper hurried forward, apologising for not having answered Miss Dimont's knock.

'OK, Elsie, it's about Helen. Come this way,' the young woman said, leading the way down a passage into a large garden room whose tall windows gave out onto the Heath.

'Beautiful view,' murmured Miss Dimont. 'Look here, I'd better explain. But first would you mind telling me how you're related to Helen?'

'She's my cousin.'

The answer, phrased as it was in the present tense, filled Miss Dimont suddenly with dread – the woman's assumption was that her cousin was still alive. Did she want to be the one to break the news of her ugly death?

'Look, I'm not quite sure how to put this, but I think I'd better get things straight. My name is Judy Dimont, I'm the chief reporter of the *Riviera Express*, which is a newspaper in Devon. Do you know Temple Regis, by any chance?'

'Heard of it,' said the woman. 'Who hasn't? A reporter, you say? What's this about?'

'I'm sorry to say that I believe Helen is dead. How are you related to her?'

'Our fathers are – were – are – brothers. Helen's father Stavros is dead, my father is out there in the garden.' She pointed to a tall man in his sixties playing croquet on the lawn. 'That's my sister with him, I'd better go and tell them. Are you sure? Are you sure it's Helen? She went missing, you know.'

She doesn't seem very upset, thought Miss Dimont. 'Someone has died,' she said guardedly, 'the police have been unable so far to identify her.'

'What does that mean?' For a moment the woman looked horrified, as if waiting to hear of some ghastly disfigurement.

'Simply that when she was found she had nothing to identify her. Look, before you go and tell your father, will you help me? Will you look at this?'

I'm taking a chance, thought Miss Dimont. I could be accused of misrepresentation, Press intrusion – oh, all sorts of things! Better soldier on, though.

'It's a dreadful thing to ask, but is this her?' She drew from her bag the folded 10 × 8 prints Terry had given her, and selected one at random.

The woman leaned forward. Miss Dimont could tell from the look on her face that she was appraising the woman in the photo, sizing her up, perhaps even matching herself against her dead cousin. It seemed a strange response.

'Yes,' came the eventual response. 'Yes, that's Helen. With that disgusting boyfriend of hers. Radish, we used to call him.'

'Hugh Radipole? Well! You're sure?'

'He took her for a drive in one of his fancy cars – she was just a schoolgirl then.'

'Would you like your father and sister to hear what I have to say?'

'Come on.' Elektra strode forward towards the garden and Miss Dimont followed. Her response seemed odd – upset, yes, to learn of the death of her cousin and yet strangely detached at the same time. The way she looked at the photograph – as if…

And then she had it – Elektra had not been looking at Helen, but at Radipole! The first glimpse was enough to tell her it was her cousin, the rest of her lingering gaze was on the man, not the girl, in the photograph.

They emerged into the sunlight to discover the croquet match had progressed away towards the end of the garden. While Elektra went over to fetch her father and sister, Judy turned to look back at the house.

And there it was – the gabled and tiled edifice which featured in one of Terry's seven prints, a picture taken roughly speaking from where Elektra was standing, telling her sister and father the terrible news.

All three came back to the terrace where Miss Dimont stood. 'My father, Aristide Patrikis, and my sister, Calista. This is – sorry, I've forgotten your name already.'

'Judy Dimont, I'm chief reporter on the local newspaper in Temple Regis, Devon.'

The man looked at her steadily. His eyes signalled his station in life – top of the tree. 'Tell me quickly,' he said. It was an order, not a request.

'Someone who I believe to be your niece, Mr Patrikis, was found shot dead in a… holiday camp in Temple Regis. She had no identifying papers, nothing to show who she was. The police have been unable to connect her with anyone, and it's only by chance that I…'

'It's not your job, is it, to do police work? Going round informing people of the death of a loved one?' His tone was patronising, final – what he said in life was written down by others, and acted upon. He did not like this journalist telling him things about his family.

Miss Dimont was undaunted. 'Forgive me, Mr Patrikis, but it is anybody's job. Families have a right to know when one of their number has died, it really doesn't matter who tells them.'

Patrikis was looking at her but, rather, looking through her. This messenger was of no importance, the message was. 'When did this occur?'

'About ten days ago.'

'You say shot.'

'Shot. She was lying on her bed in the holiday camp chalet. No possessions in her room.'

'Why has it taken so long for the family to be informed? And why,' he repeated, 'is it you who comes now?'

'She registered under a false name. She, I think purposely, left no identifying articles behind apart from the photo album. Which I suspect was an oversight – she had deliberately set out to hide her identity.'

'What name did she use?' The man seemed to be trying to bully the information out of her.

'Patsy.'

'That's not a Greek name.'

'No.'

'The police, why have they not been to see me?'

'Because they don't know yet. They've tried their best but actually it was a press photographer who made the breakthrough.'

The man ran his hand through iron-grey hair and then put his arm round his daughter's shoulder.

'What has been done with the body? Somebody, I take it, must identify her? If nobody has done so yet?'

'That would be standard procedure, Mr Patrikis. I'm very sorry to be the bearer of such bad tidings.'

'Why did you come here?'

'Sorry?'

'Elektra said you didn't know the family lived here. What were you doing knocking on our door?'

As if for the first time the man's black eyes focused sharply on Miss Dimont, making her feel most uncomfortable. He didn't like her, didn't like her questions, seemed almost insulted that someone so lowly should intrude into his private domain.

'Come on, Papa, we must do something, go to this place Regis,' said Calista, tugging at his cuff. She was clearly the favourite.

'Phone Stevens and tell him to arrange for the plane to be

in Hendon in an hour's time.' He could have been talking to an underling, favourite daughter or no. Turning to Miss Dimont he said, 'Where is this Temple Regis?'

'I think you'll find the nearest airstrip is Newton Abbot. In Devon.'

'I'll say good day, then.'

Judy and Elektra were left alone on the terrace. 'Would you like some coffee?'

'Well,' said Judy hesitantly – she was thinking of Arthur stuck in his Jaguar outside in the street.

'Well, yes. Thank you.' He would just have to wait.

'Come into the kitchen.'

Elektra led the way through a couple of large rooms to a brightly lit space large enough to cater a platoon of soldiers.

'They'll go off together,' she said, nodding as if in the direction of her father and sister. 'Stay for a while. I have to admit it's a bit of a shock. What on earth was she doing down in Devon?'

'Hugh Radipole has a hotel down there.'

'Does he? Oh yes, I forgot.'

No you didn't, thought Miss Dimont, but continued, 'Can you tell me about your cousin and Mr Radipole?'

'She loathed him. But she couldn't leave him alone. He's hardly our sort – he sold cars! – but somehow he became entangled in the family. He wouldn't go away.'

'How do you mean?'

'Well, he seduced Helen – though there's another word for it – and suddenly uncle Stavros was inviting him around all the time.'

'Here?'

‘Yes, this is Helen’s house. She inherited it when Stavros was murdered. When she went missing after he died, Papa decided he would rather live here than our house, which is on the other side of the Heath.’

‘That seems an unusual thing to do,’ said Miss Dimont, trying hard to seem conversational, not nosy.

‘Oh, we still have the other house. We move from one to the other, a month here, a month there, Papa seems to enjoy that. We keep the household staff on over there, the private staff – secretary and housekeeper – move with us when we go.’

Miss Dimont thought of her own small cottage with three bedrooms and no staff, and for a moment pictured Mulligatawny acting as secretary and housekeeper in her absence, keeping the wheels turning efficiently until her return.

‘So Stavros welcomed Radipole into his house? That seems odd.’

‘They were of a similar age, though of different wealth and background. What drew them together was Stavros’ love of cars. Big, small, new, old – he was besotted by them. He collected oddities – there was a vast garage full of them over in Maida Vale – and Hugh, er, Radipole, used to search them out for him.’

‘But he knew what was going on between Radipole and his daughter?’

‘He approved. He had Radipole under his thumb because of the money that was going his way – it was almost as if he was an employee – and so indirectly he controlled his daughter through Radipole. He was a very controlling man.’

'Most unusual,' said Miss Dimont. 'Delicious coffee, by the way.' She was thinking again about Arthur, cramped in his own bit of motoring joy, wondering how long she would be.

'Thank you. Helen – is there anything else you can tell me? I'm slightly in shock about her death. Even though we weren't that close I find the whole thing impossible to believe.'

'You weren't close even though you only lived on the other side of the Heath?'

'She was seven years older. Our fathers didn't get on well. Anyway, Helen both loved and hated her father. There was a period just before he died when she would shout and scream at him, saying some unforgiveable things, but then when he died she changed, utterly. She went round wearing black for a year, wouldn't go out, wouldn't see anybody. She went into a huge downward spiral.

'And then she just disappeared. She'd dropped hints before, to me anyway, saying she was rich at last, her inheritance from Uncle Stavros left her free to do exactly as she liked. She wanted to get away from London and go and live a completely different life.'

'In Devon? With Radipole?'

'Hardly. She ended up despising him because of the way he sucked up to her papa. No, she disappeared into thin air. To start with we thought she'd come back, but when she didn't – well, that was when Papa decided it was pointless keeping on household staff here at The Glen without them doing anything for their wages, and he moved us over here. Very soon he stopped talking about her, would hush us up if we mentioned her name. It was almost as if he thought she was dead.'

Miss Dimont looked into her cup. 'Do you know where she went?'

'Probably Switzerland. But it could have been Timbuctoo – nobody could find her.'

'Were the police involved?'

'Papa thought it was a family matter. He got some private detectives to work on finding her but they were useless.'

'But then, finally,' said Miss Dimont, thinking aloud, 'she ends up in a holiday camp next door to the man who'd been her first lover. Despite the fact she's on the run, trying to keep out of sight, she spends every evening in his bar. It's very odd, the whole thing is very odd.'

Elektra washed up the cups. 'Their relationship altered the day her father died. She was young enough to be Radipole's daughter, but suddenly she was the boss – she was the one with the money. I think when they were first together she must have been very impressed by him – he's very smooth, you know – but by the end she must have seen him for what he was.'

'Where did his money come from? He came down to Temple Regis and built this remarkable hotel – he could never have made that money selling cars.'

Elektra laughed out loud. 'You mean, did Stavros pay him to be his daughter's lover? Well, there's a thought!'

There indeed is a thought, Miss Dimont silently agreed.

'I must be going,' she said. 'May I have your number? If you like I can telephone you from Temple Regis and let you know how things are going.' She sensed Elektra had no particular expectation that her father would call.

The girl scribbled the number on a piece of paper. 'And now,' pronounced Miss Dimont, 'I'm off. Mustn't keep the chauffeur waiting.'

Elektra nodded understandingly. In her world, everyone had chauffeurs.

TWENTY-ONE

The world does not revolve around London, even if its inhabitants think so. The moment Miss Dimont stepped out of the Pullman train onto the palm-treed platform she was reminded that it does, in fact, revolve around Temple Regis. And there was Terry, sitting in the Minor, waiting for her in the car park.

'Trust you to push off just when you're needed,' he growled, but she could tell he was pleased to see her. Or thought she could tell.

'What's up?'

'Major incident over at Ruggleswick. Unbelievable. You wouldn't think that two grown men could…'

'Start at the beginning, Terry. And drive slowly.'

The photographer deliberately crunched the gears and made a jerky exit. He was in a bit of a mood.

'Unbelievable,' he repeated. 'A punch-up between Bobby Bunton and that Radipole man on the lawn outside the Marine – in front of all the guests! Well, all the guests that are left,' he added with a grim smile. 'Most couldn't stand the racket of the Devil's Dodgems, packed their bags and left. It's all-out war!'

'Good Lord,' said Judy, but not in a surprised way. She was feeding this information into her memory bank, filtering it, assessing it, trying to judge its value in the context of what she'd learned during her weekend with Uncle Arthur. 'What exactly happened?'

'I had a call from Fluffles,' said Terry with a slight smirk. 'She said she wanted those pictures I took of her but that was just an excuse. She wanted me to get over to the Marine, pronto.'

'When was this?'

'Yesterday morning. When I got there the police had been called – that Sergeant Hernaford, he's a right you-know-what – and Bunton was under arrest. They'd found a cut-throat razor in his pocket and Hernaford threatened to have him up before the beak tomorrow morning.'

'Bet they let him go,' said Miss Dimont caustically.

'Course they did! Don't want the publicity! But Fluffles was thrilled – for some reason she thought the punch-up was over her. They were shouting at each other and saying things like "Don't you dare say those things about her!" and "I'll say what I like – a whore's a whore's a whore!". Well, Fluffles lapped all this up, naturally, and wanted me to take her picture all over again. She was very excited.'

'Been a very long time since two men wanted to fight over *her*,' said Miss Dimont dismissively.

'What are you talking about? She's not a day over forty.'

'Won't see fifty again, Terry, believe me.'

'Well, all I can say is she looks wonderful on it – she was wearing this skin-tight…'

'Oh, do put a sock in it, Terry! What's the upshot?'

'Turns out it wasn't about Fluffles at all. I bumped into Cornish Pete – you know, in the band – and he was there when it happened. It was over this dead woman Patsy Rouchos.'

'That's not her name. Helen Patrikis from now on.'

'How did you find that out?' snapped Terry, and stopped the car. 'You know, I spent three hours yesterday afternoon, when I could have been sitting in the sunshine, poring over those ruddy 10 × 8s you got me to print up, trying to work out who was who and what was what. Are you telling me you know?'

'It's what I went to London for.' It came out sounding a bit superior.

Terry looked mutinous and ready to get out of the car so Judy decided it might be better to smooth his ruffled feathers. 'But if they're fighting over this dead woman, don't you see, Terry, you've got an important clue here?'

He sat with his hands on the steering wheel, deciding whether to continue the battle or subside. On the whole he rather fancied the idea of having discovered a clue that Miss Smartypants hadn't. He switched the engine on again.

'Did Cornish Pete have anything else to add?'

Terry stuck it in gear and drove off again. 'He was in the Primrose Bar yesterday lunchtime when Bobby and Fluffles strolled in – as if nothing had happened! Can you believe it? It took twenty-four hours of those dodgems to empty the hotel – Cornish Pete said some of them were leaving without paying their bills, it was chaos in reception – and there was Bunton ordering champagne as if nothing had happened!'

'And?' Miss Dimont was cross she hadn't been there.

'Cornish says Radipole comes in, spots Bobs and Fluffles, and says, "I've thrown you out once from here, I'm not going to waste any more words," and just grabbed him by the scruff of his neck and seat of his pants – Bobs was leaning against the bar – and frogmarched him through the hotel and out of the door. Gave him a good kick in the BTM for good measure!'

'But what about the whore business? This is quite important.'

'Well, Fluffles got it wrong there. She was thrilled to be fought over but it wasn't her that was the whore, it was the dead woman. Bobs had started taunting Radipole about her and Radipole went mad. Bobs is not in good shape, plus he's a lot shorter, and Radipole just laid into him. When he went down he started kicking him – vicious!' Terry was enjoying this narrative.

'Cornish Pete went over and helped pull Radipole off, Bobs was on the ground, but he was shouting, "Don't you try to blackmail me," or something like that.'

'Blackmail?'

'That's what Cornish Pete said.'

'About the wh… about the dead woman?'

'No idea.'

'By the way, Terry, where are you taking me? So kind of you to come and pick me up, but it's Sunday afternoon, it's late, I've got the Rural District Council in the morning – we're not on a story, are we?'

'You may not be,' said Terry with a grim smile, 'but I am,' and at that moment the Minor breasted the top of the hill and began its slow descent down into Ruggleswick Sands.

'I've got those photos I printed up for Fluffles and while I talk to her, you're going to chat to Bobby Bunton.' The unlovely profile of the Buntorama holiday camp appeared ahead, just beyond the deserted Marine Hotel. His dodgems were churning out '*Hoots Mon!*' at an alarming volume.

'Told Bobs you'd want to talk him through it,' said Terry. 'He wants it public, this dust-up.'

'Mr Rhys won't print it. You know that.'

'Do me a favour,' said Terry with a touch of acid. 'Just go and talk to him!'

It was rare for Terry ever to tell Miss Dimont what to do. The ordinary way of going about things in local newspapers is the reporter tells the photographer what the story is, and what sort of photograph would best illustrate the words, then the photographer takes not the blindest bit of notice and shoots what he sees fit. Neither obeys, or often even listens to, what the other's saying.

Miss Dimont's mind was full of what she had learned in London and not even the blissful train ride back to Devon had given her sufficient time to come to any conclusions about the Buntorama murder. She recognised, though, that Terry's initiative was a valuable one – getting the chance to talk to Bobby Bunton, who only a few days before had Terry kicked out of the camp, could be a huge bonus.

She didn't tell Terry that. 'And then you can buy me a ginger beer at the Marine,' she said, as if reluctantly agreeing to do him a favour.

Terry didn't care, he was looking forward to snuggling up with Fluffles. 'Come on,' he said, drawing up alongside the only decent building in Buntorama. 'They're in here.'

The King of Holiday Camps was nursing his battered ego and bruised posterior. He sat alone with a large brandy glass and a cigar, and for once seemed pleased to meet the reporter with the corkscrew curls and the convex nose. Somehow, with the prospect of revenge in print, she suddenly seemed an alluring figure.

'A glass of brandy, do!'

'No thank you, Mr Bunton, a little early for me. But thank you for seeing me.'

They went over, in some detail, the events leading up to the fracas. Miss Dimont instinctively knew it was best to let the little man get off his chest all his grievances to do with his height, his lowly birth, his lack of polish, and the fact that he'd bought all his wives and then had to pay to get rid of them, before they could get to the heart of the matter.

'I think it would help if you told me why you said those things about Miss, er,' she decided it was better not to let Bunton know the woman's true identity, 'Rouchos.'

'Whore, I called her.'

'Well, yes,' said Miss Dimont, coughing lightly. She didn't want to encourage him.

'*Whore!*'

'Yes, I believe that's the word which caused Mr Radipole to engage in violence with you. Is there any particular reason why you chose it?'

Bunton jerkily dragged the cigar out of his mouth and its ash fell on his shirt front. He was too focused to brush it away.

'You know what whores do, Miss, er... They do things for money!'

'I believe so.'

'This woman, this Rouchos woman, came to my camp under false pretences! She was a liar and a whore!'

'Can you be more specific? If it's not too much to ask?'

Bunton looked at her sideways. Perhaps he was expecting a more sympathetic, a less objective, ear.

'Radipole sent her. She pretended to be a holidaymaker but she was nothing of the sort – she was a spy, paid by Radipole to come in here and see what she could nose out.

'So,' continued Bunton, 'if you want to behave like a whore, you can expect to get treated like one.'

Miss Dimont really did not like this sort of talk at all, but felt she was at a turning-point. 'Go on,' she said, flinching at the prospect of what might come next.

'I smelt a rat when I saw her in the bar of the Marine,' he said. 'She came on strong, really strong. I only asked her if she wanted a drink, next thing I know she tells me she's staying at Buntorama and she's so glad to have met me because she had one or two little complaints to make about the accommodation.

'Well, first of all, my customers don't drink in the Marine – it's too pricey and too poncy for their tastes – so what's she doing there? Second, the complaints, as she called them, were just an excuse. I've seen it all before,' he said with a worldly smile, 'she wanted to get me in her room, and you know what for. Whore!'

He took a large swig of brandy and looked at Miss Dimont to see how his story was going down.

He really is very repellent, thought the reporter, but said, 'I can see the reason for your suspicions. So what happened next?' She dreaded the answer.

'Look,' said Bunton. 'She's a young girl. Well brought-up, I would say well-to-do. What's she doing in my place, and what's she doing playing her tricks on me? Lord knows my life is complicated enough – that Fluffles, she looks sweet but she can be poison, you know! Especially when another woman hoves into view.'

'I'm sure,' said Miss Dimont.

'She was very high-class, very hoity-toity. When we got back to the cabin she told me she'd never been in such a horrible dump in her life and gave the impression it was quite degrading to be doing what she was doing.

'So I asked her, I said, "What the hell is your game?" and she told me – I've been sent to spy on you, she said. Who by, I said. Hugh ruddy Radipole, she said. He wants to know what you're doing, what your plans are, I'm here to find out. And with that she took her clothes off. You see what I mean when I say whore?'

'Well, yes, in a manner of speaking I suppose, yes…'

'For money!' spat Bunton, helping himself to another swig.

'But surely…' began Miss Dimont, but Bunton was in full self-righteous flow.

'I've met all sorts of people Miss, er… Many could be described as dubious characters. But I've never met anybody with a complete lack of morals like her. She was cold, she was calculating, she took pleasure in what she was doing.

'She told me she was Radipole's mistress but that she hated him. She said it was her family money that bought the Marine Hotel. I doubt that's true – a load of hot air if you ask me – but I tell you, she did what she did with me out of spite. Pure malice. She said, "Tell me one thing I can tell him, anything, I don't care, one thing just to show I've done the job. Make it up, I don't care."

'This was – after. She was a very angry woman, as if somehow the world wasn't taking enough notice of her. She didn't have to, you know, with me.'

'Why did she do it then?'

'God knows. Maybe he had a hold over her about something, I just don't know. If she didn't care what story she brought back she could have got sufficient info out of me just by chatting over a drink – but she was determined to wound Radipole, and this was her way of doing it.'

'She was going to go back and boast about what you and she had done?'

'I dunno,' said Bunton, shaking his head. 'I wouldn't put it past her – she was self-obsessed, nothing mattered except how it seemed to affect her. She felt Radipole had somehow cheapened her by telling her to do this spying, and she wanted to get back at him.'

'What happened when she was found dead?'

'Well, that's just it. After the dust had settled, I had a telephone call from Radipole. Out of the blue. Remember, he'd chucked me and Fluffles out after Fluff fell over in the Primrose Bar. Ruddy snob! His people should have wiped up her spilt drink – wasn't her fault!

'Anyway, he said to me, I know who killed that Rouchos woman. And I said, "Shouldn't you tell the police?" And he said, it was you.'

'Was it?' Miss Dimont surprised herself with the directness of her question. It had to be asked. Bunton's eyes looked as though they would pop. 'Are you mad? Are you completely mad, woman? I've got the police after me because of all the hanky-panky going on in the huts and with the members of staff and – oh! all sorts of other things you don't want to hear about. Am I going to be stupid enough to shoot someone on my own premises?'

'Not you, then. Your Mr Baggs. He really looks as though he could do someone some harm – permanent harm.'

'That's why I employ him. But no, come on – I'm not that stupid. I want less trouble, not more.'

And with the blessing of the Almighty and his chum the Archbishop of York, thought Miss Dimont.

'So why did he say it? That you killed her?'

'He's not what you think, you know. He looks so suave, so top-drawer, but I know where he came from – I made it my business to find out. He said he could make it look as though I'd killed her after I found out she'd been spying on me. "You were angry," he said to me. "You know you go mad when you're angry, your staff have been telling me." Oh yes, he was paying my people to blab!

'So he was going to pin it on me. Me! With my reputation! I've been to Buckingham Palace, you know! A jumped-up car dealer, a hotelier who can't keep his guests – who the hell is *he*?'

'So what did you do? Did you say you'd go to the police?'

'Look Miss, er... I don't know about you but I have always found that least said, soonest mended when it comes to the boys in blue. I steer clear, I steer clear!

'No, Radipole was angry, very angry. Angry that I'd found out about his putting that girl in here to spy on me. But

– much more than that – when I told him what lengths she was prepared to go to get the information, he went ballistic.'

Bunton got up and strode down the room, his short legs making heavy weather of the thick carpet.

'It's very simple,' he said. 'He wants me – and the holiday camp – gone. And he doesn't mind how he goes about it. He's told me he was here first, and how dare I come and queer his pitch with all those snobby upper-class types he likes to hang around – how dare I make a noise and allow ordinary people to have their nice little cheap holiday.'

Miss Dimont could see his point. When it came down to it, both men were there to make money and neither had precedence over the other – Radipole with his sable-coated guests nor Bunton with his kiss-me-quick brigade.

'There's something else you should know. This girl, this Rouchos, told me Radipole was incredibly jealous. Possessive to the point of mania. He seemed to be her jailer, and yet why? She could get away if she wanted – she was well-off, she could afford the bus fare out of Temple Regis. Why was she hanging around with him when he was so over-protective, so clinging?'

This was all very absorbing, thought Miss Dimont, but is it taking us any further? If it wasn't Bobby Bunton who fired the fatal shot, then who was it?

'Tell me, Mr Bunton, if it wasn't you, who was it?'

There was a long pause.

'I wondered how long it would take for you to ask that question,' said Bobby. 'You know, you people on these local rags, you're slow off the mark. Slow! I've been interviewed by Fleet Street's finest in my time and I can tell you, that's the first question they would've asked. I'd give them a scotch, they'd get out their notebooks, we'd sit and have a natter and they'd plug me right between the eyes with their questions. Look at you – you haven't even got a pencil out!'

Oh dear, thought Miss Dimont. How can I tell this over-inflated egomaniac that his revelations would mean nothing to the editor of the *Riviera Express* who's never going to allow a degrading brawl between two of Temple Regis' more prominent citizens to appear in print?

'Believe it or not,' she said, cursing herself for not having provided the alibi of a notebook, 'believe it or not, I have a photographic memory, I can recall every last one of your words.' And I can, too, she thought. 'So let me ask again, who do you think killed Patsy Rouchos?'

'Who? Radipole, of course. Why did he kill her? Because he thought she was a traitor. That she'd deserted to the other side. I think she went straight out of that bedroom and told Radipole what she'd done, just to rile him up, just to show who's boss. That way she wasn't his cat's paw – she was in charge.

'She was a strange one all right. I wouldn't put it past her that she goaded him into killing her.'

Bunton swallowed the last of his brandy and looked hard at the reporter.

'The way I see it, she didn't care whether she lived or died.'

TWENTY-TWO

Betty was studying her split ends with some concern when Judy got to her desk on Monday morning.

'Bit early for you, Betty,' she said briskly.

'The Admiral dropped me off.'

'What Admiral?'

'New chap. He's been on TV.'

'I don't have a TV, is he serving or retired?' Old habits die hard when you've been in the senior service.

'Cedric, only he says Seedric, Minsell. *Sir* Seedric, actually,' said Betty. She seemed mighty pleased with herself.

'Lordy! That sounds impressive – what were you doing with him?' Judy did not say, as most people would, what were you doing with him so that he drives you to the office first thing on a Monday morning?

'He took me to the Yacht Club, I've never been there before. They do a very nice gin fizz, did you know?' Betty liked to chalk up her victories for all to see – especially with Judy, for some reason – first, an admiral. Then an admiral with a title who'd been on TV. Then the Yacht Club. Finally, gin fizzes – four chalk-ups in just a couple of sentences!

'Mm,' said Judy a trifle snootily. Most types at the Yacht Club, if they had yachts at all, used diesel rather than nature's zephyrs to propel them up and down the estuary. Few took to the open sea and those that did seem to have been awarded a silver cup just for managing to navigate past the bar.

Betty was more pragmatic. 'There's a wonderful view. And the servants who bring the drinks are really terribly nice.'

'Is he local? I don't think I've heard of him before.'

'He's taking a cottage down here, retiring quite soon. Fancies himself rather.'

'You would if you were an admiral. People salute you a lot, you get used to it. What are you doing with him? Not quite your type, I would have thought.'

'Oh! Nothing like that, Judy! Though he is very sweet. I think he took rather a fancy, if you know what I mean.'

'What would Dud say?'

Betty involuntarily touched her hair. 'No, the Admiral's *work*.'

'Picking you up after breakfast on a Monday morning?' There – she said it. Didn't mean to but it came out anyway.

'It was to make up for the dress.'

'Dress?'

'He spilt his pink gin over it by accident. He promised to pick me up this morning and drop it off at Sketchley's. He said he'd pay the cleaning bill, or take me out to supper – my choice. Such a gentleman!'

Doesn't sound like one to me, thought Judy.

'Is Lady Minsell going to be gracing the Yacht Club, too, when he's fixed up?'

'She's an invalid. Doesn't get out much.'

I bet, thought Judy. 'What's the story?'

'He's joining the board of directors of Buntorama. Bobby Bunton met him when they were both on *What's My Line?*, and you know what they say about businesses that have a lord on the board.'

'He's not a lord.'

'Well, next best thing,' said Betty, more than a little miffed Judy was so unimpressed. What she didn't know was that inwardly Judy was seething – she'd spent the best part of an hour with the boss of Buntorama last night, the man himself, and he never mentioned it once.

Or, more to the point, Judy never asked the right question. I must be slipping, she thought.

'Well, that'll be nice.'

'You seem rather cross this morning, Judy. What about a nice cup of tea?'

'Tea? I've got the Rural District Council!'

Betty quickly got out her notebook and stuck her nose in it. The RDC was her job usually, but she'd had a word with Mr Rhys and he'd let her off because she'd been so helpful over the Admiral business. She felt little remorse, because of all the boring jobs the *Express* had to cover with any regularity, the RDC was far and away the worst. Few could claim to have got through its leisurely discussions on cattle grids, tree-planting, sheep rot and silage with their eyes remaining open for the duration. Yet the *Express*'s job was to report the doings of such bodies – and woe betide the reporter who missed a word of that crucial debate on farm mud on the road (a perennial favourite).

Judy was keeping an eye on the editor's door. She was

waiting for Rudyard Rhys to make his morning appearance so she could brief him on developments in the Patsy Rouchos murder – or as she was now to be known, Helen Patrikis. It was a tremendous coup to have discovered, in the course of a short weekend, the identity which had eluded the authorities for more than two weeks. By rights her revelations should make Page One, but somehow Judy doubted Rhys's resolve: she needed time to talk him into it.

On the other hand she was expected to be in the RDC chamber in less than half an hour, and it took fifteen minutes aboard trusty old Herbert to get there. She'd weighed up how much information she would share with her editor, given his reluctance to acknowledge a murder had happened on his patch, but she did need to discuss with him the matter of informing the police. On occasion the fourth estate had been known to be slovenly in its civic duty when it came to such occasions.

Finally Rhys made his appearance, with all the speed of a Lord Mayor in procession. Nobody knew what he did with his weekends but they seemed to leave him exhausted.

'Morning, Richard.'

'Rr…rrr… Let me get my feet under the desk, can't you?' He subsided into his old revolving chair which gave out a squeak as he sat down.

'The Patsy Rouchos murder, Richard. I found out who she is.'

There was barely a flicker of acknowledgement. 'Inquest's tomorrow,' said Rhys. 'Betty's doing it.'

'Ah. Are you at all interested, Richard, to discover the true identity of the body they will be discussing in court? Or perhaps not?'

'Might be better to leave it until Dr Rudkin's had his say.' Rhys was stonewalling as usual in the face of a mighty scoop. Urgent action frightened him, though it hadn't always been the case.

'OK,' said his reporter. There was some value in this decision, though for different reasons – it meant that Fleet Street wouldn't get the story first. If Miss Dimont popped in to Inspector Topham's office and shared the news, he would be obliged to pass it on to the Coroner. By law, the Coroner would be forced to reveal Patsy/Helen's true identity – and it would be in the national daily newspapers on Wednesday. Since the *Riviera Express* didn't come out till Friday, they would have been scooped by their own scoop. Rudyard Rhys may be cowardly as an editor but on this occasion he'd made the right choice.

'I'm off to the RDC,' said Judy, with a meaningful look – four hours of mind-numbing boredom and I'm your *chief reporter*, drat it! 'By the way, I hear there's a new Admiral in town – d'you know him?'

Rhys jerked back in his chair. 'Who told you *that*?'

'Betty. He brought her in to work this morning.'

'Really?' Again the unspoken question.

'He might be interesting. I haven't got anything much on tomorrow, I could pop out and see him and see if there's a feature to be had. Apparently he's been on TV.'

'*You just leave him alone*,' barked Rhys, banging his fist on the desk. 'Betty's doing him!'

'Betty seems to be doing everything,' snipped Judy. 'Maybe you should make *her* chief reporter!'

She flounced back to her desk to retrieve her raffia bag,

then sat down. She'd seen these sudden outbursts of rage before, almost always when her editor had something to conceal. Like most men he believed in turning up the volume to drive away unwanted questions, never realising it was always a dead giveaway.

'Betty,' she said, smiling ingratiatingly across the desk, 'what's the story on the Admiral?'

Betty looked guarded. 'Oh, just that he's joined the board of Buntorama, nothing special. Page Three single column short.'

'You seem to be doing a lot of legwork for a couple of paragraphs.'

'Ha, ha! You never know what might develop, Judy. Establishing a new contact, that's all.' It sounded as false as her inexpertly applied eyelashes.

Herbert got her over to the Rural District Council offices with time to spare and with a sigh Miss Dimont took her seat in the press benches. The oak desks were as uncomfortable as they were unyielding, and she was not encouraged by a new adornment to the one she chose – the message

A SHORT COURSE OF DEATH

carved meticulously into the wood with some fine embellishments surrounding it. It must have taken hours to complete – but then, what else was a reporter to do with his time when the talk was of muck and manure?

Death proved to be shorter than usual today, however, and by lunchtime Miss Dimont was free.

Since she wasn't expected back in the office till late

afternoon she decided to take Herbert for a spin across to Bedlington in the hope of sharing a sandwich with Auriol.

The journey was, as always, exhilarating. As the dear moped manfully breasted the top of Mudford Cliffs she looked down the steep slope to the pink sand and the ivory-blue water below. Across the other side of the estuary she could see dots of white houses punctuating the red rocks and green grass. In distant water lay the skeleton of a submerged wreck – how long had it lain there on the seabed? – and, nearer to shore, the heavy breakwater which might have saved the lives of its crew had it but sailed on a few hundred yards more.

She hadn't seen Auriol since uncle Arthur dropped in on his way back to London – so much seemed to have happened since then! – and she was eager to share her latest findings with someone who might appreciate their significance. Unlike old Rudyard!

The café was still quite full with lunchtime trade and Auriol was busy, so she sat on the quay outside and drank in the sunshine. A single gull wandered over to stand at her feet, eyeing her sideways, and she looked back at him in admiration. Whatever others may think about your bad table-manners you are wise, you are brave, you are in your way very beautiful – and you are a survivor, thought Miss Dimont. If you could speak I might learn much.

'Egg? Luncheon meat? Or we could share a pasty if you like.' Auriol's lunchtime offerings were designed to please the undemanding palates of hungry holidaymakers, though she was a fine cook too.

'Anything,' said Judy, turning to her friend with a smile. 'Arthur sends his love.'

'Adorable man.'

'Lots to tell you,' said Judy, 'shall I come inside?'

'The last lot are just going. I've got some nice coffee.'

The conversation which followed was what made the two women so enjoy each other's company – an hour stuffed with information to chew over punctuated by a peppery exchange of views, a brief slide into nostalgia, and always the unspoken presence of their adored Eric. Auriol admired her friend's unstoppable brilliance, while Miss Dimont viewed with wonder a woman in her mid-fifties who could still look so beautiful.

'So you see,' Miss Dimont was saying, 'by now our dearest Eric could be doing ten years in Peterhead prison.'

'I would take him one of my cakes with a nice big file inside. He'd be out in no time!'

'On the run with Johnny Ramensky, picked up by the police next day.'

'Eric was cleverer than that.'

'He was, the fool.'

The old friends subsided into silence, then suddenly the reason she'd driven over to Bedlington came back to her. 'D'you know an admiral called Minsell? Appears on TV?'

'*Why are you asking?*' It was as if a thundercloud had suddenly obliterated the sun.

'Good Lord, Auriol, what's up? Simple question, nothing behind it!' That wasn't quite true, even so she was alarmed at her friend's sudden antagonism and awakened to its possibilities. What could have caused it?

'Just another flag officer,' replied Auriol, hastily adjusting her tone and picking up the plates with a clatter. 'There seem to be so many of them these days – more admirals than ships.

Yes, I know his name, in charge of some shore establishment. Why do you ask?' she repeated.

I won't get far with this if I tackle it head-on, thought Miss Dimont. But something's up – something Auriol knows, maybe something Betty knows, but something I don't! She did not like that.

'Oh nothing,' she lied airily. 'Just that whoever this chap is, he's turned his beady eye on Betty. She went to interview him – he's going to take a cottage down here and has accepted a directorship of Buntorama, just wondered what you knew about him. I thought I might go and do a feature on him for the paper.'

'Ohhh… he sounds pretty boring to me,' said Auriol, her eyes flicking sideways. 'Heaven knows, these days admirals are two a penny. Not as if he sank the *Bismarck* or anything.'

'You seem to know more about him than you're saying.'

'I keep wondering why you're asking,' said Auriol.

'I keep wondering why you're not answering,' said Miss Dimont.

Auriol sat down again. 'Look, Hugue, we've been friends since the year dot.'

'Yes.'

'We don't always tell each other everything.'

'Yes, we do.'

'No, we don't. You didn't tell me when that young man Valentine whatsisname kissed you and told you he loved you.'

'I did eventually.'

'Well, that's just it. There's a time and place for everything. Forget about the Admiral – let Betty do the interview, I'm sure she'll do a great job. It'll be a nice piece for the *Express* and then he can sink back into obscurity.'

'Hardly. He's on TV. He's a celebrity!'

'I really don't think serving officers should be making a display of themselves,' said Auriol without the slightest authority, since she did not possess a TV either.

'Well, I'm sorry, if he's going to come down here and plant himself on the Buntorama board *and* carry on making a display on TV, pretty soon he's going to be the most famous person in Temple Regis. Obscure he most definitely will not be. Come on, Auriol, the semaphore signals flashing in your eyes tell me you're hiding quite a big something.'

'I have orders to keep you out of the loop.'

'Oh,' said Miss Dimont, deflated. 'The Admiralty.'

'No prizes for guessing that.'

'I thought all that business was behind us. You know, those last few years in service laid me low.'

'You should have stayed in the Royal Navy. At least they stick to the rules.'

'Not always.'

'No, not always, but that stuff you were doing over in Broadway Buildings was worse. I wasn't in the slightest surprised when you resigned.'

'It was just so... demoralising. When you and I worked in Naval Intelligence, there was a purpose – a simple purpose – which was to defeat the enemy. When I transferred to MI6, some of the things I became involved in were indefensible. It's extraordinary what the mind of man can think up when he wants to create evil.'

'You were temperamentally unsuited.'

'Never said a truer word, Auriol. Of course, one does get caught up in it all. There were some early successes, but when I went back to Berlin it just came to me. I had to get out.'

'And now look at you – serene, content, accomplished, on the verge of another success by the sound of it.'

'No Eric, though.'

'Well, *I* don't have an Eric, or a David or a Robert either. We muddle along all right, don't we?'

Miss Dimont smiled but did not reply.

'Anyway, you're to leave the Admiral alone. You've got enough on your plate with the murder of this Helen Patrikis.'

'And her father.'

'For heaven's sake! One at a time, Hugue, one at a time!'

The two friends laughed and looked at each other affectionately.

'But,' said Miss Dimont as she picked up her bag, 'when it comes to the Admiral, I'll find out. I always do.'

TWENTY-THREE

Back in the office Terry was fretting about his Leica. 'Best cameras in the world bar none,' he grumbled, shaking his head. 'Why does it always go wrong?'

'Only in your hands, Terry. That old proverb – the workman and his tools.'

'What would *you* know? The best photograph you ever took was with that Box Brownie, and then you had your finger half-over the lens. Might have been an award-winning picture without that.'

He didn't mean it.

Things had moved fast. Since they met at Regis Junction twenty-four hours before Terry had got a private commission out of Fluffles to do a studio shoot ('In my fur bikini, dear, a present for Bobs!') and Judy a fascinating insight into the world of the two warring alpha males and their connection with the dead woman. Terry was eager to suggest new ideas formed by his scrutiny of the 10 × 8 prints, but Judy was striding forward in her investigation, not looking back.

'It has to be Radipole.'

'If you say so.' They were sitting at the table in the print room, where it was quiet and the lights were low so they could concentrate. The 10 × 8s sat invitingly on the corner of the table and the photographer kept glancing at them while Judy was wondering, not for the first time, whether Terry secretly used aftershave. If he did it was very discreet.

'But first take a look at these two,' he urged. 'I've had another go at this one and it's come up a bit sharper. The photo was taken in artificial light, no flash, probably with something like your Box Brownie. It's a room in a house, the light is on, but there's daylight combating the overhead light. So I'd say at a rough guess it was twilight, early evening.'

'Go on.' Judy was frustrated by Terry's meticulous deconstruction of the scene, she wanted quick results, tangible clues, not a walk round the block and a lecture on lighting. *Heaven knows he'll be telling me it was 1/25 at f8 next!*

'You'd get the same effect by using 1/25 at f8,' he was droning, 'only this was a snap, not a professional photograph.'

'Yes,' said Judy absently. She'd stopped listening.

'As we know, the original had been torn into four pieces, then for some reason stuck in the album with the pieces roughly jammed back next to each other. I took a photo of it as it lay on the page of the album, and that's what we were looking at last time. But two of the four pieces were overlapping – what I've done now is taken a pair of scissors, cut the two pieces apart and then reassembled them. And look!'

Miss Dimont looked. The picture looked pretty much the same as before. It showed the interior of a room, possibly a bedroom, though you couldn't see the bed, a wall with an oil painting, a side table and a low chair. A piece of furniture which could have been anything in one corner.

'The camera's moving,' said Terry. 'The person who took the pic was probably trying to focus on something else but they were in a hurry and missed their target. And here's the clue.'

He tapped the glossy print with his index finger. 'Down there, where the two pieces join each other. Look. A foot.'

Judy picked up a heavy magnifying glass and leaned forward. Terry was right – though it was only just visible, a naked foot protruded from the bottom of the frame.

'The first questions that come to mind,' she said slowly, 'is whose foot? And why? Why is this in the album which otherwise has family photographs?'

'You have to remember, there were other photos which had been taken out. Maybe there was a series of photos, which might have given more of a clue who the foot belongs to.'

'But,' said Miss Dimont, 'if you're taking pictures out, why not keep them all, or get rid of them all? Why leave just the one in the series – and just as important, why tear it up, then glue the pieces back in?'

'Let's leave that for a moment,' said Terry, who had no answer but was pleased she'd acknowledged his discovery. 'Take a look at this one again.'

He pulled forward the picture of the man and woman. 'It's not her father,' Terry was saying. 'This is the murdered girl – and someone who we thought was her father. Take off his sunglasses, take off the hat, and who have you got?'

'Hugh Radipole.'

'Correct. And they're in Paris. I was there myself after the Liberation and though it was teeming with people, I thought somehow that street corner seemed familiar. I got some picture books of Paris out and – hey presto!'

From a side table he drew a heavy illustrated guide to the city. The page was open at a picture of the gilded statue of Joan of Arc astride her horse.

'Joanie on a Pony, the Yanks used to call that,' said Terry. 'Now look at this.' He turned the page to reveal a similar shot, taken from a different angle. The caption read, *Statue of St Joan at the junction of the Rue de Rivoli and the Place des Pyramides*. 'They're standing facing away from Joanie, but that's where they are, all right.'

'Brilliant!' said Judy enthusiastically, though she couldn't work out whether this was a clue or not. She'd already established that Hugh Radipole and Helen Patrikis had been lovers, and where better to celebrate their love than in the City of Light?

'He took her there for the weekend, but they look as though they're hating it.'

'And each other.'

'That's love for you, Terry.'

Terry felt like saying, how would you know? But he didn't.

'And the Alvis,' he said. 'What was that you were telling me her cousin said to you? He took her for a drive in one of his fancy cars – she was just a schoolgirl.'

'Strange,' said Judy, 'that given their very bumpy relationship she would want to keep that as a memento. If you're right, Terry, that is.'

'I dunno,' said the photographer. 'You women, you're all a bit peculiar, one way and the other. Why *not* keep it? It's a very nice car.'

Judy snorted – boys and their toys again. They wandered out into the newsroom and across at the far end she saw Athene and gave her a wave. No day was complete without a ten-minute chat and a cup of her soothing tea, but there just hadn't been time. Devon's most famous astrologer waved back and the look they exchanged said, 'Tomorrow!'

Betty was at her desk, the usual pile of journalistic confetti spilling from it. She was suddenly overcome by a stab of fear. Scooping up her handbag she scuttled over to Athene's desk: 'Do you mind, dear, if I make a private call on your telephone? Most urgent.'

'I'll make the tea,' smiled Athene. Tomorrow had come sooner than expected.

The voice that answered the other end was warm, welcoming, with only the merest of accents.

'Miss Patrikis, it's Judy Dimont. From Devon. We met on Saturday.'

'I was going to telephone you,' said Elektra. 'I'm coming down, probably on Wednesday.'

'I thought your father…?'

'There's been a collision at sea. Two tankers, a great deal of oil spilled. He's flown to Crete.'

'And your sister?'

'Gone with him.'

'What's your plan when you get here?'

'I was rather hoping you'd help me decide that – this isn't something of which I have any experience. Papa told me to "take care of business" when he went out of the door but didn't specify what exactly. I suppose I must contact the police but I don't have the photographs – you do.'

'The police have the original album, but I'll come along and be by your side. Did you know there was to be an inquest?'

'What's that, exactly?'

'An official court of inquiry into your cousin's murder.'

'But… according to you, they don't know who she is.'

'They don't.'

'Well, that's a relief. Papa said whatever occurred there should be no publicity. I take it if they don't know who the body belongs to, they can't drag the Patrikis name into it?'

Heavens, thought Judy, these Greeks have a strange way of approaching the law. On the other hand, who am I to persuade her to do otherwise – this is her family matter, not mine, and she must make the decision not me.

'Where are you going to stay?'

'The secretary will find somewhere.'

'You could stay with me, though you'll find it rather different from what you're used to.'

'I went to an English boarding school. Is it worse than that?'

'A shade better.'

'Then that would be lovely. There are some things I want to tell you.'

'There's a train from Paddington that gets in at 4.30. I could meet you.'

'Oh, Stevens will drive me down, I expect.'

Huh, Judy said to herself as she replaced the receiver. Blessed chauffeurs again!

'Tea,' breathed Athene. 'You *have* been busy, Judy.'

'My dear,' said Judy, relieved to think of something else,

'the Rural District Council! Fox-hunting! They're in a complete tizzy!'

Athene wasn't at all interested in country pursuits but she was interested in Judy. 'What's happened?'

'The League Against Cruel Sports has bought some fields and woods just outside Exbridge and they're planning to turn it into a sanctuary for hunted animals,' said Judy. 'If this morning's debate is anything to go by, the RDC is ready to descend on the place, riding-whips aloft, to give them all a good seeing-to.'

'That's nice, dear.' Judy couldn't tell whether Athene had even heard what she'd said. Her aura was distinctly purplish, and she suddenly realised the deadline was looming for the most-read page in the whole of the *Riviera Express*. 'Oh! Sorry, Athene – I'm getting in your way. Your column to write!'

'That's all right, Judy, take away your tea and we'll talk tomorrow. I want to hear – those poor foxes!'

Auriol and the Admiral were sitting opposite each other in the coffee room of the Marine Hotel. Things weren't going terribly well.

'You're looking wonderful, Auriol!' Sir Cedric smiled, stretching his eyes in unspoken invitation. 'But I really don't know why I'm here talking to you. I thought we'd said it all fifteen years ago.'

'You never seemed to mind chatting to me last time around,' said Auriol comfortably. 'In fact, I'd say you quite enjoyed it.'

'We did have fun, didn't we?'

'Look, Cedric, you've been frightfully lucky. How you've managed to last so long I really do not know – Rear Admiral and a knightood? How did you swing that?' For a woman who spent her days running a harbourside café in a faraway Devon resort, she looked this late morning like a mannequin from Mayfair – granted the baking of those delicious cakes, over the years, had brought some transformation to her wartime figure, but the extra curves were beguiling. The Admiral clearly thought so.

'That's not very generous, Auriol, I've worked hard throughout the whole of my career.'

Yes, she thought, it must be exhausting giving our secrets away.

'What are you doing for dinner?'

Oh Lord, thought Auriol, here we go again… She flashed him a smile. 'Since you're going to be down here quite a lot, I should get you acquainted with the better places around town. We can start by you taking me to Amaretti's – delicious Italian food and old Tuscan wine, just your cup of tea, if I remember correctly.'

'No coupons now,' said Sir Cedric happily, 'no more Woolton Pie.'

'I think Boulestin did very well, given the rationing,' she said, referring to their habitual rendezvous in the old days. 'Tell me about Bobby Bunton.'

'Well,' said the Admiral, 'this is entirely off the record. The man's a complete rogue, but he's done some good things. I mean, I wouldn't want to stay in one of his camps but look what he's done for ordinary people. He's revolutionised the way people think about themselves and what they can expect from life with his holidays. It's cheap, cheerful, and charming – I'm all for him.'

'You like dealing with rogues.'

'Look, I shall soon be retiring. Ulla is, as you know, very unwell and the doctors' bills have been colossal. Her children are grown up and though very nice, unemployable. They are a constant drain. I've had to sell a lot of investments because Ulla expects them to live a certain life, and has no concept of where money comes from.'

'There are three, aren't there?'

The Admiral's eyes flickered. What would a woman who ran a café in an obscure corner of Devon, whom he hadn't seen for fifteen years, know about his domestic arrangements?

'I have a long memory,' said Auriol, poker-faced. 'They seemed such sweet kids back then – you showed me their photograph.' It almost sounded plausible.

'Well, Bobs is a fine fellow. Though, as I say, a complete rogue. We met on a TV show and hit it off. He asked me how to get a knighthood, so I told him – doesn't stand a chance, of course, but no need to be high-handed about it – and he took me out for a drink.

'He said he was in hot water with the authorities. They'd discovered he was stealing the church collections he took every Sunday, putting them in his pocket.'

'Good heavens – I thought he'd got the Archbishop of York to come down and give Buntorama a blessing.'

'Oh,' laughed the Admiral, 'he's a cheeky one, Bobs. He thought if he got in quick with the invitation, and the Bish accepted, nobody would dare to tell the old boy he'd had his hand in the till. So he went down to the Athenaeum, handed him his card, and invited him to Temple Regis. He's made so many headlines and made himself so popular in the tabloid press the Archbishop couldn't wait to say yes. Makes him look a man of the people.'

Auriol stiffened slightly but maintained her smile – she'd got the Admiral talking. First step.

'He is in trouble, though. The Commissioner of Police took a very dim view of the church funds matter and had a couple of his men take a look at Bunton's operations. Though it's not against the law, there's been a lot of hanky-panky going on in the camp which wouldn't look good in court, plus the people who run the funfair down here seem to be blithely unaware that there are laws in this land. Pickpocketing, short-changing, oh, all sorts of malpractice.'

'Why on earth are you getting involved, then? Think what it could do to your reputation!' Auriol did not add, nothing to what I and the Admiralty Investigations Unit are going to do to it pretty soon.

'No, he gave me his word. He said an investigation into Buntorama down here in Temple Regis could have a domino effect on the rest of his camps, so he decided the time had come for him to go legit. He explained in the early days he had to cut corners to make ends meet – he's a self-made man, after all – but the time had come to change all that. He wants that knighthood!'

'And you're going to help him get it?'

'Up to a point.' The Admiral allowed himself a wintry smile.

'You know they had a shooting down there. That's hardly going to help.'

'He thinks it's the chap who owns this place, Radipole, who did it. I doubt it myself – more likely to be one of those ragamuffins who run the funfair.'

'Either way, it's hardly going to help him to get that knighthood. And frankly, Cedric, it can hardly help burnish your reputation, either. Joining the board of a company that allows murders on the premises – these sound like they're bad people, very bad. I'm surprised at you.'

'As I said, Auriol, I can use the money. And anyway I've always enjoyed living dangerously.' His eyes twinkled.

You're a fool, thought Auriol. You know what I'm after but you think yourself far too smart to be caught. What is it about men in authority? Why do they think that they are the only ones blessed with brains?

'I saw you on the tellybox,' she lied. 'Most distinguished. Another of your fundraising techniques?'

'It doesn't pay much but gives one a reputation. I'm there to prove that not all military brass are stuffed shirts. I've done a few of those panel shows but lately I've been branching out, doing military history.'

'I heard about that. You're making a film on the building of *Dreadnaught*, I believe.'

'How interesting,' said Sir Cedric very slowly, 'that you should know that.' He looked at her hard. 'Nothing's been announced because I haven't got the go-ahead from the Admiralty yet.'

Auriol thought, well, *that* was a mistake – I shouldn't have let him know I knew he'd been up to Barrow-in-Furness. Then she thought, I don't care! Here we are, drinking coffee and making small talk and we both know what this game is. I am encircling you and your treachery, Admiral, and it is you who is pulling the noose tighter round your neck.

'I have a friend who works up in Barrow. You paid them a visit.'

'What an extraordinary coincidence,' said the Admiral, with barely veiled irony, 'I have a friend up there, too. He's called Jasper Hetherington and he's an old chum from submarine days – in charge of the whole bang-shoot. I think he's disappointed the Admiralty has given so little publicity to what he's doing, and he invited me up in the hope I might make a film about it.'

Did he also give you the plans? thought Auriol. Did he leave them on the desk and go out for a breath of fresh air while you got out your little camera? Or am I just dreaming that bit?

'How much publicity do you need about a top-secret nuclear submarine?' asked Auriol. 'Surely that's the point – the top-secret nature of it.'

'On the contrary,' said Minsell, witheringly. 'You have heard, I take it, the phrase nuclear *deterrent*? We make these weapons to deter the enemy. They need to know what we're doing, what the capability is.'

Well, they know it now, thought Auriol, thanks to you. Though how much they know is the mystery – and it's up to me to find it out.

'So we're just waiting for the BBC and the Admiralty to come to an agreement on how much we can film, and when.' He got up and laid his hand on her shoulder. 'We had some fun in the old days, didn't we? You're still a good-looking woman.'

'Not so bad yourself, Cedric,' Auriol smiled, and in truth he did still look pretty good. 'Are you planning on coming down here permanently?'

'We'll see. I think Ulla will have to go into a home. I've had my fill of Portsmouth, not a lot of fun to be had there, I can tell you, and there are a lot of old friends in Devon. Bobby found me a little cottage down here which'll do as a temporary base while we see how things pan out. I've only got a couple of months' service left, and then I think he's hoping I might become his representative down here while he moves on to his next camp. D'you know how much money he's made?'

Auriol couldn't care less but could see that Minsell was hoping for a sizeable slice of it himself. She wondered how little he was being paid by the Russians if he had to do all this extra work as well.

'So, then,' she said, getting up and smiling encouragingly at the enemy. 'Amaretti's tonight? Eight o'clock? I'll let them know.'

The Admiral put his arm round her waist and gave her cheek a peck. She felt a surge of guilt as she returned the gesture.

'Eight o'clock. And wear lots of that lovely perfume, there's a good girl.'

TWENTY-FOUR

'What the devil is this muck?'

'It's the Gevrey-Chambertin '54, sir. Which you ordered. The best we have.'

'Filth. Take it away! Take it *away!*'

Fleet Street's finest had landed, and the Grand Hotel was once again on its mettle. The wine waiter Peter Potts was run off his feet and extra staff had to be drafted in from the dining room to assist.

The rococo halls rang to the raucous jokes of the nation's purveyors of instant history, while in a back room the accountant licked his lips as he fingered the bar chits.

'That's when I bought the camel on expenses. Technically, of course, I still own it...'

'The judge had the Old Bailey cleared and ordered me to stay behind. What I told him then, well, it changed the whole course of the trial...'

'General Montgomery... it was after El Alamein. He told me – in strictest confidence, of course...'

'That Rachman, call him a slum landlord if you must, but he pours the finest single malt, I can tell you...'

The stories had been told a thousand times but burnished with a glass or two of Burgundy they came up like new. Unlike their provincial counterparts these men had travelled the world, rubbed shoulders with the rich, the famous and the notorious. They had witnessed mass destruction and taken cocktails with Gina Lollobrigida, canoed up the Suez Canal and eaten *sachertorte* in the Albertinaplatz. They were no better journalists than their provincial counterparts, but the stories were bigger, as were their expenses.

The inquest on the unknown woman coincided with the silly season – that sun-drenched period of the year when the wise Fleet Streeter takes an extended holiday because there's no news. Filling the paper becomes a heavier burden requiring extra ingenuity, resourcefulness, and the more-than-occasional recourse to fabrication. Traditionally the season would prompt a sighting of the Loch Ness Monster, involving a lengthy journey away from the office and the copious distribution of Scottish pound notes in licensed premises.

Here in Temple Regis, the press corps was at its ease. Very little would come out at the open-and-adjourn procedure, especially under the spartan reign of Dr Rudkin, the coroner, but the opening of proceedings would allow room for considerable speculation about the mystery beauty with the bullet through her heart.

Further down the corridor in the private bar, Detective Inspector Topham sat alone with his pint of Portlemouth, staring into its auburn depths and considering his future. It wasn't as if he hadn't been here before – why, when that noisy lot were last down here, after the murder of Bengt Larsson the inventor, it was just the same. There they were next door, just waiting to trample on the reputation of Temple Regis, while he sat like King Canute helplessly watching the incoming tide wash his toes.

'Time to go,' he said to himself.

'OK?' said Sid the barman, a man with an energetic elbow when it came to pint-pulling and glass-polishing but one always alert to the joys and sadnesses magnified by the drinks he served.

'Yes, Sid,' said Frank Topham, looking down at the hat beside him. It seemed to be telling him to quit. He got up and wandered over to the bar. 'When you were in the desert' – he and Sid had this in common – 'did you ever think of the future?'

'I thought of the missus. Don't know why I bothered, she buggered off with the next-door neighbour.'

'I mean,' said the policeman, 'where you'd be ten, twenty, years later?'

'The Grand's been good to me. I was a porter when I got called up, look at me now!'

Topham looked about the small room. This was the limit of Sid's ambitions, and it made him happy. Why did he, a detective inspector – highly respected and not badly paid – why did he feel only a sense of failure?

'I can't stop it, Sid,' he said. 'Can't stop the wretched advance. People who won the war seem to be turning their backs on what they won it for. It looks like we live in a golden age – the nation recovering, families back together, but it ain't so. That lot down the hall, they seem determined make their living showing how rotten people are these days – want to show life in all its grimy, grubby awfulness. I despair, Sid, I really do.'

'They here for the inquest?'

'Yes.'

'Going to have a pop at the local police for not identifying the body?'

Topham sighed. 'I expect so, Sid, I expect so.'

'Hardly your fault, Frank.'

'Whether it is or it isn't, funny enough it's not the Chief Constable I mind – though I'll be on the carpet again, I expect – or the Mayor, and he'll be sure to have his say, it's what the people in the street think of me. People in Temple Regis know who I am, and they think I can't do my job. And that makes me feel I can't do it either.'

'Think of the medals you won, Frank, the men you saved – the regiment's proud of you, boy. You're looked up to at the British Legion. Not many like you.'

'That was then. I don't know – you've got people in Downing Street saying we've never had it so good, but I feel as if the sand is shifting under my feet, giving way. People caring less about the niceties.'

Sid polished the counter in front of him. If the nation had reached its high point and was now on the slippery slope, it made little difference in here – people would still celebrate, or drown their sorrows, in his bar. They loved coming here. Not for Sid to dwell on the prospect of a people in moral retreat.

'Another, Frank?'

'Yes please.' He handed over his tankard. 'I can't let them win.'

'No.'

'I can't.'

He took the Portlemouth back to the table and sat it down beside his hat.

The headlines a couple of days later were no less than might be expected.

SLAIN IN SEASIDE PARADISE

said the *News Chronicle.*

BRUNETTE AND A BULLET

was the way the *Daily Herald* saw it.

WHO ON EARTH IS SHE?

screamed the *Daily Mirror*.

MYSTERY DEEPENS ON HOLIDAY CAMP VICTIM

was the *Daily Express'* version.

Miss Dimont read the headlines with a mixture of amusement and concern as she waited by the bandstand to meet Elektra Patrikis. Technically, she'd committed an offence punishable by a jail term – the courts don't look kindly on those who withhold information about murder victims. On the other hand, it was on the express instructions of a family member that she'd held her tongue.

Mercifully Betty had been in court to witness the skeletal Dr Rudkin deal with that insolent rabble from London, and Judy had taken the day off to spend in her garden with Mulligatawny. Recently she'd been experimenting with various different species of aquilegia to see which would cover the ancient wash-house most prettily, and the roses needed trimming. Mull watched it all through slitted eyes and outstretched paws which made him look like a sphinx. He was storing up the energy to go mousing later.

Then there were the preparations for her house-guest: though Miss Dimont was unconcerned by the riches of others, some inner voice – probably that of Mme Dimont – told her to get out the best bed-linen from the airing-cupboard and to polish up the table silver. The cottage, as always, smelt of wax polish and lavender, and the roses on the dining-room table shouted their presence out, even into the hall.

Her preparations made, she hastened to the seafront to sit by the bandstand, listening to the Temple Regis Silver Band and awaiting the arrival of Elektra Patrikis. As she listened she considered whether any actual damage had been done by her decision to stay silent – on balance, it seemed not.

While it was by no means certain that Hugh Radipole was the murderer, probably of both Helen and her father Stavros, it was looking increasingly likely. And if he was finally to be apprehended, she needed more time to be certain.

Then again, she couldn't entirely dismiss the theory that it was Bobby Bunton – or his man Baggs – who'd fired the fatal shot. Bunton was a man of uneven temperament, had taken grave exception to Helen Patrikis' contemptuous attitude to him, and had a very nasty piece of work, Baggs, ready and willing to do almost anything for his master. Had he invented that business about Radipole – saying he'd stick the murder on Bunton, simply as a double-bluff in order to point the finger at his rival?

Of the two, her instincts leaned towards Radipole, simply because he'd known both Helen and her father, and was closely involved with both. Easier to suppose one person killed them, and easy in the first case to see why – rejected by Helen, angered and humiliated by her behaviour with Bunton who was already his enemy.

But why would Radipole kill Stavros? To free Helen from her father's iron control, only to find her rejecting him? That didn't quite work, because Stavros' murder was four years ago. Why, if she'd run away from Radipole, would she come back to him now? It didn't add up.

Judy was deep in thought as the silver-grey Rolls-Royce whispered to a halt a few feet away.

Elektra opened the window and called out, 'This is lovely!'

Judy walked over and issued directions to Stevens before climbing in the back. 'I can't believe it!' said her companion. 'How wonderful this place is! My only experience of the English seaside was when I was at school, and I can assure you the coast of Essex bears no resemblance to this paradise!'

She seems much happier away from that house, thought Miss Dimont. The Rolls slid silently through the streets towards home, its spacious leather-bound interior littered with magazines, books, a fur wrap – what a way to travel!

'Stevens will stay at the Fortescue,' said Elektra, 'I am so looking forward to seeing your cottage!'

Looking forward, perhaps, to seeing how the other half lives, thought Miss Dimont, not unkindly. My home has three bedrooms, while the house you've come from could have ten times that number for all I know.

But Elektra fitted in immediately. Once Stevens had deposited the bags and the great limousine had lumbered away – that'll have the neighbours twitching their curtains, thought Miss Dimont – they sat in the garden and drank tea.

'This is just divine,' said the young woman. 'Your house is perfect, the setting perfect – I so envy you!'

'Do you really?'

'Don't be misled by appearances. We're a rich family, very rich, but with that goes the loss of certain things that you would take for granted, Miss Dimont. My father likes to surround himself by staff, and so you're never quite sure who's on the other side of the door. There's no such thing as being alone in that house – or the one on the other side of the Heath. Look,' she said, changing the subject, 'I've brought you something!'

Elektra handed over a parcel whose contents contained a boxed set of Jane Austen's seven published novels. 'Edwardian,' she explained, 'forerunners of the paperback – look, the covers are a sort of oilskin. I found them in the antiquarian bookshop on Haverstock Hill – when we met I could tell immediately you were a Jane enthusiast.'

How adroit, thought Miss Dimont – a gift that was full of thought but had not cost very much.

'They're delightful!' she exclaimed, taking out *Sense and Sensibility* and turning its pages. 'And look, the original owner has signed her name in pencil – always so fascinating to know who old books once belonged to!'

Elektra got up and walked over to the wash-house,

looking about her as she went. 'Aquilegia – and quite a few different varieties, too!'

We're going to get on very well, thought Miss Dimont. 'More tea?'

'Nearly time for a drink?'

'Ah yes,' said Judy, 'you've had a long journey.'

She made two gin-and-tonics with mint instead of the customary lemon and they went to sit in a patch of sunlight by the garden wall. Judy paid her guest a calculated compliment about the diamond ring on her right hand.

'Asscher cut? Around three carats?'

'Good lord!' said Elektra. 'How do you know that? Even I don't know what it is, and I've been wearing it ever since my mother died.'

'I used to be in the diamond trade, before the war. My father was a dealer in Antwerp. We came to Britain during the First War.'

'What a coincidence, we came from Greece in the Second. What did you do? In diamonds, I mean?'

'I used to travel round the various brokers in Paris, Madrid, Berlin, Vienna. My father became unwell and I more or less took over the business.'

'How exciting! You must have been well-off, then.'

Meaning, thought Miss Dimont, what are you doing living in a small cottage so very far from civilisation with no chauffeur at your beck and call?

'By most people's standards, yes. It's a complicated story.'

Curiously, establishing the fact that Miss Dimont understood the ways of the rich made things easier for Elektra. She smiled and stretched her legs.

'Why don't we talk about Helen? Have you seen the papers today?'

'I purposely didn't look. Stevens puts them all in the back of the car when we go on a long journey but I thought it would be too upsetting.'

'Probably just as well. I've got them here for you to have a look at if you wish, but it's pretty much as you'd suspect. All a bit torrid.'

'Was the family name mentioned?'

'No, but I'm afraid it will be eventually. It's an offence to conceal the identity of a dead person if you know who it is.'

'Papa will be here on Friday, we had a wire from Crete. He will make the identification.'

'What will you do meanwhile?'

'Oh,' said Elektra with a lazy smile, 'live the life of a normal human being. Go and have an ice-cream, maybe a donkey ride – I haven't done that since I was at school.'

'Come into the kitchen then,' said Judy, 'and tell me about Helen.'

'For your newspaper?'

'I ought to explain,' said Miss Dimont, 'that I have skills other than shorthand and typing.'

'And sizing up diamonds.'

While she prepared the supper Judy told her guest some of the murders she'd been involved in investigating.[2] It was a gentle way of introducing Elektra to the idea she was part of solving the mystery, and an important one at that.

'I think Helen was not quite a normal person?'

---

2 See *The Riviera Express*, *Resort to Murder*.

'Far from it. Very destructive, very divisive, very self-centred and opinionated. Her mother died in childbirth and as you know she was the only one. I think Stavros took his wife's death very badly indeed and my father used to tell me – I was too young – that he would say to Helen, "You killed your mother."'

'What a terrible thing to do. To a small child.'

'Yes, but somehow it was worse than that. They were very close, Stavros and Helen, and when I was older I'd sometimes hear him say it to her, only in a loving sort of way. As if it was a good thing she had done, killing her mother, so that he and his daughter could be together alone. I'd say she grew up loving him and hating him in equal measure.'

'That seems to exactly describe her relationship with Hugh Radipole,' said Miss Dimont. 'Love and hate.'

'Yes.' Elektra wrinkled her face. 'I don't really want to talk about *him*.'

Miss Dimont put down the mixing bowl she'd just picked up. 'I think you have to,' she said slowly, 'if we're to get to the bottom of who killed Helen.'

'Why?'

'I'll be frank. There are two suspects, and he's number one. He knew both Stavros and Helen. He had business dealings with Stavros and a love affair with Helen. I need to know what you know about him.'

Elektra walked over to the kitchen window, then sat down. 'There's something I have to say. I was asking myself all the way down here whether I would tell you this, but it seems unavoidable.'

Miss Dimont picked up a tea-towel to dry her hands and came to sit next to her guest. 'I think I know,' she said gently.

'You do?'

'It was when you said to me in your house, "He took her for a drive in one of his fancy cars – she was just a schoolgirl." And the way you looked at that photograph of the two of them together.'

'Oh.'

'You, too, Elektra?' asked Miss Dimont quietly.

'Helen was seventeen. I wasn't.'

'Does your father know?'

'No.'

'Did Helen know?'

'Yes, he told her. It drove her mad – well, I have to be brutally honest and say she was pretty unbalanced anyway. When she was about thirteen or fourteen, I only discovered this later, her father sent her to a psychiatrist. She was behaving as though she was Princess Margaret – impossibly grand, demanding admiration from everybody from her father all the way down to the cleaning ladies. No sympathy or interest in anyone else, demanding only the best.

'It got so bad she had to be taken away from school. She was a very, very clever child but had no friends, and the teachers couldn't handle her. Eventually the psychiatrist confirmed she was really quite unwell – narcissistic personality disorder, he called it.

'She was beautiful, in a sort of way, and very wayward. I don't suppose it was Hugh who made the running when they got in that car together.'

'Poor girl.'

'Yes, poor girl – the doctor reckoned her problem was exacerbated by the way uncle Stavros had treated her when she was little. Hot and cold, hot and cold, all the time.'

'Can you tell me about Stavros and Hugh Radipole? It seems a very odd friendship, if that's what it was.'

'Uncle Stavros was like my father – remote, autocratic, no friends. In the shipping business, everybody is your friend and everybody is your enemy – you learn pretty soon to trust nobody, and that isolates you from the rest of the world.

'One day Stavros bought a car off Hugh and they hit it off. Hugh used to bring him oddities – everything from handmade sedans to things that had been made in Weimar Germany out of pressed cardboard.

'Gradually, but it must have been later, my uncle awoke to the fact that Hugh and Helen were having an affair, but instead of shooting him or having him arrested, I think he was relieved. Hugely relieved! I think he thought, someone is going to take care of her, she's too much of a handful for me and even though I love her I want to be rid of the responsibility of her.'

Miss Dimont poured them both another drink.

'So Stavros gave Hugh the money to buy the Marine Hotel.'

Elektra stared into her glass. 'The plan was that he would take Helen away from London and away from all the problems she'd created by her weird behaviour – my uncle was a proud man, very proud of his family name, and she had become an embarrassment.'

'So what happened? When Radipole turned up here in Temple Regis he was on his own.'

'She ran away. She came back later, but preferred to go and live with her father at The Glen.'

'Hugh's reaction?'

'Very angry, very vengeful. That's when he came after me. Just to get at her.'

'So by this stage Hugh was here in Devon and Helen was in London – doing what?'

'Some very, very bad things. I'd really rather not say. She got into a lot of trouble and always uncle Stavros had to bail her out, shut people up, threaten them, bribe them. Buy them! She couldn't be trusted with money – when she had it, she'd find some gullible person or other and make them do things they shouldn't, simply for the money. It fed her narcissism.'

'What sort of things?'

'I couldn't possibly tell you, they were – horrid. She loved the excitement of manipulating people.'

'And so he starved her of cash.'

'In the end she couldn't even buy her own clothes – somebody did it for her. She didn't have a car, she wasn't allowed to take holidays alone. Yet her family was colossally wealthy – she couldn't bear it.'

'And then her father was murdered.'

'It turned her inside-out. She went from hating him to idolising him – having monuments created in his name, swearing that he would never be forgotten. She wore black for the year before she disappeared, she almost never left the house, even made the servants wear black for a time. It seemed to have driven her even crazier.'

Miss Dimont thought very carefully before putting the next question. 'Do you remember your uncle's murder?'

'Of course. We were living on the other side of the Heath.'

'Do you remember there was a burglary?'

'It was the burglar who killed uncle Stavros.'

'Maybe. Or maybe not. But did you know that it was Helen who paid the burglar to break in and crack open the safe?'

'What?' Elektra was stunned into silence. Judy nodded.

'You know,' said Elektra after a moment's thought, 'that sounds just like her. She wanted the money. Couldn't get it any other way, so she employed a burglar.'

'It seems so.'

'Who then decided to kill my uncle?'

'Yes. Or no. It may have been someone else, I don't know.'

Elektra swallowed the last of her drink. 'I hate being in that place. The Glen. Thinking of uncle Stav being killed there.'

'Elektra,' said Miss Dimont, 'please look me in the eye and tell me what your heart says.'

'All right.'

'What I say may hurt.'

'If it does, it does.'

'Do you think Helen murdered her father?'

There was a silence.

'Elektra?'

'I don't know why I never thought of it,' came the reply. 'But, since you ask it, yes.

'Yes, I think she murdered her father.'

Then who, wondered Miss Dimont, murdered Helen?

TWENTY-FIVE

So press day for the *Riviera Express* had arrived without the identity of the body on the bed being revealed. Miss Dimont, having cooked an invigorating breakfast for her guest and given out directions to local beauty-spots ('The charm of Shaldon's streets… the view of Slapton Sands as you come over the hill from Dartmouth… a sandwich lunch on the pontoon at Dittisham… the sea-tractor across to Burgh Island…') took herself off to the office.

Betty was at her desk, typing furiously. For once she'd commanded all the main stories in the paper and there was little for the chief reporter to do beyond checking proofs and writing some last-minute fillers. By lunchtime the presses would be rolling and the edition under way.

'Just popping out for an hour or so,' said Judy to Betty, 'I'll telephone in case there's anything needed. Going over to the Marine.'

Betty's head did not rise from the typewriter. She was struggling with the front-page splash, furiously hammering away in order to meet her deadline while the pear-shaped chief sub marched up and down behind her.

'Come on, come on!' growled John Ross, as if to himself – but Betty could hear him well enough and started to make mistakes. The letters in her Imperial Standard were getting stuck together, at the same time gouging holes in the copy-paper and making a terrible mess. Miss Dimont backed out of the combat zone and went in search of Herbert.

As they made the familiar descent into Ruggleswick, she wondered what was going to happen in the heavyweight contest between Hugh Radipole and Bobby Bunton. One of them had to be the murderer of Helen Patrikis and his arrest would inevitably bring about the collapse of his business.

Would it be Buntorama that prevailed in this ugly class war? Or the superior Marine Hotel? Which would be putting up the shutters?

The first thing she noticed as she switched off Herbert's little engine and pulled out his stand was the Devil's Dodgems – or the lack of them. An eerie silence had taken the place of the barrage of sound, and once again people were sitting on the terrace drinking their cocktails and making small talk.

'"Peace, perfect peace, in this dark world of sin,"' she trilled to the girl behind the reception desk.

'Sorry?'

'"No more sorrows surging round? Naught but calm is found?"'

'I don't quite…'

Miss Dimont smiled. 'You've silenced the devil and his dodgems. How did you manage it?'

The girl laughed. 'Oh! Isn't it wonderful? All we need now is for the guests to come back.'

'There are a few out on the terrace.'

'They're all we've got,' confided the girl. 'Those dodgems emptied the hotel.'

'Mr Radipole around?'

'Is he expecting you?'

'Judy Dimont, *Riviera Express*. We were having a chat the other day – just a couple of things I wanted to clear up.'

'Oh, OK. You'll find him in the Primrose Bar.'

As she made her way down the corridor she could hear in the ballroom a piano making so plaintive a noise she popped her head round the door to see what was going on. At the far end on the small bandstand Moomie Etta-Shaw was playing 'Every Time We Say Goodbye' while in the half-dark a glitterball in the ceiling slowly spangled her shoulders with shards of light. Judy waved, Moomie gave back a graceful nod.

In the bar Radipole sat awkwardly and alone, the wine glass in front of him untouched. His busy world had come to a halt.

'Hello,' said Judy in friendly fashion, 'may I join you?'

'Be my guest,' he replied with heavy irony, 'there's nobody else.'

'Blissfully quiet now,' she went on encouragingly. 'How lovely you managed to see off that Mr Bunton.'

'We came to an agreement,' Radipole said, tight-lipped. 'Don't ask.'

'I wasn't going to – I've come to talk to you about something else.'

'Oh?'

'Helen Patrikis. The woman who was murdered next door.'

The hotelier reached forward slowly, lifted the glass, and inspected its contents. He held it up to the light for several moments before saying, very slowly, 'How did you discover her name?' His voice had dropped several semitones and was almost a whisper.

'You implied you hardly knew her, you had no idea about her identity. But in fact you were her protector.'

'Yes.'

'You loved her.'

'Yes.'

'Even though – even though she was mentally unbalanced.'

'Because of it.'

'Well, I wonder about that,' said Miss Dimont, her voice hardening. 'I don't suppose the money had anything to do with it?'

Radipole moved his head slightly in her direction. 'You don't know anything about it,' he said. 'You have no idea.'

'It was Helen's money that bought this hotel. Her money.'

'Correction. It was Stavros Patrikis' money that bought the hotel. Helen had no say in it.'

'But when her father died, it became *her* hotel.'

'Again you're wrong. Stavros gave me the money in return for looking after her.' It was almost as if he was talking in his sleep, the words came slowly.

'Really?'

Radipole looked up sharply. 'What's this all about? You're a reporter on the local rag, Miss, er, what is your name?'

'Judy Dimont.'

'You'll forgive me, this doesn't sound like the sort of thing your paper could possibly be interested in. Are you hoping to sell something to one of the Sundays? If so, you can beetle off right now!'

Judy glanced around the room. A barman was counting bottles, a waitress folding napkins. There were witnesses and she was not alone. Safety in numbers.

'It's about the killing of Helen, but it's also about the killing of Stavros,' she said firmly. 'Two members of the same family murdered, four years apart.'

'What?' said Radipole, half-rising from his chair.

'You knew them both – one was your lover, the other gave you money to take care of her. You ran a moderately successful motor-car company in north London, now you're the owner of this very grand hotel. That's quite a leap.'

'What are you trying to say?'

'Despite what your hotel guests may think, you're not quite the gentleman you appear. You employed a burglar called Johnny Ramensky to crack the safe of somebody up in Scotland who owed you money, then you passed Ramensky on to Helen who paid him to burgle her father's safe.'

Radipole took a sip of his wine. 'You seem to know a lot. On your *reporter*'s salary? How d'you do it?'

'Luck,' replied Judy with a touch of sarcasm.

'I think I've heard enough.'

'I haven't finished. When Ramensky burgled the Patrikis' safe, he made the mistake of leaving the garden door open when he left The Glen. Somebody came in after him and knifed Stavros to death.'

'He said that, did he?'

'As a matter of fact he did.'

'What else would you expect from a crook like that?

"Somebody else did it" – it sounds like something from the schoolroom – "Wasn't me, teacher!" Ridiculous – of course he did it! They charged him with murder, didn't they?'

'Didn't pursue the charges. The police know his modus operandi – he wouldn't hurt a fly. Gentleman Johnny, he's called, everybody calls him that. No, there was the opportunity for you to sneak in and kill Stavros, and you took it.'

'Don't be ridiculous!' shouted Radipole. 'Why on earth should I do that?'

'You'd got the money, you'd got the hotel. The daughter had deserted you – you were worried Stavros would call in the debt since you weren't keeping to the bargain by looking after her.'

'Sheer fantasy! You can't possibly have the first notion of what went on between us back in those days. I don't know where you got this from, but you've got it all wrong!'

'I'll come back to that. Let's talk about Helen. She came down here to Temple Regis – why?'

'Somebody was after her.'

'Who? Why?'

'That's for you to find out,' said Radipole, rallying. 'She felt threatened, in danger. I'd always looked after her, I always would.'

'Despite the fact she looked down her nose at you? Despite the fact she knew it was her money that bought this place?'

'I loved her,' said the hotelier, passionately. 'I would love her still, if she were alive!'

'Even though she spent the night with Bobby Bunton, the man who's determined to ruin your business?'

'It wasn't the first time,' he said wearily, 'it wouldn't have been the last. Look, I loved her but I knew her frailties – for heaven's sake, I knew them better than anyone. I was her protector!'

'A serious personality disorder, I heard – narcissism. Is that what it was?'

'She had to prove she was irresistible to all men. No matter their age, their class, or their colour. But she always came back to me.'

'Not really.'

'Well,' conceded Radipole, 'not always, let's say.' He stared sadly into his wine.

'But you hated Bunton. Look what you did to him the other day – you took him out of here, beat him up, kicked him when he fell. That's not normal behaviour! That's revenge for him and Helen.'

'I may have got a bit enthusiastic. But no, that was more about those ruddy dodgems and the fact he was determined to drive me out of business. The man's no more than a thug – an ape! – he had it coming.'

'So you're saying you weren't upset by Helen and Bobby Bunton.'

'Look, she came down here. She was being pursued. She asked for sanctuary. She said we could make it up. I didn't believe it – she ran away three years ago, changed her identity, disappeared off the face of the earth. I tried to find her but she was determined. She was a little bit mad, you know that, but she was also extremely cunning. A year after her father was killed she did a bunk and I didn't hear from her until she showed up here a month or so ago.'

Miss Dimont sat up. 'A month? She'd been in Temple Regis for a month?'

'She was living with me in the annexe out the back. It was lovely, almost like old times. She didn't want to go out so I took care of whatever she needed. Then when that thug Bunton started upping the ante, making life difficult for me, I asked her if she'd check into Buntorama, incognito, and try to find out what was going on.'

The waitress came over and Radipole ordered another glass of wine. He thought for a moment, then said, 'You?'

'No thanks.'

Miss Dimont related Bunton's account of his encounter with Helen. 'She took him back to her chalet. Did she bring back any useful information to you after that meeting?'

'Not really.'

'*Were* you jealous of her being with him? Enough to want to kill her?'

'Kill her? You can't have been listening. I loved her!'

'You loved her so much that out of revenge for her deserting you, you seduced her cousin. Elektra. Is that love?'

'How do you know that!' Radipole looked worried, frightened even. How old had she been?

'I'll be frank, Mr Radipole.' She looked round to make sure there was still someone close by – where in heaven's name was Terry when she needed him? – 'I think you shot Helen Patrikis. I can understand why – she was unable to commit to a life with you, and you couldn't bear to be without her. Maybe she was going to run away with this person who was pursuing her, maybe not, but you knew you only had her for a fleeting moment and then she'd be gone.

'You weren't upset about her night with Bobby Bunton, but you were upset when she told you how much she admired

Bobby being a self-made man, not relying on handouts from rich Greek families.' Miss Dimont was making this up – but maybe her invention was not so wrong because Radipole did not challenge it.

'You shot her. You shot her in Bunton's holiday camp, and then you rang him up and told him you were going to pin the murder on him.'

There was a pause.

'Yes,' said Radipole. 'I did do that.

'I didn't shoot her, but I did say I could fix it so it looked like Bunton had done it. I don't know if I could have managed that, but it certainly rattled him.'

'Which is why he brought in the Devil's Dodgems. Fighting fire with fire.'

'You might say that, yes.'

The ammunition in Miss Dimont's locker was running out. She'd come to the Primrose Bar convinced of Radipole's guilt, sure that he was a ruthless killer ready to slay a father and a daughter. Now in the space of a few moments she'd changed her mind. That Radipole was a criminal there could be no doubt, but it was the sort of criminality that Uncle Arthur so often complained about – low-level cheating, wily dealing. He was the sort of man who'd move the chess pieces to his advantage while your back was turned. Nothing more.

'Why didn't you go to the police and tell them who Helen was?'

'I loved her. She told me more than anything in the world she wanted to disappear. I let her do just that. She passed out of this world without a single soul knowing she'd died. She died a nobody.'

'Doesn't sound like someone with acute narcissism to me.'

'You know nothing!' replied Radipole, angrily. 'That's exactly what it is – the thought that people are searching for you all over the world, always hoping you will make an appearance again. But that you've taken yourself to a place where you'll never be found, and the longing and waiting will go on for ever.'

'Do you think she wanted to die, then?'

'Quite probably.'

'Who killed her?'

'It hardly matters. She's dead. She wanted to be dead, and now she is dead.'

Miss Dimont looked at him. 'You don't mean that. It's a natural instinct in mankind to look for revenge when misdeeds occur. Our whole justice system is based on retribution. You would like, wouldn't you, to see the person responsible for Helen's murder brought to justice?'

Radipole got up. 'Yes,' he said, 'yes, I would. But if it's who I think it is, you'll never get them.'

Good Lord, thought Miss Dimont, here finally is the chink of light I have been looking for. Thank heavens!

'So, Mr Radipole,' she said, holding her breath as she did so, 'who *did* kill Helen?'

He looked down at her. 'Loath as I am to say this,' was his response, 'it was not that thug Bobby Bunton. I wish to God it was, but it wasn't.'

Drat it, thought Miss Dimont, that's both my suspects gone in an afternoon. I'm going home to Mulligatawny!

TWENTY-SIX

Elektra was in the garden, pinning back the clematis on the wash-house wall.

'It's getting a bit over-run,' she said, smiling, though she appeared rather nervy and the smile seemed forced. 'Have you got some secateurs?'

'I'll fetch them,' said Judy, 'did you have a nice day?'

'Heavenly. This part of the world is so beautiful – I see why you decided to settle here. Shall I make tea?'

'Straight to the drinks, Elektra, and leave the pruning. I need to talk to you.'

They settled on the old wooden bench by the apple tree and swirled their gin-and-tonics round their glasses. Elektra seemed to be finding it hard to settle despite the warm embrace of the fading sun.

'Do you mind me talking about Helen? An awful lot seems to have happened quite quickly, and I would very much appreciate your opinion.'

Elektra pushed back her thick black hair and nodded.

'For some time,' said Judy, 'I've been convinced it was Hugh Radipole who killed your cousin. He had motive enough, and the opportunity. I don't know if he owns a gun, but types like that always have one in their desk drawer somewhere.

'He's clever, and ruthless – look at what he did to you just to hurt Helen, to try to win her back.

'But in the end he's only some of the things we think he is. Behind that facade of upper-crust sophistication is a lad who left school at twelve and worked in a garage. Whose entrée to the sophisticated world he came to inhabit was through buying and selling cars. Who climbed his way out of mediocrity by seducing the daughter of a very rich man.

'His greatest piece of luck was the fact that the daughter in question was damaged goods – very damaged. Suffocated and flattened by a domineering father, her means of escape was to retreat into her own world. It seemed to the outside world she was a narcissist, in the clinical definition of the word, but I think that was just her suit of armour.

'She willingly allowed Radipole to seduce her because she wanted a father-figure she could control, unlike her real-life father. Radipole's mistake was to fall in love with her, because the only kind of relationship Helen knew or understood was to mix love with hate. That photograph I showed you from her album – they're in Paris, the capital city of love, but the look on her face is one of despair when she should be having the most wonderful time. On his, it's anger and, more important, disappointment.'

'I never really knew him,' said Elektra. 'We – well you know what we did, but it didn't mean I ever got to know him.'

'Did you love him?'

'I suppose for a moment I was infatuated. My father is just like Helen's – cold, domineering, manipulative. Brooks no opposition. I saw what had happened between Hugh and Helen and thought, maybe I can make a better job of it than she did – but he loved only her, and used to tell me so all the time.'

'That must have hurt.'

'It's why I hate him. He could have kept it to himself, but he didn't. He couldn't.'

'That painful kind of love can cause people to pull a trigger. Any sort of people. People who otherwise would never dream of breaking the law. I do understand that,' Judy said, looking sympathetically towards Elektra.

The sun was sliding behind the garden wall and they moved to a pair of garden chairs further away. From the apple tree a robin sang a long and complicated solo, taken up and echoed by his friend or partner several gardens away.

'So who was it?' said the girl. 'Who killed Helen?'

'I think you know, Elektra.'

'No… no! No, I don't know!'

'When I left you here this morning I left behind the newspapers from yesterday – the ones you didn't read on the journey down. On the hall table. They're not there now. Did you read them?'

'Well, I…'

'When we talked last night after dinner, it came to me. I was in such a hurry to discover the truth that when I came to visit you at The Glen, I left something vital out. I told you that the dead victim's name was Patsy.

'Neither of us was concerned with a fake identity, we

were both too busy looking at the photograph to see if it was Helen. We didn't dwell on the name.'

Elektra's hair was swaying though there was no breeze. Her head was down, her face concealed.

'It was only when I saw the name in print, in the papers yesterday, that the thought came to me. At the time, I was convinced the murderer was Hugh Radipole, or just possibly Bobby Bunton. Both had motive and opportunity, both no doubt had the means.

'It was only when I talked to Radipole I realised how wrong I'd been all along. Waiting for you by the bandstand, that's when it came to me, only I needed time to work it out.'

Elektra stood up. 'I don't think I want you to go on,' she said.

'There's no going back now,' said Miss Dimont firmly. 'You *did* look at the newspapers I left behind?'

'Yes.'

'And then it came to you.'

'Yes.'

'The alias Helen was living under – Patsy Rouchos.'

'Yes.'

'In ancient Greece an heiress – the daughter of a rich man with no sons – was called *epikleros*. When her father died, she was not allowed to keep her inheritance – the money had to stay in the family but in male hands. The *epikleros* was therefore expected to marry her father's nearest male relative.'

'Yes.'

'Another word for *epikleros* is *patrouchos*. Hence Patsy Rouchos – a name proclaiming to all the world what Helen was – an heiress with an obligation to marry her father's nearest relative. That relative being your father, Aristide Patrikis.'

'Such laws haven't existed for centuries. You can't possibly believe…'

'She was on the run for three years, hiding behind this false identity. Why do you think she chose that name?'

'She's an heiress. She inherited her father's millions. She was upset, unbalanced. That's sufficient, isn't it?'

'Why did she go missing? Her father died, she went into mourning. She stayed in the house, didn't go anywhere. It's not as if she ran away then, it was later. Why? Why did she wait? And then why did she flee? Why did she disappear so utterly and completely, yet bear that name which anybody with a smattering of history might work out was a very bitter joke against herself?'

'I don't know,' said Elektra, 'I have no idea. I…'

'I think you do. You know the answers. But this is very painful for you.'

The young woman burst into tears.

Miss Dimont stood up. 'I think you must face up to the truth. Your father will be here in the morning, he'll go to identify the body. At that moment, the world will know who killed Helen Patrikis. I just think it would help you – help you *very much*, Elektra – to come to terms with what happens next if we can just sit and talk it through now.'

'Get me another drink. I can't bear this.'

When Miss Dimont returned from the kitchen she half-expected Elektra to have been whisked away by Stevens in the whispering Rolls-Royce, never to be seen again. Instead the young woman had gone back to the garden bench and now sat upright in the shadows, as if ready to face a judge and jury.

'Tell me this,' started Miss Dimont. 'When Stavros was murdered, it must have been quite complicated sorting out his affairs. He was an immensely rich man, after all, and the circumstances of his death must have added extra difficulties. Is that so?'

'Yes.'

'How long did it take for his will to be sorted out?'

'I don't know – maybe twelve, fourteen months.'

'And he left his estate to?'

'Helen, of course. He left something to my father, and quite a large amount to me. But the bulk of the estate went to Helen, naturally.'

'Had you hoped for more?'

'I am already independently wealthy,' said Elektra distantly. 'My mother died when I was twelve and she left half her fortune to me. I have no need for money.'

'But Helen did.'

'Sorry?'

'She'd developed a hunger, you might say a mania, for money all the time her father slowly starved her of funds. All her friends were rich, all her relations – but she didn't have two pennies of her own to rub together.'

'That's true.'

'And so we have the motive for her killing her father.'

'That was just a theory I threw out. We had quite a lot to drink last night, you and I, it was the end of a tiring day, the long journey down here...'

'All right,' said Miss Dimont. 'Let's, just for the sake of the argument, assume that she did. She killed her father, then had to wait around for the will to be sorted out. You say it took twelve or fourteen months for the paperwork to be wrapped up – which is just about the time she disappeared.'

'Well, yes.'

'She killed him and disappeared the moment she'd got her hands on the money. She changed her name and used her wits and inheritance to make sure nobody could find her. You said you thought she might have gone to Switzerland.'

'It could have been the West Indies for all I know.'

'What was your father's reaction to her disappearance?'

'Look,' said Elektra, 'I've said enough. Why don't we leave this till morning? I'm exhausted and all this is tremendously stressful. I'm not entirely sure what I should be saying any more.'

'You won't do a moonlight flit?'

Elektra smiled suddenly.

'And miss another night in that deliciously comfortable bed? Where did you find that mattress? I must have one!'

They arrived too late at Temple Regis Police Station next morning to witness Aristide Patrikis formally identify the body of his niece. By the time Miss Dimont and Elektra had established the tycoon was in town, the deed had already been done. Now he sat at a table in a cold grey room, the soothing cup of tea before him untouched. Nearby, a wispy private secretary was looking out of the barred window, no doubt wishing he was back in Crete sorting out shipping collisions.

Patrikis sat slumped at the table, his skin showing white through the tan, his face haggard and his hands slightly trembling. Inspector Topham sat opposite, an empty notebook in front of him, a sympathetic angle to his body.

'Will you be going back to London now, sir,' he was saying, 'or would you rather go somewhere to rest after your journey? If so, there's a place I can recommend.' He was thinking of The Grand.

'No,' said the shipping man. 'My daughter…' and flapped his hand at Elektra who'd just entered the room with Miss Dimont.

'I didn't know you were already here, Papa, I'm terribly sorry.'

'Your father's had a bad shock, Miss,' said Topham. 'But the identification has been done and the paperwork is complete. If you're ready to take him away…'

'I have my own car,' said Patrikis in barely more than a whisper.

'Well, then,' said Topham, rising. 'Now that you're here, Miss Patrikis, I'll leave you to it. As I say, it's been a terrible shock and the sooner you and your father are home…'

'Perhaps you remember me, Mr Patrikis,' said Judy Dimont, sliding into Topham's seat. 'From the *Riviera Express*. I came to see you at The Glen.'

Enough of the old tycoon's swagger remained for him to nod in a dismissive way. People did not generally sit down in front of him unless invited.

'I hope the Inspector won't mind, I have just a couple of questions.'

'What.' It wasn't a question, nor an invitation to proceed.

'When your niece went missing, did you call the police?'

Patrikis looked up. He hadn't expected this after such an ordeal.

'Not immediately, no.'

'I wonder why not. After all, her father had been murdered. Did it not occur to you that she, too, might have been spirited away and something similar occurred?'

'Really, I don't think I need to…' started Patrikis.

'No, no, no!' joined in Topham. 'This gentleman has had a shock. Come on now, Miss Dimont, you shouldn't even be in here!'

Judy turned and fixed the detective with a defiant stare. 'Just give me a moment, Inspector, I think this may be of assistance.'

She turned back to the tycoon. 'Though you didn't call the police, you weren't unmoved by her disappearance, were you? You hired people to find her, a lot of people.'

'I did. I thought they'd be more effective across international borders than the British police with their…' he looked down in distaste, 'cups of tea.'

'You have some dealings with our security services, I believe.'

'All people in shipping – at least those who have fleets the size of ours – do.'

'And you asked them for help. Cups of tea or no.'

'Your MI6 has a very good reputation.'

'But she was never found.'

'No.'

'For three years, a member of one of the leading shipping families in Britain managed to disappear and despite huge efforts, she was never found. Why was that?'

'I imagine because the intelligence just wasn't good enough. Maybe she… Look – why are you asking all this?'

'She went to live in Switzerland. She took the name Patsy Rouchos. Patsy Rouchos! You understand the significance of that, Mr Patrikis, I think.'

'Sorry, I don't know what you're talking about.' He clicked his fingers at the secretary and turned to Topham. 'I think it's time to go. Will you show me the way out?'

Topham surprised himself with his reply. 'I wonder if you wouldn't mind just answering the questions, Mr Patrikis. I'm sure it won't take long.'

Miss Dimont leaned forward over the table. 'There is a long and ancient tradition in Greece, Mr Patrikis. It's called *epikleros*. An heiress may not keep the fortune she inherits from her father but must marry the father's nearest male relative. Another word for it is *patrouchos*.'

'I'm going now. I have important business to attend to – the collision of one my ships… I really haven't the time to stay here and listen to this rubbish!'

Topham raised a hand. 'One moment more, sir.' He nodded at Judy.

'After your niece finally secured the legal sign-off from her father's will, she disappeared. You went chasing after her – not for her, but for her fortune. You saw it rightly as yours, even though you are already richer than most people in this country.

'The clue was in the name she chose for herself – half of her wanted to be caught. Yet your people weren't clever enough to work that out, and so there she stayed in the mountains for three years while they scoured the globe looking for her.

She didn't even change her appearance. Most people thought with a name like that she was probably French.

'Your daughter Elektra,' went on Miss Dimont, raising her voice, 'told me you became obsessed by the money. You would sit there at night in your study calling people all over the world, seeing if they could help find her. It wasn't Helen you wanted to find, it was the money.'

'Fantasy!' roared Patrikis, for the first time looking directly at Miss Dimont.

'Several times in the past few days I've been told how wrong I am,' she replied, with spirit. 'And some of the time they've been right. But this time *I* am right.'

'Look at this,' she said, and drew from her raffia bag Terry's 10 × 8 prints. 'These are the pictures we found in Helen's picture album. She'd torn out most because she didn't want to be identified by it, but obviously the pictures meant something special to her because she kept the album by her – even when she went to Buntorama where she was shot.

'Look first at this one.' She pushed Terry's reconstructed photo of the blurry room with the foot protruding from the bottom of the frame. 'This is her father's bedroom in The Glen. Where you sleep now.'

With disdain Patrikis picked up the photograph. 'I can't see anything. It's too fuzzy. Could be anywhere.'

'Believe me, it is the bedroom. Elektra confirmed that to me. The foot you can see – it belongs to your brother. This is one of a series of pictures Helen took after she knifed your brother to death.'

'I don't believe it.'

'You knew it. Of course you knew it – it was you who

tore up the photos when she showed them to you. Did she say, "You keep away from me and my money or I'll do the same to you?" Was she proud of what she'd done, killing her father?'

'He'd always treated her very roughly.'

'Perhaps – but to kill him? Her own father?'

'She was not a normal sort of person. She was… unwell.'

'Look at this, please.' Miss Dimont showed him the family party in a restaurant. 'There are a lot of people in this picture but there you are, sitting next to Helen. You have an arm round her shoulder and she has her hand on your knee.'

'My birthday.'

'She must be sixteen or seventeen. Now look at this.' It was the photograph of Helen sitting by the pool at The Glen. 'In the corner, in the pool, that's you, isn't it?'

'Perhaps.'

'Take a look at your face.'

Patrikis picked up the photo but he was looking at the girl. Suddenly, a tear rolled down his cheek.

'You loved her?'

'Yes.'

'You loved her very much?'

'Yes.'

'You sent out search parties all over the globe, not because of her fortune, but because you wanted her?'

'She wasn't like normal people, you know. More like something which had landed on this earth, a butterfly perhaps, ready to take off without warning and disappear for ever.'

'Did she love you?' said Miss Dimont softly.

'She loved me like she loved everybody else. Part-time. Intense one minute, cold as ice the next.'

'Were you lovers? You were her uncle, after all.'

Patrikis didn't answer.

'When you found her, finally, after all those years of searching…'

'She let me find her,' he blurted out. 'She'd been living in a village high in the Alps, safe and sound. Then one day she came back to Britain, I got a message, it said she was in Devon. I came down here. She *wanted* me to find her!'

'What happened?'

'I finally discovered her in that dreadful old army camp, a cheap holiday place. Terrible! I went to her room and she was sitting on the bed. Looking so beautiful, as always. She said to me, "Look what I've come to – this! I'm spying on a disgusting old man so that I can go back and tell tales to another disgusting old man – the world is full of disgusting old men. And now *you're* here!"

'I told her not to be so silly, I wanted to marry her. She said it was as good an offer as she'd had, but the Orthodox Church would never allow it – it was against the law. I didn't care. I said we could marry under her alias and we'd go and build a house and live in her Swiss village – *I didn't care!*'

The room was silent. The secretary was still staring out of the window, Inspector Topham was as still as if he were standing to attention on the parade-ground. Elektra sat with her hands in her lap, head down.

'Why did you kill her?' asked Judy, softly.

'She gave me the gun. She said she'd bought it when she went on the run. She said, "I want to die."

'I asked what she meant. Not yet thirty, her life ahead! "You don't know," she said. "You have no idea what this madness has made me do. I changed my name because I no longer deserved to be part of the Patrikis family – the depths I have sunk to, the things I have done. We are a proud Greek family, but I am no longer worthy. I want to die."

'I told her I could help her, make her better. But it was no good, she had reached the end. "I want to die a nobody," she said, "without a name. And I want to die now. If you love me, Aristide, shoot me now."'

He looked at Miss Dimont, his eyes unseeing.

'And so I shot her. Dead.'

TWENTY-SEVEN

'The person I feel sorriest for,' said Athene as she brought round a pot of her special tea, 'is that poor old inspector. I saw him only last week in the street – the spring had gone out of his step, his shoulders were hunched, he looked as though he was completely lost. Outside the Home & Colonial, too!'

'He's back on top,' said Judy. 'No need to worry about him. He got the confession, he made the arrest. And all here in Temple Regis – he'll be a hero all over again!'

'Typical,' said Terry, with a sniff. They were all sitting round the conference table in the editor's office only, it being Saturday, Mr Rhys was not there to conduct proceedings. 'I uncover the clue that solves the whole thing – the foot – but old Topham gets the kudos!'

'I suppose you'll have next week's Page One then,' said Betty, who was supposed to be at her desk writing up the wedding reports but had wandered in – anything to get away from the wretched bridesmaids, the guipure lace and the stephanotis.

'It won't last,' said Judy, without the slightest regret. 'We know that it's *our* scoop, but the Sunday newspapers will have it tomorrow.'

'That Sergeant Gull.'

'He needs to make a bob or two on the side to support that allotment of his.'

'Have we got any biscuits?'

Peter Pomeroy nipped out and got some from his desk drawer. 'I want to give you a really strong headline next Thursday,' he said as he walked back with a tin in his hand. 'Just give the story to me now as you'll be writing it.'

'Well, it was simple really, once all the pieces were in place,' said Judy. 'Helen Patrikis was a very damaged person – damaged from early childhood because her father made her think she'd killed her mother.

'Like his brother Aristide, Stavros Patrikis was proud, powerful, manipulative and rich. With all that money he could do what he liked. He played with his daughter's emotions in the cruellest possible fashion and, as a defence mechanism, she built a wall around herself. She was diagnosed with a mental illness – narcissism – but maybe the doctors got it wrong. Maybe she behaved in that outrageous manner just to keep her father at bay, who knows. Certainly she was a very troubled person.'

'You can understand why she wanted to kill him,' said Auriol, who'd come into the office to congratulate her friend. 'Money or no money.'

'In the end,' said Judy, nodding, 'she despised him. She despised the fact that he'd given her – his supposedly prize possession – away to a car salesman. It was when she discovered that she was no more than a commodity to him – like one of his ships – that I think she hatched the plan.

'Hugh Radipole introduced Helen to Johnny Ramensky,

and she seduced Johnny into burgling the family home. While he was emptying the safe downstairs, she was in Stavros' bedroom stabbing him to death and photographing his corpse.'

'Twenty-seven knife wounds,' murmured Auriol, shaking her head. 'Unbelievable.'

'My foot!' said Terry.

'Oh shut up about your foot!' said Judy cheerily. 'And anyway it was his, not yours.'

'Go on.'

'She always went for the older man. She threw herself at Radipole just as she threw herself at Johnny Ramensky. Even Bobby Bunton, for heaven's sake! It got more dangerous when she started making up to uncle Aristide.'

'She made him love her?' asked Betty, intrigued. It was a trick she had yet to master herself.

'I think so. It was all part of the anger she felt for her father. The two brothers hated each other – they were jealous of each other's success in their separate parts of the business. Instead of being in competition with other ship owners, they were in competition with each other. One was constantly trying to outdo the other.'

'Even so,' said Betty, shaking her head. 'Her uncle. Disgusting!'

'Who knows why he allowed himself to fall for her. And in any case,' said Judy, 'we only have his word for it that he *did* love her. Maybe he was after his brother's money all along, and the girl was neither here nor there. We may never know what drove him to fire that final shot, but he's confessed to killing her and Inspector Topham's got the gun as evidence. That's enough to convict him.'

'What made her disappear?' asked Peter Pomeroy. 'I mean, when she inherited her father's wealth she could have just moved away from Hampstead – bought a castle in Scotland, anything, just to get away.'

'Aristide knew she'd killed him. He hinted as much last night. When you're that rich you have no need to go to the police, you can exact your own form of retribution on those who are inside your magic circle. When she got her hands on Stavros' money, he really truly believed it should come to him.'

'So was it money, or love?' asked Betty.

'The Greeks are a fierce and proud race,' said Judy. 'They are conscious of their history – events of two thousand years ago are as if they'd happened yesterday. Aristide Patrikis convinced himself the law of *epikleros* or *patrouchos* was as valid today as it was in the year dot. It may not exist in the statute-book, but to him it made sense – no woman should be allowed to inherit vast wealth. What, for heaven's sake, could she possibly know about what to do with it?'

'The colossal arrogance,' said Auriol, not with anger but with familiarity. She'd spent the best years of her life working for powerful men.

'Helen knew she had to get away. Uncle Aristide knew she'd killed her father. That gave him enough right, in his eyes at least, to claim the fortune – a murderer, she no longer deserved it. She went on the run, leaving clues here and there which suggested she'd gone to Australia or the Bahamas. Instead she rented a small house halfway up a mountain and decided to sit it out.'

'She must have been bored,' said Peter. 'After that fancy life in Hampstead.'

'That's, I think, when things went really wrong,' replied Judy. 'Hugh Radipole told me that when she came back to him she confessed some of the things she'd done to keep herself amused. She would buy people, and make them do things.'

'What sort of things?'

'Let's just say that after a time she realised she had lost all sense of what is right and what is wrong. Instead of using her money to do good things, she used it to make mischief in other people's lives – buying them, then tossing them away.'

Betty was trying to imagine being bought. 'It was her money to do with as she wished,' she said.

'Aristide didn't think so. But even though he spent a small fortune trying to find her, he never did – because he was looking in the wrong place. It was only when she came back to Britain that he caught up with her.'

'Yes,' said Auriol, 'that's the one thing I couldn't fathom. If she'd been so successful at disappearing herself, why come back – and how did Aristide find her?'

'Well. She came home for two reasons. First, I think the dissolute life she lived in Switzerland had left her confused and frightened and rudderless. And in her weakened state she began to believe she could see signs that Aristide was finally catching up with her. The very people she'd bought, she thought, were betraying her.'

'She was taking drugs, by the sound of it.'

'Quite possibly. She came back to Britain to be with Radipole, to seek his protection – he was the one person she thought she could rely on. After all it was her money, or her father's, which had set him up in the Marine and had turned him into a successful hotelier. Plus, though she hated and despised him, she also still loved him – a characteristic of all her relationships with men. Including her father.'

'So who gave her away?'

'Radipole did.'

'No!'

'He told me. He was paid by Aristide to blab the moment she surfaced, which he shrewdly reckoned she would. Though Radipole couldn't have known Aristide would come down to Temple Regis and shoot dead his own niece.'

'People!' said Athene, somehow capturing in a single word the iniquity of everyone involved in this extraordinary tale.

'As you say,' said Judy, shaking her head, 'people.'

Peter pushed round the biscuit tin and Athene got up to make more tea.

'I think she'd reached the end of her tether,' went on Judy. 'I honestly believe she wanted to die. Radipole said she was in a terrible state while she was living with him in the annexe at the back of the hotel.'

'Yet he still got her to go and spy on Bobby Bunton.'

'Naturally. Not a man with a great deal of heart, even if he did claim to love her.'

'Extraordinary when you think about it,' said Auriol. 'Everyone loved her – her father, even though he blamed her for her mother's death. Radipole, though he betrayed her. Aristide, even though he shot her.'

'It was a miserable life but now it's over,' said Judy. 'Perhaps we should go round to the Fort or the Jawbones and raise a glass to her. Come on, everybody!'

'Would love to,' said Betty, 'only I've still got half-a-dozen wedding reports to finish. Then I'm going to have lunch with somebody you know, Leila Davidson.'

'Good Lord,' said Judy, 'how do you know her?'

'Well,' said Betty, 'while you were off chasing after murderers, she rang up hoping to speak to you. She just wanted someone to chat to. We got talking and I ended up mentioning Dud – well, she knows him! Said her husband was a member of the same Masonic lodge, and then it all came tumbling out. We had a good old chinwag, I can tell you – honestly, those men!

'Anyway,' said Betty proudly, 'we made some decisions between us.'

'Really?' said Judy. It was a relief not to be talking about murderers any more. 'I told her about Dud and my hair. Said he was always pottering off with that stupid little leather case of his, smarming up to people, doing secret handshakes. So then she told me about her hubby – spending all the housekeeping money on those ridiculous aprons and medals and so forth, and how he was always busy learning pages of gobbledegook so he can advance to the next stage in the Craft.'

'Really,' said Judy, 'I'm so glad. I wanted to write something in support of her but I know Mr Rhys would never let it in the paper.'

'We must have talked for an hour. Then we had a drink and by the end we'd come to some very important decisions. I saw how it would be for me if I carried on with Dud – the same kind of existence as Leila, playing second fiddle to a bunch of men who want to lock themselves away in a room and play secret societies.

'So I thought, right Leila, that's it. I'm dropping Dud.'

Good heavens, thought Miss Dimont, that's a first. You've never dumped a man in your life, it's always been the other way round.

'Well done, Betty! Finally I'm free to say Dud Fensome is frightful and you can do much better for yourself.'

'And Leila – well! She went home and said to her husband, "I have met this woman who has dumped the man she loved because he put the Freemasons first. Well, I'm going to do the same. Either you dump them, or I dump you."'

'I would never have thought it. She seemed so put-upon.'

'I gave her the courage! And guess what, she won! Hubby has resigned from the Lodge and he actually said it was a weight off his mind. They're all lovey-dovey again, and I'm free of Dud! So we're having lunch to celebrate!'

'Well, Auriol, let's us go and have lunch to celebrate. Not often I solve a double murder!'

'Ah, well. Um,' said Auriol, patting her hair and rising from the table. 'Unfortunately I have some things to do.'

'Dressed like that?' said Judy suspiciously. 'Not the Admiral!'

'Which Admiral?' snapped Betty, suddenly alert. Auriol's eyes swivelled dangerously.

Crikey, thought Judy, I've put my foot in it. The beastly traitor is a double dealer even when it comes to women! 'Er, Admiral Bentinck,' she said quickly to Betty before Auriol could reply. 'Do you know him?'

Betty subsided. 'Everybody seems to have an admiral round here,' she said with a self-satisfied smirk.

'Come on, then, Athene, you'll come and have a drink?'

'No, precious, I can't. Got to go home and make up the spare room. I've got a new lodger.'

It had never occurred to Miss Dimont that Athene, so ethereal, so much a part of the celestial pantheon, could do anything quite so practical as be a landlady – after all, look at the way she dressed, haphazard wasn't the word!

'Oh,' she said feigning interest, 'anybody interesting?'

'Greville Charles. From the Riverbridge office – lovely man!'

'Well!' said Judy. 'But won't that make it difficult for his work? So far to travel every day?'

'Oh no,' said Athene. 'Didn't you hear? Oh no, you wouldn't have done – you were dealing with the murder – he's resigned. He went to see the doctor after you popped in to see him, and then handed in his resignation. He said how nice Mr Rhys had been about it and agreed it was probably better if he didn't have the stress and strain.

'It was what he's been waiting and praying for, Judy. And you did it! Up till your visit he felt it was his duty to soldier on, but honestly, it would have killed him if he'd gone on much longer. He'll come and be with me and I'll look after him, and I've got him a nice part-time job at the Kardomah, crushing the coffee beans.'

'How happy that makes me to hear that!' exclaimed Judy. And how sad, she thought.

She turned to the one person she could always rely on. 'So then, Terry, last of the Mohicans! Let's be off – which shall it be, the Fort, or the Jawbones? You choose!'

'Er,' said Terry.

Judy looked at him sharply. 'Come along now, don't tell

me you've got to go off and polish your Leica. Not on a Saturday! Not after our great triumph!'

Terry looked sheepish. 'Got a date,' he said.

'*Who?*' snapped Judy.

'Fluffles. She decided she's had it with Bobby Bunton – I think it was the business with the murdered girl that finally did it. He won't marry her – said he can't afford to, but that's a lie.'

'You can't possibly be serious, Terry! Why she must be…'

'Looked nice in her fur bikini,' said Terry smugly. 'Very nice. Especially after I put a filter on the…' and his voice burbled off into an indecipherable drone.

'Well,' said Miss Dimont, with more than a touch of pepper dusting her voice, 'I have things to do, can't sit here any longer. I have to go home and write to my mother.'

The whole room looked at her.

'I sincerely hope she won't drop dead from the shock,' said Auriol.

If you enjoyed this Miss Dimont mystery, then read on for an extract from her first adventure, *The Riviera Express*…

ONE PLACE. MANY STORIES

ONE

When Miss Dimont smiled, which she did a lot, she was beautiful. There was something mystical about the arrangement of her face-furniture – the grey eyes, the broad forehead, the thin lips wide spread, her dainty perfect teeth. In that smile was a *joie de vivre* which encouraged people to believe that good must be just around the corner.

But there were two faces to Miss Dimont. When hunched over her typewriter, rattling out the latest episode of life in Temple Regis, she seemed not so sunny. Her corkscrew hair fell out of its makeshift pinnings, her glasses slipped down the convex nose, those self-same lips pinched themselves into a tight little knot and a general air of mild chaos and discontent emanated like puffs of smoke from her desk.

Life on the *Riviera Express* was no party. The newspaper's offices, situated at the bottom of the hill next door to the brewery, maintained their dreary pre-war combination of uprightness and formality. The front hall, the only area of access permitted to townsfolk, spoke with its oak panelling and heavy desks of decorum, gentility, continuity.

But the most momentous events in Temple Regis in 1958

– its births, marriages and deaths, its council ordinances, its police court and its occasional encounters with celebrity – were channelled through a less august set of rooms, inadequately lit and peopled by journalism's flotsam and jetsam, up a back corridor and far from the public gaze.

Lately there'd been a number of black-and-white 'B' features at the Picturedrome, but these always portrayed the heady excitements of Fleet Street. Behind the green baize door, beyond the stout oak panelling, the making of this particular local journal was decidedly less ritzy.

Far from Miss Dimont lifting an ivory telephone to her ear while partaking of a genteel breakfast in her silk-sheeted bed, the real-life reporter started her day with an apple and 'The Calls' – humdrum visits to Temple's police station, its council offices, fire station, and sundry other sources of bread-and-butter material whose everyday occurrences would, next Friday, fill the heart of the *Express*.

Like a laden beachcomber she would return mid-morning to her desk to write up her gleanings before leaving for the Magistrates' Court where the bulk of her work, from that bottomless well of human misdeeds and misfortunes, daily bubbled up.

After luncheon, usually taken alone with her crossword in the Signal Box Café, she would return briefly to court before preparing for an evening meeting of the Town Council, the Townswomen's Guild, or – light relief – a performance by the Temple Regis Amateur Operatic Society.

Then it would be home on her moped, corkscrew hair

blowing in the wind, to Mulligatawny, whose sleek head would be staring out of the mullioned window awaiting his supper and her pithy account of the day's events.

Miss Dimont, now unaccountably beyond the age of forty, had the fastest shorthand note in the West Country. In addition, she could charm the birds out of the trees when she chose – her capacity to get people to talk about themselves, it was said, could make even the dead speak. She was shy but she was shrewd; and if perhaps she was comfortably proportioned she was, everyone agreed, quite lovely.

Why Betty Featherstone, her so-called friend, got the front-page stories and Miss Dimont did not was lost in the mists of time. Suffice to say that on press day, when everyone's temper shortened, it was Judy who got it in the neck from her editor. Betty wrote what he wanted, while Judy wrote the truth – and it did not always make comfortable reading. She didn't mind the fusillades aimed in her direction for having overturned a civic reputation or two, for ever since she had known him, and it had been a long time, Rudyard Rhys had lacked consistency. Furthermore, his ancient socks smelt. Miss Dimont rose above.

Unquestionably Devon's prettiest town, Temple Regis took itself very seriously. Its beaches, giving out on to the turquoise and indigo waters which inspired some wily publicist to coin the phrase 'England's Riviera', were white and pristine. Broad lawns encircling the bandstand and flowing down towards the pier were scrupulously shaved, immaculately edged. Out in the estuary, the water was an impossible shade of aquamarine, its colour a magical invention of the gods – and since everyone in Temple agreed their little town was the sunniest spot in England, it really was very beautiful.

It was far too nice a place to be murdered.

*

Confusingly, the *Riviera Express* was both newspaper and railway train. Which came first was occasionally the cause for heated debate down in the snug of the Cap'n Fortescue, but the laws of copyright had not yet been invented when the two rivals were born; and an ambitious rail company serving the dreams of holidaymakers heading for the South West was certainly not giving way to a tinpot local rag when it came to claiming the title. Similarly, with a rock-solid local readership and a justifiable claim to both 'Riviera' and 'Express' – a popular newspaper title – the weekly journal snootily tolerated its more famous namesake. If neither would admit it, each benefited from the other's existence.

Before the war successive editors lived in constant turmoil, sometimes printing glowing lists of the visitors from another world who spilled from the brown and cream liveried railway carriages ('The Hon. Mrs Gerald Legge and her mother, the novelist Barbara Cartland, are here for the week'). At other times, Princess Margaret Rose herself could have puffed into town and the old codgers would have ignored it. Rudyard Rhys saw both points of view so there was no telling what he would think one week to the next – to greet the afternoon arrival? Or not to bother?

'Mr Rhys, we could go to meet the 4.30,' warned his chief reporter on this particular Tuesday. 'But – also – there's a cycling-without-lights case in court which could turn nasty. The curate from St Margaret's. He told me he's going to challenge his prosecution on the grounds that British Summer Time has no substantive legal basis. It could be very interesting.'

'Rrrr.'

'Don't you see? The Chairman of the Bench is one of his parishioners! Sure to be an almighty dust-up!'

'Rrrr . . . rrr.'

'A clash between the Church and the Law, Mr Rhys! We haven't had one of those for a while!'

Rudyard Rhys lit his pipe. An unpleasant smell filled the room. Miss Dimont stepped back but otherwise held her ground. She was all too familiar with this fence-sitting by her editor.

'Bit of a waste going to meet the 4.30,' she persisted. 'There's only Gerald Hennessy on board . . .' (and an encounter with a garrulous, prosy, self-obsessed matinée idol might make me late for my choir practice, she might have added).

'Hennessy?' The editor put down his pipe with a clunk. 'Now *that's* news!'

'Oh?' snipped Miss Dimont. 'You said you hated *The Conqueror and the Conquered*. "Not very manly for a VC", I think were your words. You objected to the length of his hair.'

'Rrrr.'

'Even though he had been lost in the Burmese jungle for three years.'

Mr Rhys performed his usual backflip. 'Hennessy,' he ordered.

It was enough. Miss Dimont noted that, once again, the editor had deserted his journalistic principles in favour of celebrity worship. Rhys enjoyed the perquisite accorded him by the Picturedrome of two back stalls seats each week. He had actually enjoyed *The Conqueror and the Conquered* so much he sat through it twice.

Miss Dimont did not know this; but anyone who had played as many square-jawed warriors as Gerald Hennessy was always likely to find space in the pages of the *Riviera Express*. Something about heroism by association, she had noted in the past, was at the root of her editor's lofty decisions. That all went back to the War, of course.

'Four-thirty it is then,' she said a trifle bitterly. 'But *Church v. Law* – now there's a story that might have been followed up by the nationals,' and with that she swept out, notebook flapping from her raffia bag.

This parting shot was a reference to the long-standing feud between the editor and his senior reporter. After all, Rudyard Rhys had made the wrong call on not only the Hamilton Biscuit Case, but the Vicar's Longboat Party, the Temple Regis Tennis Scandal and the Football Pools Farrago. Each of these exclusives from the pen of Judy Dimont had been picked up by the repulsive Arthur Shrimsley, an out-to-grass former Fleet Street type who made a killing by selling them on to the national papers, at the same time showing up the *Riviera Express* for the newspaper it was – hesitant, and slow to spot its own scoops when it had them.

On each occasion the editor's decision had been final – and wrong. But Judy was no saint either, and the cat's cradle of complaint triggered by her coverage of the Regis Conservative Ball last winter still made for a chuckle or two in the sub-editors' room on wet Thursday afternoons.

With her raffia bag swinging furiously, she stalked out to the car park, for Judy Dimont was resolute in almost everything she did, and her walk was merely the outer manifestation of that doughty inner being – a purposeful march which sent out radar-like warnings to flag-day sellers, tin-can rattlers, and other such supplicants and cleared her path as if by miracle. It was not manly, for Miss Dimont was nothing if not feminine, but it was no-nonsense.

She took no nonsense either from Herbert, her trusty moped, who sat expectantly, awaiting her arrival. With one cough, Herbert was kicked into life and the magnificent Miss Dimont flew away towards Temple Regis railway station, corkscrew hair flapping in the wind, a happy smile upon her lips. For there was nothing she liked more than to go in search of new adventures – whether they were to be found in the Magistrates' Court, the Horticultural Society, or the railway station.

Her favourite route took in Tuppenny Row, the elegant terrace of Regency cottages whose brickwork had turned a pale pink with the passage of time, bleached by Temple

Regis sun and washed by its soft rains. She turned into Cable Street, then came down the long run to the station, whose yellow-and-chocolate bargeboard frontage you could glimpse from the top of the hill, and Miss Dimont, with practice born of long experience, started her descent just as the sooty, steamy clouds of vapour from the Riviera Express slowed in preparation for its arrival at Regis Junction.

She had done her homework on Gerald Hennessy and, despite her misgivings about missing the choir practice, she was looking forward to their encounter, for Miss Dimont was far from immune to the charms of the opposite sex. Since the War, Hennessy had become the perfect English hero in the nation's collective imagination – square-jawed, crinkle-eyed, wavy-haired and fair. He spoke so nicely when asked to deliver his lines, and there was always about him an air of amused self-deprecation which made the nation's mothers wish him for their daughters, if not secretly for themselves.

Miss Dimont brought Herbert to a halt, his final splutter of complaint lost in the clanking, wheezing riot of sooty chaos which signals the arrival of every self-regarding Pullman Express. Across the station courtyard she spotted Terry Eagleton, the *Express*'s photographer, and made towards him as she pulled the purple gloves from her hands.

'Anyone apart from Hennessy?'

'Just 'im, Miss Dim.'

'I've told you before, call me Judy,' she said stuffily. The dreaded nickname had been born out of an angry tussle with Rudyard Rhys, long ago, over a front page story which had gone wrong. Somehow it stuck, and the editor took a fiendish delight in roaring it out in times of stress. Bad enough having to put up with it from him – though invariably she rose above – but no need to be cheeked by this impertinent snapper. She had mixed feelings about Terry Eagleton.

'Call me Judy,' she repeated sternly, and got out her notebook.

'Ain't your handle anyways,' parried Terry swiftly, and he was right – for Miss Dimont had a far more euphonious name, one she kept very quiet and for a number of good reasons.

Terry busily shifted his camera bag from one shoulder to the other. Employed by his newspaper as a trained observer, he could see before him a bespectacled woman of a certain age – heading towards fifty, surely – raffia bag slung over one shoulder, notebook flapping out of its top, with a distinctly harassed air and a permanently peppery riposte. Though she was much loved by all who knew her, Terry sometimes found it difficult to see why. It made him sigh for Doreen, the sweet young blonde newly employed on the front desk, who had difficulty remembering people's names but was indeed an adornment to life.

Miss Dimont led the way on to Platform 1.

'Pics first,' said Terry.

'No, Terry,' countered Miss Dim. 'You take so long there's never time left for the interview.'

'Picture's worth a thousand words, they always say. How many words are you goin' to write – *two hundred*?'

The same old story. In Fleet Street, always the old battle between monkeys and blunts, and even here in sweetest Devon the same old manoeuvring based on jealousy, rivalry and the belief that pictures counted more than words or, conversely, words enhanced pictures and gave them the meaning and substance they otherwise lacked.

And so this warring pair went to work, arriving on the platform just as the doors started to swing open and the holidaymakers alight. It was always a joyous moment, thought Miss Dimont, this happy release from confinement into sunshine, the promise of uncountable pleasures ahead. A small girl raced past, her face a picture of joy, pigtails given an extra bounce by the skip in her step.

The routine on these occasions was always the same – if a single celebrity was to be interviewed, he or she would be ushered into the first-class waiting room in order to be relieved of their innermost secrets. If more than one, the likeliest candidate would be pushed in by Terry, while Judy quickly handed the others her card, enquiring discreetly where they were staying and arranging a suitable time for their interrogation.

This manoeuvring took some skill and required a deftness of touch in which Miss Dimont excelled. On a day like today, no such juggling was required – just an invitation to old Gerald to step inside for a moment and explain away his presence in Devon's prettiest town.

The late holiday crowds swiftly dispersed, the guard completed the task of unloading from his van the precious goods entrusted to his care – a basket of somnolent homing pigeons, another of chicks tweeting furiously, the usual assortment of brown paper parcels. Then the engine driver climbed aboard to prepare for his next destination, Exbridge.

A moment of stillness descended. A blackbird sang. Dust settled in gentle folds and the reporter and photographer looked at each other.

'No ruddy Hennessy,' said Terry Eagleton.

Miss Dimont screwed up her pretty features into a scowl. In her mind was the lost scoop of *Church* v. *Law*, the clerical challenge to the authority of the redoubtable Mrs Marchbank. The uncomfortable explanation to Rudyard Rhys of how she had missed not one, but two stories in an afternoon – and with press day only two days away.

Mr Rhys was unforgiving about such things.

Just then, a shout was heard from the other end of Platform 1 up by the first-class carriages. A porter was waving his hands. Inarticulate shouts spewed forth from his shaking face. He appeared, for a moment, to be running on the spot. It was as if a small tornado had descended and hit the platform where he stood.

Terry had it in an instant. Without a word he launched himself down the platform, past the bewildered guard, racing towards the porter. The urgency with which he took off sprang in Miss Dimont an inner terror and the certain knowledge that she must run too – run like the wind . . .

By the time she reached the other end of the platform Terry was already on board. She could see him racing through the first-class corridor, checking each compartment, moving swiftly on. As fast as she could, she followed alongside him on the platform.

They reached the last compartment almost simultaneously, but Terry was a pace or two ahead of Judy. There, perfectly composed, immaculately clad in country tweeds, his oxblood brogues twinkling in the sunlight, sat their interviewee Gerald Hennessy.

You did not have to be an expert to know he was dead.

TWO

You had to hand it to Terry – no Einstein he, but in an emergency as cool as ice. He was photographing the lifeless form of a famous man barely before the reality of the situation hit home. Miss Dimont watched through the carriage window, momentarily rooted to the spot, as he went about his work efficiently, quickly, dextrously. But then as Terry switched positions to get another angle, his eye caught her immobile form.

'Call the office,' he snapped through the window. 'Call the police. In that order.'

But Judy could not take her eyes off the man who so recently had graced the Picturedrome's silver screen. His hair, now restored to a more conventional length, flopped forward across his brow. The tweed suit was immaculate. The foulard tie lay gently across what looked like a cream silk shirt, pink socks disappeared into those twinkling brogues. She had to admit that in death Gerald Hennessy, when viewed this close, looked almost more gorgeous than in life . . .

'The phone!' barked Terry.

Miss Dimont started, then, recovering herself, raced to the

nearby telephone box, pushed four pennies urgently into the slot and dialled the news desk. To her surprise she was met with the grim tones of Rudyard Rhys himself. It was rare for the editor to answer a phone – or do anything else useful around the office, thought Miss Dimont in a fleeting aperçu.

'Mr Rhys,' she hicupped, 'Mr Rhys! Gerald Hennessy . . . the . . . dead . . .' Then she realised she had forgotten to press Button A to connect the call. That technicality righted, she repeated her message with rather more coherence, only to be greeted by a lion-like roar from her editor.

'Rrr-rrr-rrrr . . .'

'What's that, Mr Rhys?'

'Damn fellow! Damn him, damn the man. Damn damn damn!'

'Well, Mr Rhys, I don't really think you can speak like that. He's . . . dead . . . Gerald Hennessy – the actor, you know – he is dead.'

'He's not the only one,' bellowed Rudyard. 'You'll have to come away. Something more important.'

Just for the moment Miss Dim lived up to her soubriquet, her brilliant brain grinding to a halt. What did he mean? Was she missing something? What could be more important than the country's number one matinée idol sitting dead in a railway carriage, here in Temple Regis?

Had Rudyard Rhys done it again? The old Vicar's Longboat Party tale all over again? Walking away from the biggest story to come the *Express*'s way in a decade? How typical of the man!

She glanced over her shoulder to see Terry, now out of the compartment of death and standing on the platform, talking to the porter. That's *my* job, she thought, hotly. In a second she had dropped the phone and raced to Terry's side, her flapping notebook ready to soak up every detail of the poor man's testimony.

The extraordinary thing about death is it makes you repeat things, thought Miss Dimont calmly. You say it once, then you say it again – you go on saying it until you have run out of people to say it to. So though technically Terry had the scoop (a) he wasn't taking notes and (b) he wasn't going to be writing the tale so (c) the story would still be hers. In the sharply competitive world of Devon journalism, ownership of a scoop was all and everything.

'There 'e was,' said the porter, whose name was Mudge. 'There 'e was.'

So far so good, thought Miss Dimont. This one's a talker.

'So then you . . .?'

'I told 'im,' said Mudge, pointing at Terry. 'I already told 'im.' And with that he clamped his uneven jaws together.

Oh Lord, thought Miss Dimont, this one's *not* a talker.

But not for nothing was the *Express*'s corkscrew-haired reporter renowned for charming the birds out of the trees. 'He doesn't listen,' she said, nodding towards the photographer. 'Deaf to anything but praise. You'll need to tell me. The train came in and . . .'

'I told 'im.'

There was a pause.

'Mr Mudge,' responded Miss Dimont slowly and perfectly reasonably, 'if you're unable to assist me, I shall have to ask Mrs Mudge when I see her at choir practice this evening.'

This surprisingly bland statement came down on the ancient porter as if a Damoclean sword had slipped its fastenings and pierced his bald head.

'You'm no need botherin' her,' he said fiercely, but you could see he was on the turn. Mrs Mudge's soprano, an eldritch screech whether in the church hall or at home, had weakened the poor man's resolve over half a century. All he asked now was a quiet life.

'The 4.30 come in,' he conceded swiftly.

'Always full,' said Miss Dimont, jollying the old bore along. 'Keeping you busy.'

'People got out.'

Oh, come ON, Mudge!

'Missus Charteris arsk me to take 'er bags to the car. Gave me thruppence.'

'That chauffeur of hers is so idle,' observed Miss Dimont serenely. Things were moving along. 'So then . . .?'

'I come back to furs clars see if anyone else wanted porterin'. That's when I saw 'im. Just like lookin' at a photograph of 'im in the paper.' Mr Mudge was warming to his theme. ''E wasn't movin'.'

Suddenly the truth had dawned – first, who the well-dressed figure was; second, that he was very dead. The shocking combination had caused him to dance his tarantella on the platform edge.

The rest of the story was down to Terry Eagleton. 'Yep, looks like a heart attack. What was he – forty-five? Bit young for that sort of thing.'

As Judy turned this over in her mind Terry started quizzing Mudge again – they seemed to share an arcane lingo which mistrusted verbs, adjectives, and many of the finer adornments which make the English language the envy of the civilised world. It was a wonder to listen to.

'Werm coddit?'

'Ur, nemmer be.'

'C'rubble.'

Miss Dimont was too absorbed by the drama to pay much attention to these linguistic dinosaurs and their game of semantic shove-ha'penny; she sidled back to the railway carriage and then, pausing for a moment, heart in mouth, stepped aboard.

The silent Pullman coach was the *dernier cri* in luxury, a handsome relic of pre-war days and a reassuring memory of antebellum prosperity. Heavily carpeted and lined with exotic African woods, it smelt of leather and beeswax and smoke, its surfaces uniformly coated in a layer of dust so fine it was impossible to see: only by rubbing her sleeve on the corridor's handrail did the house-proud reporter discover what all seasoned railway passengers know – that travelling by steam locomotive is a dirty business.

She cautiously advanced from the far end of the carriage towards the dead man's compartment, her journalist's eye taking in the debris common to the end of all long-distance journeys – discarded newspapers, old wrappers, a teacup or two, an abandoned novel. On she stepped, her eyes a camera, recording each detail; her heart may be pounding but her head was clear.

Gerald Hennessy sat in the corner seat with his back to the engine. He looked pretty relaxed for a dead man – she wondered briefly if, called on to play a corpse by his director, Gerald would have done such a convincing job in life. One arm was extended, a finger pointing towards who knows what, as if the star was himself directing a scene. He looked rather heroic.

Above him in the luggage rack sat an important-looking suitcase, by his side a copy of *The Times*. The compartment smelt of . . . limes? Lemons? Something both sweet and sharp – presumably the actor's eau de cologne. But unlike Terry Eagleton Miss Dimont did not cross the threshold, for this was not the first death scene she had encountered in her lengthy and unusual career, and from long experience she knew better than to interfere.

She looked around, she didn't know why, for signs of violence – ridiculous really, given Terry's confident reading of the cause of death, but Gerald's untroubled features offered nothing by way of fear or hurt.

And yet something was not quite right.

As her eyes took in the finer detail of the compartment, she spotted something near the doorway beneath another seat – it looked like a sandwich wrapper or a piece of litter of some kind. Just then Terry's angry face appeared at the compartment window and his fist knocked hard on the pane. She could hear him through the thick glass ordering her out on to the platform and she guessed that the police were about to arrive.

Without pausing to think why, she whisked up the litter from the floor – somehow it made the place look tidier, more dignified. It was how she would recall seeing the last of Gerald Hennessy, and how she would describe to her readers his final scene – the matinée idol as elegant in death as in life. Her introductory paragraph was already forming itself in her mind.

Terry stood on the platform, red-faced and hopping from foot to foot. 'Thought I told you to call the police.'

'Oh,' said Miss Dimont, downcast, 'I . . . oh . . . I'll go and do it now but then we've got another—'

'Done it,' he snapped back. 'And, yes we've got another fatality. I've talked to the desk. Come on.'

That was what was so irritating about Terry. You wanted to call him a know-it-all, but know-it-alls, by virtue of their irritating natures, do *not* know it all and frequently get things wrong. But Terry rarely did – it was what made him so infuriating.

'You know,' he said, as he slung his heavy camera bag over his shoulder and headed towards his car, 'sometimes you really *can* be quite dim.'

*

Bedlington-on-Sea was the exclusive end of Temple Regis,

more formal and less engagingly pretty than its big sister. Here houses of substance stood on improbably small plots, with large Edwardian rooms giving on to pocket-handkerchief gardens and huge windows looking out over a small bay.

Holidaymakers might occasionally spill into Bedlington but despite its apparent charm, they did not stay long. There was no pub and no beach, no ice-cream vendors, no pier, and a general frowning upon people who looked like they might want to have fun. It would be wrong to say that Bedlingtonians were stuffy and self-regarding, but people said it all the same.

The journey from the railway station took no more than six or seven minutes but it was like entering another world, thought Miss Dimont, as she and Herbert puttered behind the *Riviera Express*'s smart new Morris Minor. There was never any news in Bedlington – the townsfolk kept whatever they knew to themselves, and did not like publicity of any sort. If indeed there was a dead body on its streets this afternoon, you could put money on its not lying there for more than a few minutes before some civic-minded resident had it swept away. That's the way Bedlingtonians were.

And so Miss Dimont rather dreaded the inevitable 'knocks' she would have to undertake once the body was located. Usually this was a task at which she excelled – a tap on the door, regrets issued, brief words exchanged, the odd intimacy unveiled, the gradual jigsaw of half-information built up over maybe a dozen or so doorsteps – but in Bedlington she knew the chances of learning anything of use were remote. Snooty wasn't in it.

They had been in such a rush she hadn't been able to get out of Terry where exactly the body was to be found, but as they rounded the bend of Clarenceux Avenue there was no need for further questions. Ahead was the trusty black Wolseley of the Temple Regis police force, a horseshoe of spectators and an atmosphere electric with curiosity.

At the end of the avenue there rose a cliff of Himalayan proportions, a tower of deep red Devonian soil and rock, at the top of which one could just glimpse the evidence of a recent cliff fall. As one's eye moved down the sharp slope it was possible to pinpoint the trajectory of the deceased's involuntary descent; and in an instant it was clear to even the most casual observer that this was a tragic accident, a case of Man Overboard, where rocks and earth had given way under his feet.

Terry and Miss Dimont parked and made their way through to where Sergeant Hernaford was standing, facing the crowd, urging them hopelessly, pointlessly, that there was nothing to see and that they should move on.

The sergeant spoke with forked tongue, for there *was* something to see before they went home to tea – there, under a police blanket, lay a body a-sprawl, as if still in the act of trying to save itself. But it was chillingly still.

'Oh dear,' said Miss Dimont, conversationally, to Sergeant Hernaford, 'how tragic.'

''Oo was it?' said Terry, a bit more to the point.

Hernaford slowly turned his gaze towards the official representatives of the fourth estate. He had seen them many times before in many different circumstances, and here they were again – these purveyors of truth and of history, these curators of local legend, these *nosy parkers*.

'Back be'ind the line,' rasped Hernaford in a most unfriendly manner, for just like the haughty Bedlingtonians he did not like journalists. 'Get BACK!'

'Now Sergeant Hernaford,' said Miss Dimont, stiffening, for she did not like his tone. 'Here we have a man of late middle age – I can see his shoes, he's a man of late middle age – who has walked too close to the cliff edge. When I was up there at the top last week there were signs explicitly warning that there had been a rockfall and that people should keep away. So, man of late middle age, tragic accident. Coroner will say he was a B.F. for ignoring the warnings, the *Riviera Express* will say what a loss to the community. An extra paragraph listing his bereaved relations, there's the story.

'All that's missing,' she added, magnificently, edging closer to the sergeant, 'is his name. I expect you know it. I expect he had a wallet or something. Or maybe one of these good people—' she looked round, smiling at the horseshoe but her words taking on a steely edge '—has assisted you in your identification. He has clearly been here for a while – your blanket is damp and it stopped raining an hour ago – so in that time you must have had a chance to find out who he is.'

She smiled tightly and her voice became quite stern.

'I expect you have already informed your inspector and,

rather than drive all the way over to Temple Regis police station and take up his *very precious time* getting two words out of him – a Christian name and a surname, after all that is all I am asking – I imagine you would rather he did not complain to you about my wasting his *very precious time*.

'So, Sergeant,' she said, 'please spare us all that further pain.'

It was at times like this that Terry had to confess she may be a bit scatty but Miss Dimont could be, well, remarkable. He watched Sergeant Hernaford, a barnacle of the old school, crumble before his very eyes.

'Name, Arthur Shrimsley. Address, Tide Cottage, Exbridge. Now move on. Move ON!'

Judy Dimont gazed owlishly, her spectacles sliding down her convex nose and resting precariously at its tip. 'Not *the* Arthur . . .?' she enquired, but before she could finish, Terry had whisked her away, for Hernaford was not a man to exchange pleasantries with – that was as much as they were going to get. As they retreated, he pushed Miss Dimont aside with his elbow while turning to take snaps of the corpse and its abrasive custodian before pulling open the car door.

'Let's go,' he urged. 'Lots to do.'

Miss Dimont obliged. Dear Herbert would have to wait. She pulled out her notebook and started to scribble as Terry noisily let in the clutch and they headed for the office.

Already the complexity of the situation was becoming clear; and no matter what happened next, disaster was about to befall her. Two deaths, two very different sets of journalistic values. And only Judy Dimont to adjudicate between the rival tales as to which served her readers best.

If she favoured the death of Gerald Hennessy over the sad loss of Arthur Shrimsley, local readers would never forgive her, for Arthur Shrimsley had made a big name for himself in the local community. The *Express* printed his letters most weeks, even at the moment when he was stealing their stories and selling them to Fleet Street. Rudyard Rhys, in thrall to Shrimsley's superior journalistic skills, had even allowed him to write a column for a time. But narcissistic and self-regarding it turned out to be, and of late he was permitted merely to see his name in print at the foot of a letter which would excoriate the local council, or the town brass band, or the ladies at the WI for failing to keep his cup full at the local flower show.

There was nothing nice about Arthur Shrimsley, yet he had invented a persona which his readers were all too ready to believe in and even love. His loss would be a genuine one to the community.

On the other hand, thought Miss Dimont feverishly, as Terry manoeuvred expertly round the tight corner of Tuppenny Row, we have a story of national importance here. Gerald Hennessy, star of *Heroes at Dawn* and *The First of the Few*, husband of the equally famous Prudence Aubrey, has died on our patch. Gerald HENNESSY!

The question was, which sad passing should lead the *Express*'s front page? And who would take the blame when, as was inevitable, the wrong choice was made?

ONE PLACE. MANY STORIES

Bold, innovative and empowering publishing.

FOLLOW US ON:

@HQStories